AMBUSH

BOOKS BY JAMES PATTERSON
FEATURING MICHAEL BENNETT

Haunted (with James O. Born)
Bullseye (with Michael Ledwidge)
Alert (with Michael Ledwidge)
Burn (with Michael Ledwidge)
Gone (with Michael Ledwidge)
I, Michael Bennett (with Michael Ledwidge)
Tick Tock (with Michael Ledwidge)
Worst Case (with Michael Ledwidge)
Run for Your Life (with Michael Ledwidge)
Step on a Crack (with Michael Ledwidge)

For a complete list of books, visit JamesPatterson.com

AMBUSH

JAMES PATTERSON
AND JAMES O. BORN

GRAND CENTRAL
PUBLISHING

NEW YORK   BOSTON

Copyright © 2018 by James Patterson
Manhunt copyright © 2017 by JBP Business, LLC.

Grand Central Publishing
Hachette Book Group
1290 Avenue of the Americas, New York, NY 10104
grandcentralpublishing.com
twitter.com/grandcentralpub

Originally published in hardcover and ebook by Little, Brown & Company in October 2018
First trade paperback edition: July 2019

Grand Central Publishing is a division of Hachette Book Group, Inc. The Grand Central Publishing name and logo is a trademark of Hachette Book Group, Inc.

MICHAEL BENNETT is a trademark of JBP Business, LLC.

The publisher is not responsible for websites (or their content) that are not owned by the publisher.

The Hachette Speakers Bureau provides a wide range of authors for speaking events. To find out more, go to www.hachettespeakersbureau.com or call (866) 376-6591.

Library of Congress Control Number: 2017946204

ISBNs: 978-1-5387-1378-5 (trade paperback), 978-0-316-41469-2 (ebook)

Printed in the United States of America

LSC-C

10 9 8 7 6 5 4 3 2 1

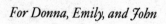

For Donna, Emily, and John

CHAPTER 1

I WATCHED THE eight-story apartment building on 161st, about half a block from Melrose Avenue. Nothing special about it. Old window air-conditioning units dotted the facade, but the place had a certain charm. Of course, over years of surveillance in unsavory neighborhoods of New York City, I've learned to adjust my expectations.

My partner, Antrole Martens, and I were sitting in his Crown Victoria. By tradition, the most beat-up car in our homicide unit went to the rookie on the squad. Despite its faint odor of vomit, Martens had handled the assignment of the shitty car with grace in his six years with the NYPD. He understood he had to earn his place in the unit, but there was no doubt he was on his way up. I thought he was exactly the kind of cop we needed in a command position.

I wanted this arrest to go well for him. I could still remember my first arrest in Homicide. A pimp named Hermine Paschual. He'd stabbed a john who'd argued about the price. At the time, I thought I was changing the world.

Now it was my job to make sure things went right. I said, "How sure are you about this tip?"

He smiled. "Sure enough to drag your ass out here with me."

"Let your kids get a little older and life get a little busier, and we'll see how serious you take anonymous tips."

Antrole laughed. "That's why I'm stopping at two kids. Thinking of you managing ten makes my head spin."

"Imagine what it does to me." Just then, my phone rang, and I looked down to see that it was my oldest girl, Juliana. I always answered the phone the same way when one of my daughters called.

"Hello, beautiful."

"Hey, Dad!"

There was no teenage disdain today. She was excited about something.

"What's going on, sweetheart?"

"I've got big news. But I have to tell you in person."

"How about at dinner tonight?" I smiled when I heard her giggle. She was not a giggler by nature, so this had to be something good. Harvard flashed in my brain. Although I would've preferred Columbia, a few blocks from our apartment on the Upper West Side.

Juliana said, "I can't wait. I'll tell the whole family at once. I gotta go. Bye, Dad. Love you."

Before I could even say "Love you" back, the connection was dead.

Antrole deadpanned, "Can we squeeze some police work in

now? After all, this tip was called in to you. I just happened to answer the phone at your desk."

"Let's call Alice and Chuck to come with us. Maybe Harry, too."

Antrole said, "Why the party? We can grab this dope ourselves. We get all the glory, and it'll be easier to talk to him."

"He's a suspect in a murder."

"And we're NYPD detectives. I thought in the old days you guys used to make arrests by yourselves."

"Yeah. We also used to get shot more frequently."

"Am I going to have to shame you into coming with me? Besides, if we have a few minutes alone with this guy, who knows what he'll tell us?"

"I hate it when rookies make sense. Let's go." His excitement was contagious.

CHAPTER 2

EVERYONE OUT IN the neighborhood made us for cops as soon as we started walking down the sidewalk. It wasn't as if we were working undercover, but a young black guy in a sharp suit and an older white guy wearing a sport coat to cover his gun—we could've been in uniform and not been any more obvious.

Our suspect had shot a customer who stiffed him on a bag of heroin in front of a grocery store in Midtown with plenty of witnesses. A poor business plan all around.

The tip said the suspect was in apartment 416. I didn't trust the elevator to make it up all four floors without some sort of issue, so despite Antrole's objections, we took the stairs. It gave me a minute to talk to my headstrong partner.

I said, "Nothing fancy. We knock and hope he answers. Maybe we try the door to see if it's locked. Otherwise we come up with another plan that may or may not involve the SWAT team. Got it?"

Antrole nodded.

At each landing, I took a moment to get a feel for the surroundings. Antrole probably thought I needed to catch my breath, but this climb was nothing compared to the basketball games I played with my kids. I took it slow because every apartment building has its own aura. Sometimes it's because of the tenants, and sometimes it's because of the area. Either could kill you if you weren't careful.

On the fourth landing, I said, "You ready for this? It doesn't matter what happens—you've done a good job getting us this far. Now we have to use our heads."

"You don't have to talk to me like I'm some kid out of the academy. I have four years' patrol experience and two years in the detective bureau. I'm only new to Homicide. Homicide detectives are not the only ones who make arrests."

"I don't *have* to talk to you like that, but I enjoy it. That's one of the advantages of being senior."

I appreciated the smile that spread across Antrole's face. Feeling out a new partner is always an ongoing process, but this guy was all right.

He said, "This suspect might be the key to some of the unsolved homicides connected to the heroin dealers up this way."

"Could be." Antrole was looking at the big picture—rare with new homicide detectives. He showed a ton of promise.

The fourth-floor hallway was empty. That was always good. I paused at the stairwell and just listened to the sounds of the apartment building for almost a full minute. Nothing unusual. Latin music from one apartment. Someone talking loudly in another.

As we carefully made our way down the hallway, I heard a TV playing a daytime talk show in another apartment.

The cheap carpet was uneven over a wooden floor that broadcast sound. A wide set of windows at the end of the hallway took the edge off the gloomy vibe of the building.

Then we found ourselves in front of apartment 416. Antrole slipped to the other side of the door and drew his Glock service weapon. I pulled my pistol, too, though I thought it was a little premature.

We listened at the door, and I put my hand against it to see if I could feel any vibration. Unexpectedly, it pushed open a few inches.

I looked to Antrole, who angled his head to see into the apartment.

That was odd. Drug dealers in this neighborhood rarely left their doors unbolted, let alone open. It was nice to catch a break once in a while.

From my angle, I could see the suspect we were looking for sitting on a couch under a wide, dirty window. His head leaned back on the rear of the couch. He wasn't moving. I motioned to Antrole that I saw someone inside.

The young detective nodded and turned before I could tell him to wait.

A shadow passed the open door, and I heard someone inside. It was a single word. Some kind of command. I wasn't even sure what language it was. But the subsequent gunfire was unmistakable.

The door appeared to explode, and Antrole jumped to the other side of the doorway, his gun up.

I crouched quickly and fired a couple of rounds into the

apartment. I didn't see a target—it was just to keep the shooters behind cover. We had to move and move quickly.

The gunfire didn't slow down.

This was an ambush.

CHAPTER 3

ALEXANDRA "ALEX" MARTINEZ aimed her Canon EOS 5D Mark III digital SLR camera at the tallest of the three young men, dressed only in tight white underwear. The abs of all three looked like ice trays, and their arms had just enough meat on them. But the tallest of the three, Chaz, was special. The camera loved Chaz.

Alex realized she was barking at the model next to Chaz when he got too close. It was like having a Matt Groening character pop up in a Renoir.

The top of this building in the Morrisania neighborhood of the Bronx provided an interesting urban backdrop and conveniently put her in position for another assignment. Photographing nearly naked models was fun, but it didn't pay the bills.

This wasn't a coincidence. Alex had planned the photo session to the last detail, including the location. Just as she did everything else.

She checked her watch. They'd been at it for more than two hours, but she could wrap it up just about any time she wanted. That was the advantage of being prepared: you usually got the shots you needed quickly.

Then she heard it. A couple of pops, seeming to come from the next block.

The models craned their necks, looked over the side of the building in the direction of the sound. She could look down on 161st Street and see the front of the building the gunfire was coming from.

She turned away from her crew as a smile crept onto her face. It was even more gunfire than she'd anticipated. Michael Bennett had been executed.

CHAPTER 4

ANTROLE AND I crouched low. Gunfire had a way of triggering the instinct to ball yourself up as small as possible. The ambushers kept firing high, as if they expected us to still be standing. It was a classic mistake. The holes along the door and the wall gave me an idea of where the shooters were in the room.

Both Antrole and I started to return fire with our Glocks. The shooters had lost the element of surprise, and our police training and tactics gave us the upper hand now. I saw a shadow move near the door and peppered it with .40-caliber rounds. Splinters and debris filled the open doorway.

A bullet pinged off a metal door frame across from me. It struck a Pokémon sticker between the eyes. I hoped the shooter wasn't a good enough shot to have aimed for it.

A splinter the size of a toothpick lodged in my left hand. Pain shot up my arm, and blood spread across my fingers.

Now I could hear the shouts and cries from people in the other apartments, which distracted me from whoever was shooting at us. But only for a moment. A door opened a crack, and a head popped out. All I could see was gray hair.

Antrole shouted, "Police! Get back inside."

Someone yanked the old man back into the apartment.

Antrole backed against the far wall of the hallway and scooted to my side of the door just as a wave of shots hit the spot where he had been crouched. Shouting at the civilian had given away his position.

He hunkered down next to me with his pistol up, and I felt the tide turning. All we had to do was move down the hallway and wait for the cavalry to arrive. Calls to 911 had to be flooding in about now. Time was on our side.

Then a shotgun blast blew a hand-size hole just above my head. Jesus Christ. It felt like it had come from a bazooka. I choked on some of the drywall dust launched into the air and blinked to clear it out of my eyes. Sweat gathered on my forehead, and I felt myself pant.

The shotgun racked on the other side of the wall. The shooter would fire again at any second.

Antrole yelled, "Clip."

He was reloading, so I needed to keep my gun up. Our training would save us.

I saw a shadow pass the hole in the wall where the shotgun had done its work and fired twice as Antrole opened up on the doorway again. Someone hit the floor hard on the other side of the wall.

Bullets hit the wall all around us after Antrole fired. He stumbled awkwardly onto the floor.

I looked down and saw that Antrole had been hit in the leg. Blood was pumping out onto the cheap carpet, making the washed-out colors in the fabric come alive with red.

I leaned in close and said, "Can you walk?"

"If it will get us away from here, hell, yes."

It felt like maybe the gunfight was over. No one was shooting, a welcome change.

Something flew out the door and bounced back off the wall. It made an odd thumping sound on the floor right in front of the door. I saw it roll around in odd arcs on the ground.

Too late I realized it was a hand grenade.

CHAPTER 5

MY EYES FOCUSED on the old-style army pineapple grenade, almost hypnotized.

Instinctively, I reached down and grabbed Antrole by the collar. He raised his pistol and fired at whoever had tossed the hand grenade from the other side of the door. It was tough pulling 180 pounds across the rough, cheap carpet, an exercise in physics and friction.

I couldn't tell how many shooters were left inside the apartment, but Antrole was laying down fire to keep their heads down. At least one of them was still active. I could hear him scuttling around the apartment, then he fired a round through the wall.

Someone at the other end of the hallway popped out of an apartment and started to run. A young man in a white T-shirt disappeared down the stairwell. It distracted the shooter in the apartment, too. For an instant, everything went quiet.

When I had dragged Antrole a few feet down the hallway, his collar gave way and ripped completely from his coat. I tumbled backward onto the floor and felt a sting of pain, a finger on my left hand turned awkwardly. I desperately reached out to grab my partner again. It felt like I had dropped him down a well. I shouted something, but by now my ears were ringing so badly I don't even know what I said.

That's when it happened. The grenade detonated.

A giant wave of light and heat. I don't know that I'd ever experienced anything close to it. I couldn't even say it made a sound, my ears shut down so fast.

I felt pain on my forehead, but only for a moment.

Then everything went cloudy.

Then it went dark.

CHAPTER 6

ALEX STOOD WITH the nearly naked men on the edge of the building, looking toward the sound of the gunfire. She casually raised her camera and focused it. She knew exactly which building the sound was coming from.

She knew which building it was because she had chosen it. Just as she'd set up this photo shoot.

It was one of several contracts she had taken here in New York City for a Mexican drug cartel. Fashion photography provided her with a cover for the way she made her real income.

Alex snapped photo after photo, watching the flash of the explosion through her lens almost a second before the sound of it reached her ears. It was a low, hollow thump. But first she saw the windows blow out and a burst of flame shoot into the air. It was spectacular.

She heard Chaz say, "Damn, did you see that?" A smile crept across her face again. An explosion like that would solve a lot of problems. No loose ends. In her business, there was nothing worse than a loose end.

CHAPTER 7

THINGS WERE HAZY, as if I'd walked into fog. I felt like I was in a tunnel, with sound echoing everywhere. Then I heard voices. They sounded distant, until I saw a face right above me.

It was a uniformed patrol officer, a woman with short brown hair. She was helping someone near me, a paramedic. I couldn't follow what they were doing.

The paramedic had sweat dripping from his long nose as he looked down at me. I felt pressure on my forehead. He looked down and said something comforting, or at least I thought so.

I tried to ask about Antrole and warn them about the shooters, but when I attempted to speak, nothing came out.

The paramedic patted my chest. It looked like he said, "Relax—it will be fine."

The young patrol officer couldn't mask her emotions as well. She looked worried. Even scared.

Then I faded out again.

The second time I opened my eyes, things were much sharper. There was a bright light above my head, and I was lying flat on my back. I heard the sounds of normal life around me. Someone walking in a hallway. A quiet discussion in the corner. Nothing frightening, like screaming or angels singing.

Before I could say anything or ask any more questions, I saw Mary Catherine's face above me. She looked like an angel. She was so beautiful. Immediately I felt better.

When I saw my grandfather Seamus, I knew I was still alive. He was too mean to die. He was in the official uniform of the Catholic Church. As a priest at Holy Name, he had access to any hospital in the city.

I didn't like the look of concern on Mary Catherine's face. I knew I was the cause of it, and that was the last thing I wanted to do to the woman I loved.

I took a breath and tried my voice. It cracked, but I said, "How is Antrole?"

I knew the answer, but I had to ask anyway. I saw the hand grenade and felt the blast. I remembered his collar tearing away and the feeling of losing him down a well.

Mary Catherine shook her head and leaned away from me.

Seamus stepped up and said, "I'm afraid your partner was killed in the blast. The doctors say you were incredibly lucky."

I lifted my right hand and flexed, just to make sure I could. I wiggled my toes and felt the blanket on them.

Seamus said, "Everything's there—don't worry. You have a concussion, a bunch of stitches in your head, a broken finger on your left hand. They want to look at your back and spine more closely tomorrow."

Suddenly I felt the pain in my left hand when I tried to move my index finger. My back was sore, but I didn't say anything.

Mary Catherine took my hand and kissed me on the forehead. I had so many painkillers running through me that I barely felt her lips.

I looked up and said, "Do the kids know?"

"Yes. We knew it would be on the news. We made arrangements for the kids to be driven home. Juliana and Jane are making dinner and ensuring that everyone does their homework. There's nothing you need to worry about."

But that's what I did. I was a father. I worried.

Then I remembered Juliana's phone call. "What was Juliana's big news? Please tell me it has nothing to do with a wedding dress or falling in love with a boy across the country."

Mary Catherine gave me a smile. That's what I needed. "No, nothing like that. My guess is that Jane will be the first one to give us that kind of news."

"Please don't tell me she's decided not to go to college and wants to travel the world alone."

Seamus said, "Don't be an ass. That girl is saddled with your practical nature. She has big news, and you're going to be happy no matter what it is. Your job is to just be proud."

"I'm always proud, but I can be worried, too. I'm a father."

"And I'm your grandfather, and I never worried that much about you."

It didn't matter how old I got—my grandfather still treated me like I was an eighth grader. And somehow, though I would not admit it openly, I liked it.

Mary Catherine indulged me. "Juliana landed a TV role.

It's a locally produced drama. She's very excited about it, so no matter what she says, don't ask questions about who's producing it or what she's expected to do. Ease into it a little bit. It is a legit production company, even if it's not very big."

I supported my children in everything they did. I also tended to get involved in everything they did. This was no different. I looked up at Mary Catherine and said, "I'm happy for her and can't wait to see her on set."

CHAPTER 8

AFTER I TALKED to Mary Catherine and Seamus, Harry Grissom came into the room. The lanky lieutenant looked like he could've been a gunfighter in the Old West. His weather-beaten face gave no hint that he'd worked in New York City for the past twenty-five years, though his Brooklyn accent did. His droopy mustache hid a knife scar only long-time colleagues knew about.

I knew his presence meant that he was worried about me, but like the professional he was, he got right to the important questions.

"Who gave you the tip?"

I shook my head. "Antrole took the call."

"Why didn't you call for backup?"

I shrugged. What was I going to do? Throw my late partner

under the bus? Finally I said, "It didn't seem like a great tip at the time. You know how it is."

Thank God he'd worked the street and really did know how things happened, what good cops had to do just to make a case. If you went by the book on everything, nothing would get done.

Harry shook his head. "This whole thing's screwed up. Your suspect, Emmanuel Diaz, was dead hours before you got there. Two of the shooters are dead, and one is in the ICU with a couple of bullet wounds and shrapnel from the grenade."

"So it was an ambush?"

"We're not sure. Who knows what went on? You might have interrupted a rip-off, and they were searching the apartment. To be on the safe side, the NYPD is not releasing any details about you or Antrole. The hospital staff know to keep things quiet."

"I like the sound of that."

"It might keep the media circus away from you for a few days."

Then the swinging door to my room opened, and I had a quick peek at an attractive young woman with a baby in her arms, holding the hand of a little boy in the hallway. I recognized Antrole Martens's wife, a Wall Street banker, and their two young children from photos on his desk.

Antrole's world revolved around his family. It hurt to know what they were going through right now.

I wanted to call out to her, but the door closed. All I could do was lie there in silence.

CHAPTER 9

ALEX MARTINEZ WAS back in her comfortable hotel room after a quick drink with the crew and models from the shoot to show them how happy she was with their work. The drink also provided cover if anyone was to ask questions about the shooting that occurred just down the street.

She had gently fended off an awkward invitation from Chaz, the model, to come back to his loft in SoHo, as he downplayed the fact that he had two roommates in a tiny apartment. But Alex had far too much on her mind to be able to concentrate and enjoy an evening with an underwear model. He was a beautiful young man, but not that beautiful.

Now she sat on the edge of the bed reviewing the photos she'd taken earlier while the big flat-screen TV bolted into the wall played the local news. She had dozens of shots of underwear models, plenty of suitable material for her client. But she was more interested in the photos she took of the building where the explosion occurred. The shots of the explosion coming from the building on 161st Street were remarkable.

Her favorite caught the plume of flame at its apex. It was at least three meters out the window, with sparkles of glass around the flame catching the sun just right. She couldn't have planned a better photo. It made her appreciate how hard wildlife photography would be. Patience was the key. Patience, and a lot of shots with a good lens.

The photos of the explosions were striking, but they didn't provide her with any information she could use on her job. She needed to know if her target, Detective Michael Bennett, had been killed in the explosion in order to officially close out her contract.

When Alex heard the TV news anchor mention a shootout, she looked up. They were calling it the Battle in the Bronx. It might not have made the news if it were just gunfire, Alex thought. But add an explosion to the mix, and it caught their attention.

The anchor revealed that there were several fatalities, but there was no mention of police officers down or even injuries. That was frustrating. She did learn that one of the suspected gunmen was in critical condition at New York–Presbyterian Hospital in Washington Heights.

Alex had hired some local gunmen from a Dominican gang. They came highly recommended, and she liked to distance herself from some of the action. It confused local homicide detectives when there was evidence of a gang with multiple weapons. They didn't think *lone assassin* in a case like that.

All she wanted to do now was close out the contract and return to her ranch, in Colombia. At least for a little while, until she had to come back to New York and finish her other business.

Her stomach growled, and she realized she had forgotten to eat. She needed to get out, relax a little bit, and wait for the information she needed to become public.

Alex stepped into the bathroom and combed out her long, dark hair. At five feet six, with muscular shoulders and other curves, she knew she'd never be a model, but she appreciated what God had given her to work with.

Her version of self-reliance would terrify most people. It required constant physical fitness and mental sharpness, without slipping. And right now, self-preservation meant she had to get the hell out of New York as soon as possible.

CHAPTER 10

DESPITE MY ARGUMENTS, the doctors wouldn't release me from the hospital that night, and it was too late to let the kids visit me. A day without seeing my kids was torture. When I told the doctor that, all she said was, "Then this is our version of waterboarding."

Dr. Carole Fredrick looked like she was fifteen, but I could tell by the way she handled me that she was a veteran of emergency-room medicine and experienced at dealing with stubborn patients. Even patients who were with the NYPD and had an army of children to back them up if they needed it.

Dr. Fredrick said, "And please don't think you can change my mind. I have a three-year-old at home, and I can assure you that if she can't make me budge on a decision, neither can you."

I believed her.

They set me up in a semiprivate room where my obese

roommate was unconscious when I arrived. I didn't know if that was a permanent state or one that just occurred nightly, but it was clear that the man wasn't stirring for the rest of the night.

Mary Catherine tucked the blankets around my chin like I was a child. She began updating me about the kids, speaking so softly it was hard for me to hear.

Seamus said, "You don't need to keep it down on account of his roommate. That guy is sawing wood." He chuckled as he looked over at the man.

I said, "Is that any way for a priest to talk?"

"What? I'm not hurting his feelings. I'm not even saying anything bad. It's just that we don't have to worry about disturbing him."

I looked at the thin, eighty-one-year-old man who'd been a pillar for me throughout my life. After my grandmother died, he sold his bar and, to everyone's surprise, was admitted to the seminary. He became a priest with life experiences unlike anyone else in the Catholic Church, but his new vocation had not changed the man he was one bit. All it did was alter his clothing. He was still obnoxious and opinionated. He was also loyal, caring, and more devout than any man I knew. He loved each one of my ten adopted children as if he had been there at their births, and he cared for my first wife like she was his daughter. When she died of cancer, he was as lost as I was. And now, years later, he had accepted Mary Catherine into the family wholly and unconditionally.

I said, "It's getting late. Why don't you guys get some sleep? I'll be home sometime tomorrow."

Mary Catherine said, "I'm staying here tonight."

"In that chair? I don't think so. Get a good night's sleep, and I promise it will be better for all of us tomorrow."

Mary Catherine took a sharp tone, which always brought out her Irish accent more acutely. "I won't sleep a wink tonight, whether I'm lying in our bed or sitting in that chair. So please stop arguing with me."

I knew when I was beaten. I had to be satisfied that at least Seamus was going to go home and rest.

Mary Catherine moved to the edge of my bed and carefully brushed hair away from the stitches in my forehead. I liked the feeling of her fingers playing with my hair and the warmth of her body close to mine.

After a few minutes, I said, "Thank you for staying. This is nice."

"Yes, it is. I'm sorry you have to get blown to smithereens just so I can have a few quiet moments with you."

"You know that's not true. I always have time for you."

She smiled and said, "I know you do. It's just that with the kids and everything else, alone time is a precious commodity."

"You know, if we went on a honeymoon, we'd have plenty of time alone together." I said it casually but was afraid I was crossing a line. We had discussed dates for our wedding, but I kept getting the feeling Mary Catherine wasn't quite ready.

She said, "If we went on a honeymoon while you were in this kind of condition, I'm afraid you wouldn't survive."

Somehow I managed to chuckle. The movement hurt my back.

She said, "Let's not talk about a date just yet. We've got plenty to work out before we take on the planning of the wedding."

It was hard to argue with logic like that. I was about to suggest she climb under the covers with me when the door to my room burst open.

A tall African American nurse with stylish glasses and a somewhat severe expression stared at us.

The middle-aged nurse said, "I know I'm not seeing a visitor in a semiprivate room more than an hour after visiting hours are over. Tell me that's not what I'm seeing."

Mary Catherine stammered, "You don't understand—"

The nurse didn't let her finish. "No, sugar, *you* don't understand. I can't show any favorites. Even if this young man is a hero and risked his life for the city today, it's my job to make sure pretty young things like you don't throw off his schedule. Now, you need to head out of here, get a good night's rest, and come back at 10:00 a.m. Not before. Wait until at least ten o'clock."

I had to smile. That was how you handled someone. She could've been a cop or a priest or a teacher. Thank God she was a nurse.

CHAPTER 11

ALEX SLIPPED INTO Aretsky's Patroon well after the usual dinner crowd had gotten settled. The popular steak house near 46th Street and Third Avenue was one of her favorite stops in the city. There was no denying her South American heritage. She was a meat eater.

Deciding that a seat at the cozy bar was her best bet, Alex slid onto an empty stool at the end of the bar with no one near her. She ordered a glass of 2010 Carmignano from the thin bartender, whom she recognized. He gave her a quick smile and even managed to wink his drooping right eye.

After she ordered her favorite dish, the roasted veal chop with fennel and vegetables, she relaxed for the first time all day. She liked the comfortable atmosphere of the bar. Sports memorabilia hung high on the walls. A bat from Derek Jeter over the door. One of Wayne Gretzky's hockey sticks from his last game as a New York Ranger behind the bar.

She sipped her wine and thought about her life back in Colombia. That was where she wanted to be. In the open spaces, with people who loved her. Not in a crowded, dirty city with people she was paid to kill.

She was a little bothered that she couldn't find the information she needed to close her contract on Michael Bennett. The Mexican cartel liaison she dealt with, who constantly bragged about his contacts, wasn't able to help her, either. She learned a new lesson about depending on the cartel's contacts. She hadn't developed her own for this job and was in the dark. She didn't like the feeling.

Her cartel contact knew only that one of the gunmen she had used was at New York–Presbyterian in the ICU.

Alex wasn't going to let that ruin her night. She lingered over her delicious meal and even chatted with the bartender a little bit. He had an eastern European accent, but his name tag said LARRY.

She watched the couples come and go through the restaurant. This time of the evening it was a decidedly younger crowd, stockbrokers from Wall Street and other young people who thought they would rule the city one day.

Those kinds of ambitions had never interested her. She had wanted to do something creative since she was a little girl. It wasn't until she was older, after her father was murdered, that she discovered you could be creative in any number of jobs.

Her father's death, from a single gunshot wound to the head, had affected her in so many ways. Most of them she preferred not to explore too deeply. She'd get nothing of benefit by hanging on to the past.

Her fashion photography had provided a welcome outlet for her creativity. And, surprisingly, she could mix her two occupations with some frequency. It was easy to scout locations for both a photo shoot and a contract. They didn't necessarily have to be two different places.

Once she had finished most of what was on her plate, just as her mother had taught her to do, Alex raised her hand to catch the bartender's attention. She noticed that in addition to his drooping right eye, Larry had a shuffle in his gait. He seemed a little young to have suffered a stroke. She wondered if the secret police in his home country were anything like the police she had dealt with in Colombia over the years.

She pulled a simple Yves Saint Laurent leather wallet from her purse. Before she even had it opened, Larry raised his hands.

He had a broad smile when he said, "It's already been taken care of."

"What? By whom?"

"The man at the end of the bar by the door."

Alex turned to see an attractive man a few years older than she was, wearing an expensive suit, raise a glass of Scotch and smile.

She plopped a fifty-dollar bill on the bar and said, "Then this is for you."

Larry didn't offer much resistance.

She turned toward the door and walked out with her confident stride. As she was about to reach the man sitting at the end of the bar, she turned her head slightly, smiled, and said, "Thank you for dinner."

Then she kept walking. The guy was lucky he didn't try to stop her. She had things to do.

CHAPTER 12

THE FLOOR NURSE had made the hospital policy clear to Mary Catherine, and my fiancée left without too much fuss. Although I liked having her with me, I felt better knowing she was home and would have a chance to sleep. Besides, it would be more comforting to the kids in the morning if she were there.

The drugs felt like they were starting to wear off, but I wasn't tired. Instead I found myself staring up at the stained ceiling. I replayed my last moments with Antrole Martens over and over. The sickening sound of the hand grenade as it rolled on the rough, carpeted floor. The stinging of the dust in my eyes from the bullets winging through the wall. The sound of people in the other apartments as they scrambled for their lives. A gunfight could be a complicated and devastating business for a cop. Losing a partner was something you never got over.

I heard my phone ringing somewhere in the room. My son Eddie liked to change the ringtone every few days. For the past week, it had been Robert Plant belting out the words "And she's buying a stairway to heaven."

It took me a few moments to realize it was close to me, in the drawer of the night table right next to my head. I fumbled with the drawer and snatched the phone up.

I didn't recognize the upstate New York number, so I answered it with "Michael Bennett."

A woman's voice said, "Mr. Bennett, this is Kathy Morris. I'm the inspector at the Gowanda Correctional Facility."

Inspectors investigated crimes at prisons. I had a flash of fear about Brian, who was housed at the facility.

I blurted out, "Is Brian okay?"

The inspector said, "I'm sorry to say that your son Brian has been stabbed."

I thought I might black out for the second time that day.

CHAPTER 13

AFTER I'D HEARD all the information Inspector Morris was willing to divulge, I lay back down and considered my options.

It was hard to picture my little boy being stabbed. Brian had suffered severe lacerations to the face and two puncture wounds to his abdomen. It had been an official report delivered in clinical terms, but I knew what a knife attack looked like. Knife wounds are ugly and shocking, even if you don't know the victim. Thankfully the administration had shown some common sense and immediately moved him by ambulance to a hospital near Buffalo.

Brian was serving a term for selling drugs. It was a mistake that would affect him, and me, for the rest of our lives. He never could explain why he did it. Just that he got in deeper and deeper, then couldn't get out.

He had worked for a lowlife who used kids to sell his shit. Brian was lucky. Some of the kids selling synthetic drugs, including meth and ecstasy, had been killed.

The cartel that ran the business had used a fifteen-year-old boy named Diego to handle competition and potential witnesses. I tracked Diego down to the library on Columbia University's campus, where we chatted for a few minutes before he pulled a pistol and tried to kill me. Unfortunately, I was forced to shoot him. It troubled me still.

This was no coincidence. The ambush on Antrole and me was connected to Brian's attack. I just had to think clearly to figure it all out.

Now the question was, how could I escape and make my way to Buffalo? There was no question I was going to see my boy. There would only be a problem if someone was foolish enough to get in my way.

I found my pants folded across the chair at the back of my room with my shoes underneath it. I had no idea where they came from or who had bothered to fold them. My shirt was nowhere to be seen. I can imagine what the person who found it thought when he or she saw Antrole's blood splattered across it.

My police ID was in the same drawer as my phone. I had what I needed.

I borrowed a shirt from my roommate's closet. The color matched my khaki pants, but it was way too big. I tucked it in as best I could, looking like a kid wearing his father's long-sleeved shirt.

Pain shot through me as I adjusted the shirt, then pulled my belt tight to give my back some support. It didn't help much.

The room dipped and spun a couple of times as I got dressed, but the longer I was on my feet, the steadier I felt.

I peered out my door and didn't see anyone at the nurses' station. Why would I? It was the middle of the night and nothing was going on. I slid down the hallway quietly, like a ninja. At least in my current state it felt like I was a ninja. I took the elevator all the way down to the lobby. Once there, I walked through as if I were just another visitor. Why not? Security was intent on keeping people out of the hospital, not in.

Out on the street, I realized my plan wasn't completely thought out. What now? I couldn't walk to Buffalo. Then I remembered Eddie teaching me about my new apps. I grabbed my phone and hit the Uber app, and a few minutes later a black Dodge Charger pulled up in front of me. It felt like magic.

As I hopped in, all I said was, "Need to go to Buffalo."

The tubby white guy behind the wheel turned and said, "I can't drive to Buffalo."

"Sure you can. Just head north on I-87. I'll guide you the rest of the way in."

The driver had no sense of humor and said, "Let me rephrase that. I *won't* drive to Buffalo. It's too far."

I took a moment to think, then gave him the address of my apartment instead.

The Ford twelve-passenger van we used to tote around my army of a family was in its usual spot in a parking garage across from our building. The family tank would be my chariot on the ride to Buffalo.

The spare key was under the rear bumper, conveniently, though it wasn't easy to grab it when my muscles were stiff and pain made me groan with the slightest bend. Now I was sure the painkillers had worn off completely and I could drive safely. Unfortunately, that meant I was in incredible pain. Life is trade-offs.

I couldn't twist in the driver's seat and bumped a support pillar backing the van out. But just like when I stood after lying in the bed, the longer I was behind the wheel, the better I felt.

All I could think about was Brian and getting to him.

CHAPTER 14

THE HOSPITAL IN Buffalo looked like any other hospital, and God knows I'd seen too many of them recently, but once I got inside it had a very different feel from a New York City facility. It was quiet, and security was lax. An elderly woman at the information desk told me Brian was in room 315.

I slipped up to the third floor with the intention of heading right to Brian's room. As I came down the hallway, a short man in uniform stood up from a plastic chair pushed against the wall. A true roadblock.

He held up a hand and said, "Where are you going?"

I muttered, "Room 315."

"Why?"

I tried to push past him. That's when I noticed that the patch on his shirt showed he was from the department of corrections. I understood his concern, so I said, "I'm Brian

Bennett's father." I thought that would settle the matter.

The lean little guy said, "No visitors."

"But—"

In a louder voice he said, "No visitors. Let me be clear. You cannot see him until he's secure in another state facility. Got it?"

I could feel the anger rise to my throat. Suddenly my back didn't hurt quite as much, my finger wasn't throbbing, and my head didn't feel like I'd been hit with a frying pan. Now the only thing I needed was to see my son. And this little jerk was standing in my way.

The DOC man said, "You can check on his status in a few days. But you need to leave before you're charged with trespassing." He gave me another look and said, "And you might want to shower first." He sniggered, looking over his shoulder at a uniformed Buffalo police officer. I noticed the SWAT tag under his badge. He was about my age and in good shape.

The cop gently took my right arm and guided me in the opposite direction, toward the elevator. I could tell he knew me. Someone had talked about the cop's kid who'd been stabbed while he was on the inside.

When I looked over my shoulder, all I could see was the smirk on the DOC man's face. He kept it until the elevator doors closed and blocked my view.

CHAPTER 15

AS SOON AS the elevator doors closed, the Buffalo cop said, "You don't know me, but I owe you big-time." He held out his hand and said, "I'm Jeff Hutcheon."

I shook his hand but didn't say anything. It had to be a mistake.

"The case you made a few years back. When the guys took the hostages at the First Lady's funeral and killed the mayor."

I'd never forget that case. It was Christmas. Maeve, my wife, died around that time. My life was in ruins, and that case haunted me. Until I figured out that prison guards from upstate had staged the whole event, with the help of an FBI agent. They'd played the NYPD like a cheap guitar.

Hutcheon said, "My cousin was one of the prison guards. The whole family was embarrassed. He's doing his time in a federal pen in California now. But I know that entire case forward and backward. I recognized your name as soon as that department of corrections prick started bragging about whose kid was being held. They hired us as extra security."

I said, "All I wanted to do was visit my son." My voice was still weak.

Hutcheon smiled and said, "And you're going to. I guarantee it."

Five minutes later, following the instructions the cop gave me, I stepped out of the elevator and back onto the third floor. The first thing I heard was raised voices. As I walked down the hallway, I saw that the cop who'd talked to me was leaning against the wall, holding the attention of the department of corrections man.

The cop said, "I'm telling you we're going to need more overtime for this detail, and you guys need to start paying up."

The DOC man sputtered, trying to explain that he didn't control the money. The cop leaned in closer and put his hand on the man's shoulder.

Standing in front of Brian's room was a second Buffalo officer, who motioned for me to step forward. As I walked past Hutcheon while he was berating the department of corrections man, he raised his eyes to me for a moment and winked.

A smile spread across my face. I needed the help right about now.

The cop by Brian's door patted me on the shoulder, then opened the door. I stepped into the room, where the TV played softly and gave me enough light to see Brian asleep in his bed.

I stepped forward and had to stifle a yelp. He had bandages wrapped around his face and forehead as well as his left arm. He looked like he belonged in the film *The Mummy*.

I took a seat right next to his bed and leaned in to get a better look. I didn't care what the State of New York said—he still looked like my little boy asleep in the bed. I could just see the rough edges of the stitches on his cheek at the edge of the gauze bandage.

It hurt me both physically and emotionally to see my oldest son like this. Since his arrest and conviction, I had lived in a half fog of worry. The DA wanted to make an example of a cop's kid who had made a mistake. The example haunted me every day.

As if sensing I was there, Brian turned his head, then opened his eyes. The smile he gave me made everything I'd gone through worthwhile.

I said in a low voice, "Surprised to see me?"

His voice was a little scratchy. "Not at all. I knew you'd come."

He reached across with his right hand and took hold of mine. I carefully leaned down and touched my forehead to his. I almost cried, but I didn't want to upset him.

After a few minutes of silence, Brian lowered the covers and lifted his gown to show me the two red stab wounds on his abdomen, covered by thin gauze. In total, he had gotten thirty-six stitches.

"I was scared, Dad. Really scared. It was two guys I barely knew. They passed me on the rec field and just started to slash and stab. It just happened that one of the corrections officers was standing nearby and was on the ball."

I tried to limit my professional questions, designed to figure out who did this and who ordered it. Brian explained that he didn't know much except they were both Mexicans who claimed to be part of a cartel. No one at Gowanda messed with them.

Brian told me again about the war between the Mexican cartel and the Canadian mob over territory. He'd warned me about the brewing feud when he first went to prison. He wondered if he was just caught in the middle.

Most people associated the word *mob* with Italians from New York, but the term applied to a lot of organizations. The Canadian mob was mostly made up of French Canadians who were loosely affiliated but banded together when threatened by outside groups.

Then Brian said, "But it doesn't matter what happened to me. I'm worried they might come after you or the family. It's all my fault. I brought all this on." He started to cry.

That made me cry. I tried to tell him not to worry about it, that it wasn't his fault, but I wasn't so sure. Maybe this was all related to retribution for his working in the drug business and my trying to ruin that business. I knew drug cartels could be ruthless.

I said, "Brian, you're not responsible for other people's actions. You're a good kid who made a mistake. I'll fix all this. I promise."

His eyes turned up toward me. "Really? Do you think you can?"

I squeezed his hand gently. I couldn't put into words how much it hurt to see my son like this. Not only the bandages but also the agony over what he had put the family through.

Being a father was so much harder than being a cop.

CHAPTER 16

ALEX MARTINEZ HAD done reconnaissance on NewYork–Presbyterian, attached to the campus of Columbia University. The hospital had a stellar reputation. If she thought the gunman would die of his wounds, she wouldn't bother to follow up. But chances were he'd survive the injury. And that meant he was a risk.

She had come to the hospital earlier to pay a visit to the main security room. She told the uniformed guard she'd lost her wallet, so he sent her to the lost and found department, in the empty administrative office—where the camera feeds were. She disconnected the main cable on the other side of the wall, counting on the fact that it would take an hour for someone to figure it out.

Now, in the late afternoon, no one seemed to notice her as she walked down a fifth-floor corridor, pushing a gurney.

She was dressed in billowing blue scrubs designed to hide her shape, and a blue surgical mask covered her face. The outfit would make a description more difficult later. She knew exactly what room the gunman was in and how many nurses were on duty. This was the slow time for the nurses. There were three on duty, and one of them was in the cafeteria on the first floor.

She'd waited until the other two were busy in patient rooms. This was her chance. Alex had a flutter of nerves. No amount of preparation could compensate for a freak coincidence.

She saw the corrections officer sitting on a folding chair in front of the gunman's door. He paid no attention as she came toward him with the gurney.

Alex did not take killing lightly. There had to be a clear reason and purpose behind taking a life. Usually that reason was money.

Her heart beat faster as she scanned the man for weapons. All he had was an ASP baton on his belt, but he was fit and muscular. She knew she'd have to act decisively.

Just as she started to squeeze past the uniformed corrections officer, he stood up to give her more room. She liked good manners.

He smiled and said, "Can you manage okay?" He made sure she got a good look at his biceps as he held up his hands to let her pass.

She nodded and said, "Aren't you nice." Alex noted his relaxed demeanor. Perfect.

When the gurney was past him and she was inches from the officer, she pulled a Taser from under the sheet on the gurney.

The guard stared at her for a moment, trying to make sense out of what he was seeing.

Alex jerked the trigger and fired the weapon before he had worked out what was in her hand. The two tiny darts that carried the charge lodged in his neck and chin. He tried to reach up, but the charge came too fast and too strong.

He made a short gurgling sound Alex could just hear over the crackle of the Taser, sending the electrical current coursing through his body.

After a moment, he dropped right across the gurney.

Alex calmly stepped forward and jabbed him in the neck with a hypodermic needle filled with a relatively small dose of ketamine. He'd be out for twenty minutes.

It was easy to push him the rest of the way onto the gurney. There were only a couple of pillows underneath the sheet.

Then she turned the handle to the gunman's room and was inside in an instant. The door banged open as she dragged the gurney into the room.

Alex glanced at her watch. Two minutes had gone by since she started pushing the empty gurney. She was well within her time frame. She took a breath to keep calm and centered, then turned toward the bed.

The Dominican gunman was about thirty and had both his arms strapped to the side of the bed. A plastic oxygen mask clung tightly to his face. He looked over, and, for a moment, appeared hopeful. He must've thought it was a rescue attempt.

She stepped across the room with another hypodermic needle in her hand. This one she had filled with a homemade concoction that included sedatives and cyanide. Fast and absolute. Like the judgment of God.

The gunman's eyes grew wide, but he didn't say a word.

Alex said, "I am very sorry to have to do this. I can't risk what you might say when you recover." She injected the solution into his IV bag.

The young man knew exactly what she was doing. He started to thrash in the bed and make a mewing sound underneath the oxygen mask. She watched the milky white substance quickly work its way through the tubes and into the man's arm.

Alex patted his forehead and brushed his hair with her fingers, trying to keep him calm. She softly said, "It's okay. Just calm down."

In less than a minute, he had stopped thrashing, lulled into a stupor, then his breathing stopped altogether.

On her way out of the room, Alex turned the corrections officer's head to make sure he had an open windpipe. He was breathing regularly, and his pulse was strong.

All in less than three and a half minutes.

CHAPTER 17

ALEX KEPT THE surgical mask on as she hurried out of the room. The corrections officer didn't move. She'd remember that dose of ketamine.

As Alex reached the end of the hallway, the elevator directly in front of her opened. She was surprised to see another uniformed corrections officer with a pistol in a holster on his hip.

This guy was taller and older than the corrections officer she had just dealt with. That might mean he had more experience and common sense. He smiled at her, then looked down the hallway.

She held her breath.

The corrections officer looked right at Alex and said, "Where's the officer who's supposed to be guarding that room?" He had a hint of annoyance in his voice.

Alex stayed very calm and said with authority, "He followed a doctor and the patient down to the CAT scan room."

She stayed right in front of him, hoping he bought her story. She casually reached behind her back and gripped the Taser, tucked into the pants she was wearing beneath the surgical scrubs. It would be a little messy to Taser this officer right in front of the elevator. But she'd do it.

Then she had an idea.

Alex said, "Come with me, and I'll show you exactly where they went." She waited for his response. If he hesitated too long, she would just use her Taser. It was either that or her stiletto into his brain. She didn't really want to spend the time on either option.

The corrections officer said, "They should've told me. But okay, I guess it's no big deal if I meet them in the CAT scan room."

She stepped onto the elevator with him.

He wasted no time in asking, "What's your name?"

She was ready to answer. "Nancy Gorant." Her reconnaissance had included finding a nurse that was about her height with similar hair. It would muddy the waters later.

"How long have you worked here, Nancy?"

Alex knew to say, "A little over four years."

When the elevator opened on the main floor, she pointed in the opposite direction from where she was headed and told the officer, "The CAT scan room is all the way down this hallway, then take a left and go to the end of that hallway. You should see it on your right at the very end."

Alex watched him walk away in the direction she had pointed. Her plan had worked.

She left her mask on and exited by the main door. No one would get a clear view of her face.

They wouldn't be able to see the smile underneath the surgical mask as the feeling of satisfaction swept over her.

CHAPTER 18

RETURNING HOME WAS trickier than I expected. I was greeted by the combined force of Mary Catherine's and my grandfather's anger over my foolish idea to drive all the way to Buffalo while I was still recovering.

The doctor was mildly annoyed, but she seemed like a doctor used to dealing with stubborn cops.

It was all worth it to see Brian and ease my mind. Even if only temporarily.

Now I was ready to spend an extra couple of days with the family, who seemed to like having me around during the day.

Chrissy, the youngest, still liked to lay her head on my lap while I read to her or she watched TV. Shawna, a year older, was content to just hang near me. I liked that.

Trent and Eddie tested my ability to play rough. They quickly realized I was more fragile than usual when a stitched wound on my stomach started to leak blood. The wrestling match ended quickly, but I appreciated that my boys still enjoyed roughhousing with me.

The twins, Fiona and Bridget, were involved in a project on the dining-room table. It was some kind of quilt that Bridget had started, but she had quickly gotten in over her head. Mary Catherine rescued her and recruited Fiona to help her finish.

Ricky enjoyed making me special lunches that always had a decidedly Cajun flair. For a kid who'd been raised in New York City, Ricky knew his way around jambalaya and gumbo. If you would've told me one of my kids would get upset because he couldn't find fresh okra in the city, I would have thought you were crazy.

But I had slowly reconciled myself to the fact that both Jane and Juliana, my pretty teenage girls, had their own lives. All I asked was that they remain good students and study during the week so that they would have time to go out on weekends.

Juliana had been sitting quietly in the recliner at the end of the couch, petting our cat, Socky. I could sense that she was waiting for a chance to talk with me without an extra set of ears around.

Her long dark hair twisted over her shoulder and made me realize just how beautiful she was. When we adopted her, she was only two months old, and even when she was just a toddler, her bright brown eyes and brilliant smile always lit up a room when she walked in.

I stood up, gently nudging Chrissy to the side. I said to her and Shawna, "You can watch TV for thirty minutes."

Chrissy's eyes lit up. "Anything we want?"

"Within reason. If you're going to go off our usual routine of TLC or public TV, try sticking to a cartoon or something that won't make you stay up at night." I knew that would be enough to hold these two in place.

I caught Juliana's eye and motioned her out to the balcony.

It felt good to step out into the fresh air. The wound on my head was healing, and the cool breeze on my face made it feel better. I wrapped an arm around Juliana. Holding my daughter near reminded me of her mother.

Maeve had built this family. There was no way I would ever let it fall apart.

I started the conversation. "I know you want to talk to me about your TV job. And I want to say how proud I am of you and how lucky that producer is for having found you."

Her smile was enough reward for holding back my five hundred questions. She wrapped an arm around me and gave me a quick hug.

Juliana said, "Thanks, Dad. With everything that's going on I was worried what you thought about it."

"I heard about your audition. They picked you out of two hundred young actresses."

"I did the audition on a whim. I couldn't believe they picked me. All the filming will be in Brooklyn, and it won't interfere with school in any way."

"You know I'm going to be visiting the set, right?"

"Come on, Dad. It's not like I'm a baby."

"You're *my* baby."

"So I'll be the only member of the cast who has a chaperone?"

"I don't know about that."

She looked at me, thinking I meant I wouldn't be visiting the set. Instead I said, "Maybe other cast members will have chaperones as well."

You can't always be the fun dad.

CHAPTER 19

NO MATTER HOW annoyed my children might be with me, it was a rule that we eat dinner together as a family every night. We were lucky to have an excellent chef in Mary Catherine, and recently she had been assisted by Ricky.

Tonight Ricky had shown her how to make a lovely lasagna. I could tell who had made the dinner before they said anything. Mary Catherine focused on meat and potatoes, reflecting her Irish upbringing, while Ricky was developing a talent for seasonings. It was a miracle that I didn't weigh six hundred pounds.

The other family tradition was my grandfather's grace before every meal. He had a knack for hitting just the right tone and subject. He spent his days as an administrator at Holy Name, but occasionally he would deliver a sermon, and there were few priests who could match him—though I would never flatter him by saying so.

We all joined hands around the long table, which held an empty chair for Brian. He would stay in Buffalo for at least another few weeks, and I planned to visit regularly.

Seamus started the prayer. "Dear Heavenly Father, thank you for this wonderful meal. Thank you for letting us all be here together. Thank you for looking after Michael on his dangerous job and safely bringing him back to us once again.

"Please protect our Brian as he recovers from his injuries. And dear Lord, please look after our beautiful Juliana on her grand adventure."

Everyone mumbled, "Amen."

When I raised my eyes, I saw that Juliana was smiling broadly at her great-grandfather. When you're one of ten children, any extra attention is a big deal.

When she looked across to me, her face returned to a scowl. I understood that. Someone had to be the tough guy.

Sitting next to Juliana, her sister Jane had her back and gave me a similar look. Why not? Whatever they could talk me into letting Juliana do, Jane would be able to get away with soon as well.

At least the acting gig was scheduled around her school and counted toward a course in acting.

I avoided the silent confrontation by looking at Seamus and saying, "Anything big going on at Holy Name? Have to perform any exorcisms? Anything unusual?"

Being a subversive himself, Seamus rarely reacted when I prodded him. As he had often told me, I was a good person, if not necessarily always a good Catholic. That was the important thing.

He said, "Now that you mention it, I do have a new assignment along with all my other duties."

Mary Catherine said, "What's that?"

Seamus said, "I'm mentoring a new priest at the church. He was transferred from Bogotá, Colombia. He's green, but he has some interesting ideas about handling the kids. And I like being able to shape people's attitudes when they're new to the priesthood."

He looked across the table as if challenging me to comment. I refrained from saying how much he liked shaping people's attitudes about everything.

CHAPTER 20

ALEX MARTINEZ WAS tired of wasting time on the cop. These big jobs with multiple hits could be draining. She didn't like juggling hits like this, but she was in it for the money, and this job paid well.

Taking a break from Bennett, she focused on another hit. One of the Canadians she'd been hired to deal with was back in town. She'd spent the day understanding where he went and what he liked to do. There wasn't much planning to this particular job.

Alain Coush was a young French Canadian in his early thirties who lived just outside Quebec. During the day he wore shorts and sleeveless T-shirts, obviously trying to show off what weights and a decent amount of steroids had done for him.

But now, out on the town for the evening, he looked more

like a character out of a 1980s comedy. His shirt was open at least three buttons, and he wore several thick gold chains. He didn't appear to be as interested in his job as she was in hers. If he really had been brought to New York to scare some of the Mexican cartel members, Alex would've expected him to do some surveillance of his own. Instead he just looked like he was trying to meet women.

She hated a poor work ethic.

He had driven a rented Ford Mustang from the hotel across town to this Irish pub almost two hours earlier. Alex had watched him park two blocks away and followed him at a discreet distance to the pub.

As she passed his car, with her target more than a block ahead, she casually stuck a toothpick in the driver's-side door lock, then broke it off.

She entered the pub about ten minutes after he did.

Again, she was not impressed with his work ethic or his self-preservation skills. He sat down with a group of his friends and started drinking dark ale and eating potato skins and fried chicken wings. It was a happy bunch, and no one noticed her sitting by herself at the end of the bar, pretending to be engrossed in her phone.

When she sensed that the party was about to break up, she slipped out the door a few minutes before he did. She knew where he was headed. She was good at her job. Even if he wasn't.

She had uncovered a few rumors about the burly Alain. He was known to be a little rough and crude with his victims. He didn't seem to care if they were male or female. He was the kind of guy who may have enjoyed his work a little too much. There was no art in it for him.

Alex watched him come down the street, then casually fell in behind him. Everything was in position. Even the street was empty of pedestrians. That was the sort of thing you couldn't plan for. She just needed him to hold still for about three seconds, then she could do what she needed to do.

It felt good to be active, not worrying about what happened to the cop, Bennett. No matter what happened tonight, she had a flight booked for Colombia in the morning. She needed to get home to her ranch and people she could trust. She could always come back later and finish up the rest of her contracts with the cartel.

She reached into her purse and felt the small Kahr 9mm pistol. It was either that or a stiletto on jobs like this. It depended on the target. This guy was tough, and a gun was the safer choice.

The French Canadian was almost to his Mustang. She kept walking at a normal pace as he came up to his car and tried to insert the key into the driver's-side lock.

Breaking off a toothpick in a lock was an effective old trick.

It drew all his attention and held him in place. Alex heard him curse under his breath as he tried to force the key into the lock.

When he glanced up and saw her standing there, he still wasn't alarmed. Idiot.

He gave her a smile and said, "Hello there."

She could barely make out his accent as he spoke in English. "Hello yourself."

"Aren't you the pretty one."

Alex knew those were the last words he'd ever utter. She silently raised the pistol and sighted down the barrel. The two

9mm rounds slipped through the barrel and silencer with just a popping sound. Both rounds hit her target in the face, and he dropped to the sidewalk without a sound.

She walked past him, glancing down to make sure the shots were as devastating as she thought. Blood leaked out of the two holes in the Canadian's face on the sidewalk. One was in his cheek, and one was just above his left eye.

She took a quick photograph as proof that he was dead and was on her way. One more contract closed, and now she could think about how she would get to the airport in the morning.

Those were the kinds of problems she liked.

CHAPTER 21

I HAD TO make myself useful if I was just going to be around the house, so I let Mary Catherine sleep in and managed to feed all the children and get them to Holy Name on time. Even the principal, Sister Sheilah, seemed to be happy with my performance. Believe me, that had not happened often in my life. I sometimes had the feeling that I was her white whale. The one that had gotten away. She had tried to break me as a child, and sometimes it felt like she was trying to break me as an adult.

But the kids liked her. Sure, she was tough and a disciplinarian, but there was something about the way she made things run and how she treated the kids that made her almost lovable to them. The conspiracy theorist in me made me think it was just another way to get to me. Make my kids love her so that it annoyed me. My grandfather was the only one I liked to share those theories with.

So I decided I would. I pulled my giant Ford van around the block and parked in front of the church's administration building.

As soon as I stepped in the door, a priest I didn't recognize greeted me and said, "How may I help you?"

He looked to be a few years older than I was and in excellent shape. I detected a slight accent and looked past him to find my grandfather. I said, "I'm Michael Bennett, Seamus's grandson."

A smile spread across the priest's face as he said, "The detective with an army of children."

"That's me."

"I'm Alonzo Garcia. I'm the new priest here."

"*You're* the priest Seamus is mentoring?"

"The very same."

I blurted out, "But you're..." I managed not to say the word *old* aloud.

A smile spread across his face as he said, "Much more handsome than you expected?"

We both laughed.

Father Alonzo said, "I'm new to the priesthood. The church thought a man like your grandfather, who had a similar experience, might be of some use."

"You owned a bar, too?"

He chuckled. "Hardly."

I was hoping for some elaboration, but I let it go. For now.

I followed the priest back into the spacious offices, which had boxes stuffed in every corner. He picked up a cup of hot tea he had been brewing and set it on the desk in front of Seamus.

My grandfather said, "I see you two have met." He coughed, then blew his nose.

Father Alonzo put a plate with a sliced orange on it in front of my grandfather before he could say anything. I liked that.

We'd all been worried about Seamus's health in the past few months. He had lost weight since his heart attack, and he tended not to look after the details of his life, such as needing to drink enough fluids and eat enough fruit.

We all chatted for a few minutes, and Father Alonzo invited me out to the athletic fields to look at the soccer game going on in the back. He was clearly proud of teaching some of the students at Holy Name new ways to approach the most popular team sport in the world.

As soon as we were outside, he turned to me and said, "Your grandfather can be quite a stubborn man."

I let out a snort. "No"—then I remembered who I was talking to—"kidding."

Father Alonzo said, "He stays up too late, doesn't get any rest during the day, and doesn't eat nearly as much as he needs to."

Now we were talking as we circled the soccer field. My grandfather had come out separately from us and was on the sideline.

It was a spirited and competitive game. I was impressed. I had seen a lack of enthusiasm about soccer for years here at the school.

Two boys, about ten, got into a shoving match after a ball had rolled out-of-bounds. I was impressed with Alonzo's casual intervention as he sent one boy running to the goal and the other to the opposite side of the field.

Then my grandfather shouted after them in Spanish. I had never heard him speak any Spanish before, despite the fact that almost a third of the students were Hispanic.

Seamus looked at me and smiled. "I showed Alonzo some of the important aspects of leading a flock, and he's been teaching me Spanish. It seems to be working out well for both of us."

I had to agree.

CHAPTER 22

TWO DAYS LATER, at exactly nine in the morning, I entered the office building that housed Manhattan North Homicide. It was on Broadway near 133rd Street, across the street from an elevated number 1 train. There was nothing to indicate that the building, owned by Columbia University, housed specialized units of the New York City Police Department, including Homicide and Intel.

We sometimes joked that Intelligence was where the really smart cops went—smart enough to go there so they wouldn't get in fights or be shot at.

The unit was so good at its job that it often gave a heads-up to the feds about changing crime trends or specific threats. Of course, that was something the FBI would never admit.

I still felt tired and moved a little slowly. This was what I needed. I had to get back into the rhythm of life.

It took almost twenty minutes to reach my office, on the seventh floor. I was greeted by everyone from the building maintenance man to the inspector, who kept his office there. A quick word and handshake or just a pat on the back made me feel comfortable, happy to be back.

An officer-involved shooting touches all cops. A fallen cop reminds each of us of our mortality and that being a cop is more than just a job. I understood it was hard for the public to comprehend something like that. Most people didn't have jobs that occasionally involved someone trying to murder them.

I couldn't help but look over at Antrole's empty desk. No one had touched anything. Photographs of his family still sat on the corner. It wouldn't surprise me if no one moved them for months. No one is too eager to move on after a cop dies in the line of duty.

The public information office of the NYPD had released Antrole's name to the media. I was simply listed as "another detective who sustained injuries." I was good with that.

I was also good with the fact that I had returned to work. Being busy kept my mind off things. It also made me feel like I could make a difference in the world. At least in New York City.

I hadn't been at my desk five minutes when Harry Grissom stopped by to say hello, then asked me to follow him into his office. He closed the door behind us, then leaned on the edge of his desk when I took the chair in front of it. I had learned over the years that this was a sign he was worried about me. If he was mad, he'd sit in his chair behind the desk. But when he was concerned about a detective's state of mind, he thought leaning on a desk made the meeting feel more personal.

He said, "You didn't have to rush back to work."

"I was out long enough. I feel fine. I got my head on straight. You don't need to worry about that."

The lanky lieutenant just stared at me. He was hard to read. I was glad we never played poker. Finally he said, "I want you to ease back into operations. Don't take on any specific cases. Take a good look at all the homicides in Manhattan and the Bronx. See if you can find any important patterns. That's the sort of thing we should do more of."

I was able to suppress a smile. My lieutenant, the senior officer in my unit, was breaking the rules without saying it overtly. He was allowing me to look into the ambush that killed my partner by trying to find out if it was connected to any other homicides. He didn't say it. He couldn't. But he was giving me leeway to work in both Manhattan and the Bronx.

Because a cop was involved in the shooting, Internal Affairs was working with Homicide on the case. They wouldn't want me anywhere near it. I was a witness and was too close to Antrole to ever officially be allowed to directly investigate the ambush.

I took my new mandate seriously and quickly gathered all the information I could on every homicide for the past three months. Most of them would be considered "usual." A domestic that ended with the wife stabbing the husband. An armed robbery of a jewelry store where the robber panicked and shot the sixty-eight-year-old wife of the owner. The usual series of drug killings. Nevertheless, there were a few that caught my eye.

The first, of course, was the killing of the Dominican gunman who had survived our ambush. He was in the hospital and expected to make it. The cop on duty said someone Tasered him, then he was immobilized with a heavy dose of tranquilizer.

The details on the killer were sparse. The cop thought it was a female but couldn't swear to it because he never saw her face. It could've been a short man. The baggy surgical scrubs and his foggy memory from the tranquilizer didn't help with his description.

I also noted that someone had disabled the video surveillance at the hospital. That was not the sign of a rash and hasty killer.

CHAPTER 23

IN THE AFTERNOON, I drove south to Brooklyn. It wasn't until I was across the Brooklyn Bridge that I realized how rarely I came into this borough. The place had really seen a renaissance in recent years. This was where all the hot new restaurants were opening, and it was continuing the slow process of attracting TV and film studios. There were soundstages and great locations all over the area.

Here in Brooklyn Heights, there were only a couple of the kinds of warehouses a movie studio would use. The area didn't compare to Red Hook or Gowanus, where there were plenty of warehouses that attracted trendy new businesses.

I found the address that Juliana had given me and paused outside for just a minute. This didn't look like an elaborate modern soundstage. It was an old warehouse in Brooklyn Heights.

No one greeted me as I entered the front door, and no one tried to keep me from walking through the corridors. I could see activity in the main room. As I walked back, a man carrying a long boom microphone nodded hello.

"Am I headed the right way to the set of *Century's End?*"

The chubby man hooked his hand and pointed his thumb toward the main room.

I thanked him and kept walking. It may have been a small crew, and there may have been no security, but the set was impressive. It looked like a popular nightclub from the nineties, with a dance floor and wraparound bar.

No one was filming, and most people were just milling around the set. Juliana had told me it was a drama about young people in New York during the 1990s. I wasn't sure I wanted my daughter pretending to be someone on the bar scene in the nineties. I was a young person in New York at the time. It may have been fun, but it's not what you want to think about your kids doing.

I heard the familiar squeal of "Dad." It was an excited sound, and she was happy to see me, despite her objections to a visit. I turned with my arms open to give her a hug.

As she jumped up to hug me, I caught a quick glimpse of her costume. A low-cut cocktail dress. Really low-cut. I didn't know how to react. I didn't want to make her self-conscious. Unthinkingly I slipped off my sport coat and draped it over her shoulders. She frowned at me but kept it there.

Part of me knew that I wanted everyone to see my gun and badge clearly. Sometimes it helps as a father if you're big and everyone knows you're a cop.

I said, "You said you'd be finishing up soon, so I thought I might give you a ride back home. Save you the effort of riding on the subway."

Juliana said, "Thanks, Dad." She took a moment to introduce me to the director. He was a little older than I was and couldn't have cared less that there was a visitor on the set. He gave me a bored nod and told Juliana to be back on set tomorrow.

As we walked off the set, I was already thinking of how I would ask Mary Catherine to come by and hang out during the filming. It was the only way I would ever get some peace.

CHAPTER 24

THE NEXT DAY, I sat at my desk and looked at several cases that had caught my attention. My review of homicides in Manhattan and the Bronx included the murders of two Canadian tourists.

One had occurred before the ambush and one just after. At first glance the two cases seemed unconnected, until you noticed that both men had criminal records for narcotics trafficking in Canada.

That fell in line with what Brian had told me earlier about the Mexican cartel battling with a Canadian group for control of the synthetic drug market in the northeastern United States. Other sources had said the same thing.

The first homicide had occurred near Times Square, and the victim was described as a "tourist." My research told me he was a moneyman for the Canadian mob. He'd been stabbed once through the heart. According to the medical examiner's report, the wound was caused by a straight four-inch blade. The word that stuck in my head was *stiletto*. No one in forensics had ever used that term. They used clinical terms like *blade* and *instrument*.

I talked to the detective handling the case. I remembered him from other cases. Nice fella, but maybe not as driven as most homicide detectives.

When I got him on the phone he said, "That was a nasty one. Coroner said she thinks the perp was a male between five seven and five ten."

"How did she come up with that?"

"The angle of the strike along with the power behind it. She thinks it was someone who really knew how to use a knife or a sharpened spike."

Again I thought, *Stiletto.*

I said, "You got anything about the victim or motive?"

"Yeah. The victim was just a tourist from outside Toronto. I figure he was a robbery victim."

"Did you see his criminal history?"

"I did—so what?" He was annoyed that someone else was snooping into his case.

"Don't you think that could've played a role in the murder?"

The detective said, "No. He was the victim, not the suspect."

I let it go. Then I said, "According to the report, he still had his wallet and money on him when the body was found."

"Yeah—so?"

"What kind of robber goes to the trouble of killing you but doesn't bother taking your money?"

"The kind who gets spooked by something or didn't mean to kill the victim."

"How could being stabbed in the heart be an accident?"

"I don't know. I'll tell you when we catch the robber."

I knew I wouldn't get much useful information from this guy.

The second homicide occurred a few blocks from Bryant Park. The victim was a known enforcer for the Canadian mob named Alain Coush, and he had just left an Irish pub. He'd been shot twice in the face. There were no witnesses and no leads.

I knew the detective on that case well. Her name was Cassandra Max, known as Cassie to her friends and Maximum Cass to anyone who got on the wrong side of her. She was as intelligent and hardworking as anyone—a rising star and considered one of the sharpest homicide investigators in the city. Her ability to speak Spanish and Creole, which she learned from her parents, made her even more valuable. When I met with her, she said, "We got nothing, but I'm still canvassing the area and seeing if we can find any security video." She flipped open a notebook. "I'd say it was a professional. Someone jammed a toothpick in the car's lock. Looks like when the victim tried to open the door the killer stepped up and shot him."

I liked that no-bullshit attitude and work ethic. I'd stay in close contact with her because something would get done on this case.

But even if these murders were part of a pattern—how did they fit in with the ambush that killed Antrole or the attack on Brian?

CHAPTER 25

AFTER MY DAY of research and reading hundreds of reports, I decided to stop by Holy Name to check on my grandfather.

As soon as I walked into the office, I could hear Seamus and his new friend, Father Alonzo, debating one of the deep philosophical questions of our day: whether American football or soccer is more entertaining.

My grandfather smiled when he saw me and motioned me to the seat in front of his desk. He said, "You look troubled, my boy. What's the problem?"

"Just busy at work. I've been looking at a couple of murders connected to the drug trade. No one understands that research can be as tiring as walking a beat."

Seamus said, "Can you tell us about the cases?"

I gave them a quick rundown about the two Canadians and

how they were killed. I left out some of the gruesome details, but they got the gist. I finished, "So it might be a long shot, but I'm working out if there's any connection to the ambush on Antrole and me. I have this feeling that all this violence is connected, including the attack on Brian."

I was surprised when Father Alonzo leaned forward.

He said, "I don't mean to intrude on business that does not involve me, but I have seen things like this before."

"Where have you seen murders like this?"

"Colombia. It makes Chicago seem tame." He paused, then asked, "The murder that did not involve a gun. Was it a single blow with some kind of a knife? Perhaps to the heart, or under the chin into the brain?"

That caught me by surprise. "Yes. A single blow to the heart."

"And the gunshot murder appeared to be well planned? Perhaps some kind of distraction was used?"

Now I was stunned. "Yes. It appears the killer broke off a toothpick in the victim's car door lock. The theory is it gave the killer enough time to stop and aim carefully." Alonzo nodded. I continued, "But I can't tie either of those murders directly to the ambush. There's nothing about either murder that lines up with the attack that killed my partner."

Father Alonzo said, "It's very common for Colombian contract killers to hire local muscle in certain situations. Especially if the killer is from out of town. And I know many hit men that use a sharpened stiletto whenever they can. It goes back to training they received in Bogotá by one particular martial-arts instructor. Many wannabe cartel members trained there over the years. It was a badge of honor to say that was where you obtained some of your skills. Even some police trained there."

I said, "That's excellent insight, Father Alonzo. Do you have any other surprises?"

"I'm sorry. I have been completely involved in the Church for some time now. Aside from the occasional racy confession, I am completely cut off from any kind of outside vice or violence. But if you need a soccer coach, I'm your man."

"And I'm sure you don't want to share how you know any of these kinds of details."

"Just observant. Hoping to help."

It was clear he was going to leave it at that.

I kept my eyes on the fit fortysomething priest with my best police stare. His brown eyes didn't leave mine.

When I had more time, I had to find out how this affable priest knew so much about the drug trade.

CHAPTER 26

IT'S HARD TO be anything but grateful when a woman like Mary Catherine greets you at the door after a long day. She gave me a kiss that would've been longer if Chrissy and Shawna hadn't run up, chattering like monkeys, waiting for their father to pick them up.

I appreciated the enthusiasm and bundled both girls over my shoulder as I started to march through the apartment, greeting the older children as I went. I was impressed that Jane, Ricky, and Eddie were all studying in the dining room. Books and papers were spread across the table, and all I got was a cursory nod as each of them looked up.

Bridget and Fiona were practicing some sort of stretching routine on the floor of the living room. A PBS yoga person from the nineties was giving slow, deliberate instruction on TV.

A few minutes after I got home, Juliana practically skipped

through the front door. Her excitement was contagious. It immediately drew Jane away from her studies.

My oldest daughter squealed, "I got it. I got it."

When I looked over, I saw that she was holding something in her hand. It looked like a credit card, but I couldn't tell what kind.

I dropped the little girls onto the couch and followed Mary Catherine to Juliana. She held up the card in front of me and said, "I'm official. I got my SAG card. You only get that when you're a professional actress."

This was exciting news. When she held the card in front of me, I had to stare for a minute. All I could say was, "Who is Jules Baez?"

Juliana gave me a sly smile and said, "That's my stage name. No two stage names can be the same."

Mary Catherine said, "There was another Juliana Bennett?"

"No. I just felt this was more unique. The director helped me figure it out. He said it gave me more of an edge."

I had to ask, "Why do you need an edge?"

"Jules Baez just sounds *edgier*. It's subtle, Dad. You need to be in the industry to understand things like this."

I was about to respond when I felt Mary Catherine's hand on my shoulder. She had a way of gently calming me down and distracting me.

We let Juliana hurry into the dining room as all the kids gathered to see her fantastic new Screen Actors Guild identification card.

Mary Catherine eased me back into the living room and said, "She's excited. Let her have her moment. I know you're uncomfortable with her using a different name and wanting to be edgier, but you have to remember who she is. She's a good girl who has never given you any problems. We need to trust her judgment. At least in something like this."

I nodded. My fiancée had an outstanding connection to the kids. She read them as well as any parent I had ever seen. I'd be an idiot not to listen to her.

After dinner, the kids settled back into their studying routine. I was happy to see that Juliana had joined her younger brothers and sister at the dining-room table. Wearing her glasses, focused on algebra, she was my girl again, and I felt a wave of relief.

I joined Mary Catherine on the balcony, and we looked out toward the river. She leaned her head against my shoulder and said, "I hope you realize what a good dad you are."

I thought about Brian. "I've made some mistakes."

"Isn't that what we humans are supposed to do?"

She never failed to make me feel better when I was a little troubled. I kissed her on the top of her head and said, "Have you given any thought to a date for our wedding?"

She turned and gave me a smile. Then there was a squeal inside the apartment. Nothing out of the ordinary, just the usual sounds of kids.

Mary Catherine turned from the railing and said, "What on earth?" Then she hurried inside without answering my question. I took a few moments to be alone on the balcony.

CHAPTER 27

ALEX MARTINEZ DROVE her Chevy Silverado pickup truck from the parking garage near the El Dorado airport, in the northern section of Bogotá, all the way to her ranch outside the smaller town of Melgar, about two and a half hours to the southwest.

She could smell some of the animals at the Zoológico Cafam Melgar as she passed by. The simple municipal zoo carried a much different odor from her ranch. She attributed some of the smell to the presence of primates. Whereas she appreciated the smell of a horse, a primate was just a little too close to human.

Alex could barely contain the excitement she felt about returning home. All the major cities—New York, Paris, Mexico City—were just too crowded. The more time she spent in these places, the less human she felt.

The front gate to the ranch was open. They were expecting her.

She waved from the truck without slowing down as the families in the first two houses stepped outside to wave to her. She found a way to employ both husbands and both wives as well as provide an education for all six of the children. Sometimes it wasn't easy.

A mile later, she slowed down in front of the main house. She could see the broad shape of her housekeeper, Maria, and her rail-thin husband, who handled all the maintenance around the house. Right next to them were the two people she really wanted to see.

She slipped out of the pickup truck, and her feet had not even touched the ground when tiny arms wrapped around her waist to give her a hug. She dropped to her knees to embrace both her daughters at once.

Clemency was six and liked to conduct herself with some dignity. Her neatly brushed hair hung straight back, as usual. Her little sister, Gabriela, who was just turning four, had her usual disheveled look, which warmed the heart of every adult she met.

Alex just took a moment and got lost in the emotion of her two girls hugging her. Every time she left, she felt she had been gone too long.

She walked toward the house with a girl hanging on to each hand. She wanted to hear everything that had happened and all that they had learned.

Maria embraced Alex and kissed her on the cheek as if she were her own daughter. Maria's husband gave a stately bow. The older man had spent many years in the military before being forced out under suspicion of being associated with a drug cartel. She'd asked him about it once. He'd laughed and said, "If I worked with a drug cartel, would I be fixing your toilets now?"

The other six men and women, who worked in the stables near the house, kept their distance but gave Alex a polite wave. She was home, and she felt it. She didn't think anything could dampen her mood.

As soon as Alex was inside and the girls were dutifully running one of her bags into her bedroom, she felt her phone vibrate. When she looked down at the text message, she immediately recognized the number. It was her contact with the Mexican drug cartel.

The text message was simple and to the point: Michael Bennett is alive.

CHAPTER 28

ALEX MARTINEZ UNDERSTOOD how much she missed her daughters when she was away. Today she was getting an idea of how much Gabriela and Clemency had missed *her*.

They were ready to ride, each in her own style.

Clemency wore everything perfectly. English riding boots halfway up her calves, her riding pants tucked neatly into the boots. And Gabriela looked just like an outlaw from a 1950s movie. Right down to the red bandanna tied around her neck. Her wild dark hair poked out from underneath the tiny Stetson.

Alex helped the girls saddle their own horses. She wanted them to be self-sufficient as well as understand how to keep the horses calm and healthy. She showed Gabriela the proper way to ease the bit into the horse's mouth. The little girl focused on the lesson completely.

Clemency lately had favored a colt named Samuel. Alex didn't think her daughter got the joke that someone had named the horse after the famous gun manufacturer Samuel Colt.

Gabriela had recently been riding a pony named Biscuit. Alex could see why. The little horse had a wild mane and was full of energy. They were made for each other.

When Alex was growing up, her British riding instructor had always referred to horses like Biscuit as a Welsh cob. That was not a term you heard frequently in Colombia. Out of respect for the man who was very important during her formative years, Alex still called Biscuit a Welsh cob.

As much as she relaxed at times like this, she always stayed aware of her surroundings, conscious of how many enemies an assassin makes during his or her career. Her 9mm Beretta hung in a bag from her saddle, always within easy reach. One of the habits she had picked up since she stumbled into her profession as a young college grad.

The girls' father, Rafael, never agreed with her choice of jobs. That might have helped push him out the door to shack up with a cruise-ship dancer. The girls got postcards from all over the world now but rarely saw their shiftless father, who lived off a trust fund.

Gabriela giggled, which made Alex twist in the saddle to see what her daughter found so amusing.

Biscuit was sniffing the hindquarters of Clemency's colt, Samuel.

Alex looked ahead again to hide her smile.

Clemency trotted up, then had to fight to control Samuel.

Alex said, "You're doing great, Clemmy, but think of you

and Samuel as one. You're part of him, and he's part of you. Let him feel your confidence."

Clemency nodded and immediately tried a quick turn and sprint, her long, dark ponytail flowing behind her.

Now Gabriela caught up to her mother.

"How am I doing, Mama?"

"Wonderful, baby. You and Biscuit are perfect together."

Alex was distracted by another rider coming from the direction of the ranch. She tensed and unbuckled the pouch holding her pistol.

Then she recognized the rider and called out, "Manny."

Her slim thirty-three-year-old cousin smiled as he approached.

Alex leaned over and kissed him.

He said, "You look beautiful, as always."

The girls both raced up to greet her cousin, whom they called Uncle Manny.

Manny said, "I propose a race. Your mama and me, to the far hill and back. You two will be the referees in case she tries anything funny."

Alex didn't wait for a signal. She urged Mitzi into a full gallop, and Manny fell in behind her immediately.

Manny rode a gelding from her stable named Reynaldo. The horse was big, more than fifteen hands high, but he had a smooth gait.

Alex looked ahead slightly, avoiding gopher holes and other dangers to a galloping horse. She urged Mitzi on with a nudge from her feet. She'd never used a whip or spurs in her whole life.

Manny matched her step for step, kicking Reynaldo harder, but nothing more.

Reynaldo had the stride, but Alex had the experience.

Alex circled the oak tree at the crest of the hill. She looked up to see the girls cheering about four hundred meters ahead. Sweat was dripping into her eyes, and she felt her legs tiring under the stress of riding and standing up slightly in the stirrups.

Alex hated to lose. Especially to her cousin Manny.

Alex smiled at the girls' squeals as she crossed the finish line ahead of Manny.

They both eased the horses to a trot, then returned to the giddy girls.

Manny said, "Once again, your beautiful mother has demonstrated to you that women can compete with men anywhere."

Alex beamed at the victory and the girls' excitement.

After a few minutes, they sent the girls ahead so they could talk about their shared profession.

Alex said, "Any interesting jobs coming up?"

Manny shook his head. "I'm taking a break. I was almost caught by the Brazilian national police after I completed a contract in Rio. Some oil company executive hired me to deal with one of his rivals. The job itself wasn't that hard, but any time you take a contract not related to the drug business, the police tend to take notice. I barely made it back here without having to explain why I put two bullets in the back of the man's head."

Manny looked at her. No humor in his tone. "I've heard about your New York contracts. People in the United States don't like it when cops are killed. It's not like Mexico, where a payoff will keep people quiet. In the States they'll do everything they can to find you. You've got the girls. This ranch. All those people you take care of. I've only got me."

"And your mother."

"Okay, but no children."

Alex sighed. "What can you do? It's the business. I'd prefer to stay here with the girls."

"I would prefer that as well. Let *me* finish the contract."

She laughed. "Always trying to protect me. I appreciate it, Manny, but I can complete any contract you can. Besides, there are still a couple of Canadians in New York I need to deal with as well."

"When do you leave?"

Alex said, "Tomorrow I'm meeting with my liaison to the cartel. I'll see what he has to say before I make any decisions."

Manny laughed and said, "That is so you. No decision, no matter how small, is ever taken lightly. I wish I had your discipline."

Alex sighed. "No, you don't."

CHAPTER 29

I GOT HOME in the evening just before dinner. I was beat. I guess I wasn't as fully recovered as I thought. Just like everyone from Mary Catherine to the doctors had told me. And oddly, I still had a hard time admitting I was stubborn.

The younger kids each darted into the hallway to greet me, as they always did. I doled out hugs and kisses that immediately wiped away my exhaustion. The older kids gave me courtesy nods, and Ricky even said, "Hey, Dad."

Dinner smelled like a traditional Irish roast with maybe a splash of spices from Ricky.

As I stepped into the dining room, ready to greet Mary Catherine, I was surprised to see the athletic form of Father Alonzo helping to move some glasses into the living room.

"Hello, Michael. I hope you don't mind that your grandfather brought me along for dinner."

"No, of course not. In a family this size one more person is barely noticed."

Just then, Chrissy ran up with our cat in her arms.

"Something's wrong with Socky."

I took a closer look. "What do you mean, sweetheart?"

Shawna and Trent joined the medical consultation.

Chrissy was hesitant.

I asked, "What is it?"

"It's Socky's...um...uh...butt."

I checked, and sure enough, there was a piece of string poking out slightly. I leaped into action. I looked at Trent and said in a mock official tone, "Find me an open operating table with newspaper covering it."

My son sprang to attention and called, "Yes, sir." He gave me a quick smile and wink.

Trent led me into the living room, where he had cleared the coffee table and spread newspaper over it. He helped me hold Socky, who seemed to like the attention, as I conducted a thorough examination.

Eddie joined us out of curiosity as the girls knelt down to comfort the cat.

I used a napkin to grasp the string and pull. The foot-long string slid out easily, although afterward Socky squirmed free and fled.

I held up the string and said to the girls, "Voilà. The operation was successful."

Mary Catherine stepped into the living room and said, "Quit acting like a child in front of our guest." Then she saw the string I was holding and said, "I wondered where the pork-loin string went last night."

I smiled and said, "I hope you're not going to use it again." I was rewarded with a hail of laughter from the girls.

Father Alonzo laughed, too, and said, "You're a lucky man to spread such joy."

I smiled. He was right.

As dinner simmered and the children cleared their homework off the dining-room table, I joined Seamus and Alonzo on the balcony.

Both priests sipped on glasses of red wine, and Seamus passed one to me. I accepted and brought it to my nose, hoping it wasn't my Talisman Weir Vineyard Pinot Noir. Sixty bucks was a lot for a cop to shell out for wine. I'd been saving it for a special occasion.

Alonzo was perceptive. He said, "I hope you like the wine. I took it from the Communion box at Holy Name."

I just stared at him for a moment, speechless.

Alonzo said, "I'm sorry—just a poor joke. We picked it up at the liquor store down the street."

I wasn't used to a priest with a normal sense of humor.

We chatted for a few more minutes. Alonzo complimented me on how well behaved the children were. It's hard to not like someone who compliments your children.

I tried to get a little more of his background. He was raised in Bogotá, educated in Mexico City.

Alonzo said, "I had quite a full life before God set me on the right path. I'm trying to use my experience in a different way, dealing with everyday people."

"What motivated you to join the Church?"

Now Seamus interrupted. "Michael, my boy, those aren't the kind of questions we ask people who've come into the Church. No one cares that I used to own a bar."

I said, "No one would know if you didn't tell people every ten minutes."

Before he could answer with a sarcastic comment, Juliana stepped into the room and said, "Mary Catherine says dinner will be ready in about ten minutes."

Father Alonzo greeted Juliana and tried to make conversation, asking her, "Have you given any thought about where you want to go to college?"

She avoided looking at me when she answered. "I have a lot of options on the table right now. I'll start to narrow them down near Christmas." She backed out of the room before I could comment.

Alonzo tried again, asking me, "So have you and Mary Catherine picked a date?"

I looked down at the tile and just shook my head. "You ever been married, Alonzo? I mean, before your marriage to the Church?"

He said, "I was engaged once."

"What happened?"

"The usual. Who knows? There are thousands of possible answers. The easiest explanation is that she fell in love with another man. A man who could provide her with things I couldn't. But now I have the Church."

Seamus clapped him on the shoulder and said, "And you've got me."

Alonzo smiled and said, "Oh, joy."

That was the hardest I had laughed in months.

CHAPTER 30

THE NEXT DAY at the office, I wasted no time, walking up to Harry Grissom and telling him some of what I had deduced about the string of killings. These weren't business-as-usual drug rip-offs and grocery store robberies. There was a pattern to it—I just hadn't figured out what that pattern was. I needed to keep digging and wanted Grissom's blessing to start rummaging through old homicide cases.

He pulled me over to a corner near a window where no one in the squad bay would hear us. Then he looked at me with those droopy eyes and said, "What've you got?"

I'd known this hardened cop for too long not to come right to the point. "I think the ambush was part of a bigger drug war that's going on. I don't know why anyone would want me or Antrole dead, but the way our original suspect was murdered and the tip that came in to us makes it look like it was a setup from the very beginning."

Grissom just nodded as he considered it.

"I've also found two murders of Canadian nationals here in the city in the last week. Both victims had a past involving narcotics and were known to be associated with the Canadian mob. I have intel from a couple of sources that says the Canadians are clashing with a Mexican cartel over control of the synthetic drug market."

The lieutenant interrupted me. "Are you saying there's a drug war involving Canadians?"

"Yes, that's exactly what I'm saying."

"That will be one of the quietest, most polite drug wars in history." He took a moment to think, then said, "You can keep on your assignment, trying to discover patterns in these homicides. But I don't want you to start coming up with crazy conspiracy theories. You know as well as I do that the majority of the murders in New York are somehow related to drugs. I want to find Antrole's killer just as badly as you do. But I don't want you raising such a fuss that someone asks why you aren't assigned any current homicides. Is that clear?"

"Crystal."

"Then I expect you to get on with your assignment. If that assignment happens to lead to viable suspects in Antrole's murder, then everyone is happy. If not, I wasted my best detective on a foolish assignment. I've been accused of worse."

I watched Grissom as he padded back to his office. I often wondered if he tried to be inspiring or just had a way about him that pushed you to your limits. Suddenly I felt energy. I needed to line up some leads and feel like I was doing something.

That's how a cop should always feel.

CHAPTER 31

ALEX ENJOYED THE ride from the ranch up to Bogotá. She and the girls sang songs, then played silly games like "I spy" and "I'm thinking of an animal." That was Gabriela's favorite game because she loved animals and it was just twenty yes-or-no questions. Her sister was nice and usually picked a simple animal that Gabby could identify.

Alex's mother laid a guilt trip on her about being away so much. Alex didn't bring up the fact that she worked hard to pay the bills, which included her mother's comfortable condo in the suburbs of Bogotá.

That was all just a prelude for what the real purpose of the day was. She left the girls at her mother's condo for an hour and drove to Alcalá Park, between the highway and 19th Road.

It was a quiet park with enough trees to make finding a

shady spot to sit easy. It also wasn't a particularly busy park during the week.

As soon as she entered the park, she saw the man she needed to speak to sitting on a bench as far away from the parking lot as possible. She casually strolled toward him so she wouldn't draw attention to herself and to let the man know she was in no hurry. He had an inflated view of himself. Many men in his position did.

Alex walked past him, feeling his eyes all over her, then sat on the far end of the bench. She didn't say anything.

He was a well-dressed, extremely handsome thirty-five-year-old with a trim body. His Tommy Hilfiger shirt was clearly his attempt to look casual, but he looked like someone out of a catalog. She would've used him in an ad that called for a father and son.

The man simply said, "Alex, nice to see you. I occasionally forget that you could be a model as well as a photographer."

She took a moment and said, "What brings you all the way from Mexico City?"

"Business. Always business. As long as Colombia controls the transportation and access to our product, I will make a dozen trips a year to your lovely country."

Alex couldn't get a sense of what Oscar was thinking. She suspected he was annoyed that she had not completed her contracts in New York. But he showed no sign of it. A wealthy man like him, who enjoyed getting his hands dirty occasionally, knew how to hide his emotions.

Finally Oscar said, "Some of the Canadians on your list are back in New York. And Detective Michael Bennett is alive. I believe my text to you covered that fully."

"Yes. And I've considered the contract carefully. Isn't it dangerous for your operation to kill a New York City detective?"

"This has more of a personal element in it."

"Such as?"

"Does it matter? You've already been paid half up front to eliminate him. You need a reason to collect the other half?"

Alex gave him a careful smile. "I was just curious. It won't be an easy job to complete. Bennett has proved quite resourceful."

Oscar slowly bobbed his head. "Don't get me wrong—I agree with you. But I am only a cog in a big organization. I am the liaison to you and several others. But I heard from some of my associates that Detective Bennett shot and killed a young man in a library not too long ago."

"Sometimes police have to do things like that."

"But this young man worked for us. His mother is related to someone higher up in the cartel. Apparently she asked for us to deal with the cop who shot her son, Diego. It's really a matter of honor. But none of that should concern you. All you need to worry about is that Bennett needs to die. The sooner the better."

"I agree. I will head back to New York in a few days. I'm still in contact with some of the Dominicans I used for the ambush."

"Did they prove reliable enough for you to use them again?"

"They screwed up the first time, but they have a certain reputation to uphold as well. Besides, they're expendable. That's why I pay them so well."

Oscar smoothed his dark hair and said, "That's funny. That's the same way we feel about you."

CHAPTER 32

SO FAR, I wasn't impressed with Juliana's new career. It felt like my daughter was using it as an excuse to distance herself from the family. Her stage name was only part of the puzzle. She was spending a lot less time at home and barely spoke when she was there.

I took another ride into Brooklyn and strolled onto the set.

A cameraman nodded to me as I walked past. Although no one had paid me any attention the first time I visited, it was clear that everyone knew who I was. I kept my sport coat on, covering my pistol this time. There was no sense in being obnoxious.

I saw a chair with a sign that said JULES BAEZ. It made me cringe, but there was nothing I could do about it.

I heard a loud voice yell, "Quiet on the set." Someone else made another announcement, then slammed the handle down on a board indicating what scene they were working on. It was just like I had seen in movies. Even for me, it was kind of exciting.

Then I saw my little girl turn toward a tall, handsome young man. Two cameras were close to them as they filmed what looked to be a tender scene. Now that I saw how professional the production was, despite the cheesy studio, I felt better.

I watched as Juliana and the young man did a quiet scene where he told her about his dream to be on Broadway. This was not a show I'd watch if my daughter wasn't in it.

The scene ended.

The director yelled, "Cut. That was perfect."

Someone else called for the set to be changed, and I watched Juliana as she walked toward me with the young man.

"Hey, Dad." She gave me a mechanical hug.

I took a breath and said, "You looked great up there, sweetheart."

That brought out a big smile.

Juliana said, "Dad, this is Cade."

The young man stuck out his hand and gave me a firm handshake as he looked me in the eye and said, "It's nice to meet you, Mr. Bennett."

"So you know Juliana's real name."

"Oh, yes, sir. My real name is Carter Javits. But around here I'm Cade Jason. I'm trying to go by that all the time now."

"Your parents must be very happy."

Juliana cut in. "I have to get my stuff." She looked up at Cade and said, "I'll see you later tonight."

I said, "What's going on tonight?"

"Cade is taking me out to dinner." She wandered off to gather her purse and school clothes.

I decided it was time to get to know this young man. "Is this your first acting job?"

Cade said, "No, sir. I've had a few bit parts here and there since I graduated three years ago."

"What high school did you graduate from?"

"I graduated from Stony Brook University three years ago with my degree in communications."

Like any father, I did the math in my head quickly. He had to be twenty-five or twenty-six. I played it cool. "Would you like to eat with us tonight, Carter—I mean, Cade?"

Juliana saved him. "Thanks, Dad, but we've already set up our plans."

With that I was served notice that my daughter had grown up.

CHAPTER 33

ALEX MARTINEZ TOOK Avianca flight 244 directly from Bogotá to New York. It was a flight known for being watched by the DEA. Now that drugs came in by the truckload across the border, the flight had lost some of its mystique.

That night, Alex wasted no time checking into an older, funky hotel she liked, the Skyline Hotel on West 49th. There was something about the retro feel of the place that gave it charm. And the hotel had a decent indoor pool.

In the morning, Alex immediately started researching her next target.

Alicia Toussant was an attractive middle-aged Canadian woman who financed much of the violence the Canadian mob used to keep people in line. She was here in New York gauging her organization's efforts to control the synthetic drug market.

Alex preferred not to take contracts on women, but she felt

that if a woman was in some kind of nasty trade like drugs, then all bets were off.

Alex knew that no one would show her mercy if she was ever targeted because of her job.

After only a short time conducting surveillance on the woman, Alex discovered that Ms. Toussant had a security man who stayed well out of the way and out of sight. It was the mark of a true professional, not drawing any extra attention to herself.

Alex first noticed the man when she started following the Canadian from her hotel. She appreciated her choice of the Hotel Giraffe on Park Avenue South and 26th, which was under the radar but boasted a good restaurant and comfortable atmosphere.

The man was dressed in casual clothes, his loose shirt probably covering some kind of weapon. He was in his midforties and had a little extra weight on him. He wasn't there to scare people; he'd been chosen because he was discreet and knew his business. Alex wouldn't take any chances when the time came.

Alex knew the hotel and the area well. It would be difficult to get into the woman's room at the Giraffe. That meant she had to find a spot in the open to do it—rarely a good idea in New York City.

She conducted the rest of her surveillance a little farther back than she normally would to keep both the bodyguard and Alicia Toussant in view.

The Canadian seemed to have hourly meetings. She was a hard worker. Alex admired that. They were all short face-to-face meetings with white or Hispanic men. Alex didn't care what each meeting was about. Because some time after sunset tonight, any agreements struck would be null and void. That's how things worked in the narcotics business.

Later in the day, Alex followed while Ms. Toussant strolled down Fifth Avenue. Alex had enough photographs of her to create a pretty good biography in pictures. It was the necessary preparation for any assignment.

Only once did Ms. Toussant have any contact with her bodyguard. She bought something small from a jewelry store, then turned and walked directly to him. He stuck whatever she had bought in his left front pants pocket.

Alex noticed that the sun was setting and some of the city lights were slowly coming on. Her target turned and started to stroll back toward the Hotel Giraffe.

Alex fell in behind the bodyguard. She had both her stiletto and her 9mm pistol in her Vera Wang purse, which had a strap that slipped over her shoulder comfortably. She was as ready as she would ever be.

First she had to deal with the bodyguard.

CHAPTER 34

ON THE WALK back to the hotel, Alex formed a plan in her head. It was tricky because there were two targets, though she was only getting paid for one. She would've preferred to kill Alicia Toussant without having to deal with the bodyguard. But killing him, too, was just a good business decision.

Then she saw an opportunity she couldn't resist. Her target, Alicia Toussant, strolled into Madison Square Park. She stopped and sat on an ornate cement bench. She pulled out an iPhone and relaxed on the bench. It looked like she'd be there awhile.

Immediately Alex changed her plan and started to ease up behind the bodyguard, who was standing behind a chest-high wall at the edge of an intricate water fountain.

Alex glanced around and realized the park was relatively quiet. The bodyguard gazed up at the Flatiron Building in the distance. Then he returned his gaze to his employer. It almost looked as if he was spying on someone from the bushes. He was just being professional and maintaining his surveillance of the entire area.

That was his mistake.

He never even noticed Alex as she came up behind him with her stiletto already extended.

Just as she stepped up next to the bodyguard, he turned, giving her the opening she needed. She shifted her weight and drove the stiletto straight up under the man's jaw so that the sharpened steel crashed through his mouth and nasal cavity, then directly into his brain.

Alex would call his expression *confused.* He didn't understand what had happened or why he couldn't move. His eyes focused briefly on her, and he gurgled a question for a moment.

Then she moved her left arm behind him and eased him carefully to the ground. He was now just a sack of bones and skin. Against the wall, with the bushes near him, his body was barely visible.

Alex ran her hands over his waistline and found a Browning 9mm pistol in his waistband. She slipped it into her purse.

Just as Alex was about to leave the body, she reached down into his left front pants pocket and retrieved the tiny box that his boss, Alicia, had given him earlier.

She opened it and found a pair of beautiful pear-shaped diamond earrings. They were at least two carats. They were remarkable. For a moment, Alex wished she were a thief instead of a killer. She slipped the earrings back into the man's pocket.

When Alex stood up and peeked over the wall, she could see Ms. Toussant still sitting in front of the fountain.

Maybe this wouldn't be as hard as she thought.

CHAPTER 35

ALEX WAS POLITE and waited until her target completed her phone call. When the woman slipped the iPhone back into her purse, Alex calmly walked toward her and sat down on the same bench.

Alex said, "Hello, Ms. Toussant."

That got the woman's full attention. She turned her pretty face, framed by light brown hair, and focused on Alex.

She said, "Do I know you, dear?" She had a slight French accent.

Alex said, "No. I'm not someone you would normally do business with."

"But you *do* work for someone. That means you're not here for a friendly conversation." The woman looked over Alex's shoulder toward the wall where her bodyguard had been waiting.

Alex calmly pulled the man's 9mm pistol from her purse

and said, "If you're waiting for the man who owns this to come to your rescue, you'll be in for a surprise."

The Canadian remained calm and said, "Are you just going to shoot me? No warnings or attempts to find out information?"

"I'm afraid not." Before Alex could say anything else, the Canadian financier swung her left hand, knocking the pistol away, and came back with a right elbow that caught Alex low on the chin.

The blow knocked her off balance and almost completely off the bench. She twisted into a crouch as she slid off the bench to face the Canadian woman.

The Canadian threw a knee just as Alex looked up from her crouch. She was able to move, and the knee just grazed the side of her head. She had underestimated her target.

The Canadian didn't waste any time throwing another kick, then pulling a straight razor from God knows where. She whipped it at Alex's face.

Alex felt the blade just miss her nose as she jumped back. That thin blade would've sliced her nose in half. She desperately tried to regain her balance before the Canadian disfigured her. Or worse.

A police siren blasting in the distance distracted them both for a moment.

As soon as Alex realized it was a block away, she hopped back and raised the pistol. Just as her target advanced with the razor poised for another strike, she pulled the trigger. Without a silencer, the shot sounded like a cannon. But the echo would make it hard to tell exactly where the shot came from.

The bullet struck the woman just above the bridge of her

nose. She crumpled straight to the ground right in front of Alex.

Instead of checking the body, which was perfectly still on the hard concrete next to the fountain, Alex looked up to make sure no one was rushing toward her.

Alex backed away from the body, then turned and walked quickly away. The few people on the edges of the park paid no attention to her.

Alex kept moving onto Broadway. She looked straight ahead as she passed the Flatiron Building and continued. She turned right on 21st. Looking around quickly, she pulled out the Browning pistol she had used to kill the Canadian financier and tossed it into the back of an idling garbage truck just before it rumbled away from the curb.

Thank God for lucky opportunities.

Alex worked to control her breathing and made sure her jaw wasn't broken. It was sore but intact.

If nothing else, it would confuse the cops for a while that there were two bodies at the same scene killed by different methods. She started to smile thinking about the detectives who would have to figure that puzzle out.

CHAPTER 36

I FINALLY DECIDED that if I wanted to understand murders associated with the drug trade, I needed to understand the drug trade a little better. My best contact in the NYPD narcotics unit was a sergeant stationed right in my building.

Sergeant Tim Marcia was a few years older than I was, and no one would mistake him for anything but a cop. At six one and beefy, he'd kept the same mustache since the mid-1990s. He was about as straight a shooter as anyone would ever meet, and he understood the drug world better than anyone else.

I sat in the passenger seat of his seized Range Rover. The narcotics unit often used cars it seized from drug dealers to conduct surveillance or undercover operations.

We drove up into the Bronx so Sergeant Marcia could talk to a couple of his informants. He treated them more like he was a big brother or mentor than a cop. I liked that.

Near Yankee Stadium, I sat in the Range Rover while he chatted with a young Puerto Rican man just outside the SUV.

Sergeant Marcia said, "You sure that's it? You haven't heard any other rumors?"

The thin young man shook his head and mumbled, "No. Nothing at all."

Sergeant Marcia put a playful headlock on the young man, then said, "Don't be late for class. And don't make your mother worry about you tonight. Be home by ten."

The young man smiled and waved as he walked off.

When Sergeant Marcia slipped back into the car, I said, "That's not exactly how the movies portray your job."

"Everyone has his own style. I never pretended to be Popeye Doyle from *The French Connection*. I would rather fix a few lives while making a case than run a big operation that disrupts an entire neighborhood."

"I couldn't agree more. What did your young friend have to say?"

"He says there's been a disruption of the synthetic drug market. Everyone was making a fortune on ecstasy and meth, and now they're back to selling pot and coke. My snitch says there's been some Canadians trying to dump extra meth on the market, but the Mexican cartel has told people to steer clear."

I said, "Sounds like my son Brian got the straight scoop." I wouldn't have chosen these circumstances, but I'd been grateful to see Brian in the Buffalo hospital at least twice a week.

Sergeant Marcia said, "I don't want to admit that a Homicide puke came up with an explanation for what's going on in the narcotics trade. This is embarrassing."

"You help me find this killer, and I'll never tell a soul."

Sergeant Marcia laughed. "We go back too far. I have too much on you. You won't tell a soul no matter what happens."

"But you'll help me just the same?"

"I'm insulted you even have to ask. We'll figure this out, and I'll write an official report saying that we got the original information from Brian. Maybe we can use that as a way of showing the court how much he's cooperated. Who knows? Maybe we can cut that crazy sentence down a little bit."

That was the mark of a true friend.

Sergeant Marcia said, "Synthetics are a part of the drug trade I don't have a lot to do with. All my experience is with heroin and cocaine. I can predict what those users and dealers will act like. The synthetic drugs like ecstasy attract a new kind of seller and affect all users differently. I knew the Canadians were heavily involved in that market, but they tend to stay under the radar, and we haven't made any serious arrests.

"It's just semantics when we're talking about drugs. People are going to use them whether they're in the form of prescription pills or black tar heroin. Sometimes I feel like we should just legalize all drugs and take the consequences."

"What kind of consequences?"

"A surge in overdose deaths. A much higher percentage of the population that doesn't contribute anything to society. A bunch of drug dealers looking for a different crime they can commit because the government has taken over their jobs. Who could tell what would happen? I don't even like to think about it."

Listening to the narcotics sergeant, I remembered an old-timer in Vice talking about how the Dutch handled some of their crime problems. He had said, "The Dutch had a problem with prostitution, so they legalized it. Then they had a problem with drugs, so they legalized them. Let's hope they never have a problem with homicide."

CHAPTER 37

ALEX REACHED A few conclusions after her first day following Michael Bennett. The detective was as busy as any man who ever lived. Between work and a huge family, Alex wondered when the man slept. She would probably not use her stiletto unless she could catch him by surprise, because he was tough and in shape. A gun would be the safest avenue.

That was why she was meeting with these two Dominicans at a White Castle off Webster Avenue in the Bronx. She would've preferred a busy Starbucks in Midtown, but she understood what they were doing. They wanted to meet her on their turf.

Alex sipped a coffee while the men worked their way through a plate piled high with tiny hamburgers. They spoke in Spanish, but in this neighborhood, that wasn't any shield against someone listening in. Their Dominican accents were a little difficult for Alex to understand, but she had explained who the target was and where they might intercept him. Then she said, "I want just the two of you involved. The fewer the better."

The older, pudgier man, with tattoos running up and down his arms, said, "We'll need a driver. My cousin Julio will do it. But…"

Alex was losing her patience. "What? What's wrong now?"

The man said, "A cop is a big deal. We took the job before, but now it's going to be a second cop. There's heat building."

"You told me your crew was the toughest in the city. That any one of your men would die rather than be dishonored and not finish a job. I've already paid you a lot of cash up front."

The man interrupted her. "And we have three men dead because of it."

"That's not my issue. That's why I hired you as contractors."

"What about Cesar, who was killed in the hospital? Did you do that so he wouldn't talk?"

Alex had lost her cool. She snapped, "Give me back the money."

"What? I don't have it just lying around."

"If you're not going to give it back, do your job. Do what I tell you or I'll make sure no one ever hires you or any of your crew again. Is that what you want?"

The younger man started to say something, a vein on his forehead popping out. But the man with the tattoos put a hand on his chest.

"We'll do it. And we'll expect *you* to come up with the rest of the cash quickly when it's done. Then we'll be square. At least as far as money is concerned."

"What's that supposed to mean?"

"We have some questions we'd like answered. After we get paid."

"Once I close out my contracts and you've done what you've been paid to do, I'll talk with you all you want."

The man picked up a tiny hamburger and popped it into his mouth. He washed it down with a big gulp of soda. Then he looked at Alex and said, "You'll have me, Laszlo here, and my cousin Julio whenever you need us."

Alex eyed Laszlo. He was the surly, emotional type that made this job miserable sometimes. She hoped his older friend could keep him in line.

CHAPTER 38

AFTER MEETING WITH the Dominicans, Alex used the entire afternoon to gather more information on Bennett. By following him to meet his grandfather—who, she learned, was a priest—she had the opportunity to photograph the churches in the neighborhood where Bennett lived and his grandfather worked. She loved the architecture of churches and relished the opportunity to mix pleasure with business.

Late in the afternoon, when she was tired of waiting for Bennett to emerge, Alex strolled into Central Park. She eyed a cop on horseback who was checking her out, then was distracted by a group of tourists riding horses with a guide. Horses right in Central Park!

Clemency and Gabriela could ride better than any of these adults, Alex thought. She knelt down and snapped half a dozen quick photos of the group with the sun casting wild beams of light through the trees. It was a wonderful sight.

Then she heard a man's voice say, "Are you a spy conducting surveillance or just a fan of horses?"

The voice startled her, and she turned quickly, rising to her feet. She stared for a moment. It was the policeman sitting atop his bay horse, more than sixteen hands tall. The horse's placid eyes took her in.

Alex said, "Excuse me?"

"I said, are you a spy or just into horses?"

"Both." She hated to lie.

It was hard for a man not to look sexy on top of a horse, but this policeman also had broad shoulders and a square jaw. He looked like a recruiting poster. He gave her a smile, showing his perfect white teeth.

Alex felt herself flush slightly. She liked the way his eyes stayed on her face. It showed a good upbringing.

She stepped closer to him and ran her hand along the horse's graceful neck. "What's his name?"

"Traveller."

"Just like Robert E. Lee's horse."

The cop stared at her, then said, "That's exactly right. Almost no one gets that."

"I bet the horse people do."

"The horse people and the Civil War nuts."

On impulse, she said, "How do I rent a horse here?"

"You know how to ride?"

"I've been around horses my entire life."

The cop said, "What do racehorses eat?"

Alex smiled. "That's the oldest joke around. Fast food."

"Okay, that's one. What goes in the horse's mouth?"

"The bit." She tried to look insulted, but this guy was too adorable.

The cop said, "Finally, the most important question. Will you go out with me?"

She couldn't help but laugh. "Let's see how the ride goes."

"Fair enough."

Suddenly not only Alex's day but also her whole trip started to look brighter.

The cop's name was Tom McLaughlin, but his friends called him T-Mac. He'd been raised in Quantico, Virginia, where his father was stationed in the Marines. That's where he developed his love of horseback riding.

Alex couldn't remember the last time she actually enjoyed herself this much on an assignment. Time flew while they rode through the park.

Alex said, "Is it hard to get an assignment in the NYPD horse unit?"

"It's called the Mounted Unit. And you'd be shocked how many cops want to get in. There's only about fifty-five horses now. We go all over the city for PR and sometimes crowd control. We also patrol the park. I love it, except I never get weekends off."

He had a simple, direct way about him, and Alex found him interesting.

When he asked for her phone number, she gave him the number to her burner phone, which would be good for the length of her stay in New York. A stay she hoped would be long enough to see this handsome cop again.

She said, "I'll only be in New York another week or so. But I would enjoy a nice dinner. Steak and horses are two of my favorite things."

T-Mac gave her a dazzling smile and said, "Mine, too."

CHAPTER 39

I GOT THE call about a double homicide down in Madison Square Park around nine o'clock. Mary Catherine understood that I had a certain duty, no matter what time of the day or night I was called. She just reminded me to take it easy, since I was still recovering from my injuries.

There's a certain Zen to doing the job you're trained for and understand so well. I even had a twinge of excitement as I hopped in my city car and headed south. This time of night, I made it to the crime scene pretty quick.

Sometimes I forget about the turnover in the NYPD. I didn't recognize a single one of the young uniformed officers maintaining the perimeter of the crime scene. It was at the lower end of the park near a massive water fountain. I had my ID and a badge on a chain around my neck. I didn't wear a jacket, so everyone saw the second badge clipped next to my gun on my belt.

As I approached the fountain, I saw exactly who I was looking for. Cassie Max was on one knee by the edge of the fountain looking back toward some bushes and a low wall. Her short black hair was covered by a scarf as she focused her attention on the far side of the fountain.

As soon as she saw me, a smile whipped across her face and she sprang to her feet.

Cassie said, "It's nice to see that senior detectives still come out after dark."

"When I was younger, the word *senior* was code for 'old.'"

"Nothing's changed." She gave me a sly smile that conveyed her wit and intelligence. Then she said, "I called you as soon as I realized this victim was Canadian. When I saw she might be connected to the Canadian mob, I knew you'd be interested."

"It looks like you get all the homicides in parks."

"They can be a convenient place to kill someone."

"What about the second victim? Is he a Canadian as well?"

"No. He's a local thug named Anthony Chichee. He has half a dozen arrests for assault and is the suspect in two homicides. He's known as an enforcer and bodyguard for hire."

I said, "So what have you figured out so far?"

"The woman, Alicia Toussant, was shot one time just above her nose. The bullet never exited. The medical examiner's people took both the bodies about twenty minutes ago. I was just trying to line up where the shot was probably taken from. There's a spent casing over there." She pointed to the edge of the concrete.

"Depending on the weapon the killer was using, I suspect whoever took the shot was standing about ten feet away."

"Same caliber as your murder near Bryant Park?"

"It was a nine, but so are about seventy million others. If the killer is as professional as I think, I doubt we'll match up the slugs."

I took a few seconds to scan the entire crime scene. Experience had taught me that you sometimes thought of a new angle when you just looked around.

I said, "I don't think anyone wants to hear about a turf war here in the city. It sure looks like someone has got it in for Canadians, and my sources say it's one of the Mexican cartels."

"I'll leave it up to you to look at the big picture. I just want to find the killer here and in Bryant Park."

"Was the second victim also shot?"

"No. He was killed up close. I suspect it was before Ms. Toussant was shot. Someone shoved a sharp-edged weapon up through his jaw and into his brain."

Instantly I realized the other connection to murders in the city. I didn't need to take a look at the ViCAP database to tell me what I already knew. I said to Cassie, "Would you call that sharp-edged weapon a stiletto?"

She thought about it for a moment, then nodded.

I said, "Then I can guarantee that these murders are connected to what I'm looking at."

CHAPTER 40

I STAYED AT the scene with Cassie Max until almost the middle of the night. I didn't bounce any more of my conspiracy theory off Cassie. She needed to focus on this individual homicide scene. Cleared murders are the currency of a homicide detective.

No detective wanted a double homicide to go cold. The fact that there were two victims meant that there were almost twice as many leads to follow up on. Twice as much media coverage. And twice as much pressure from above to clear the case.

I was confident in Cassie's abilities and intended to work with her as I developed more leads myself.

I managed to wake up and get into the office early, and at midday decided I needed to check on my grandfather. It also gave me a break from the mountain of reports I'd been reading.

I came in through the administrative offices of Holy Name and found my grandfather absolutely motionless at his desk, with his head to one side. His mouth was open, but he wasn't snoring.

I approached from the door slowly, feeling a wave of fear rise up in me. I said his name several times softly. I carefully placed my hand near his mouth and nose, hoping to feel his breath.

I wasn't sure, so I leaned in closer. As I did, his right eye popped open.

"What the hell are you doing?" His voice was clear and his accent sharp. That meant he was alert.

I hopped back, trying to hide being startled. I also didn't want him to think I was afraid he had died at his desk.

I said, "Just came by to say hello."

Seamus said, "Do you sneak up on everyone you want to say hello to? Go say hello to Alonzo back at the indoor basketball court. I want to finish my nap."

I thought that was sound reasoning and headed through the rear of the gymnasium attached to the school.

There was a spirited basketball scrimmage going on as Alonzo shouted encouragement from the edge of the court. When he saw me, he handed his whistle over to one of the assistant coaches.

He extended his hand as he said, "How are you, Michael?"

"Good." I almost had to shout over the noise of the game in the enclosed gym.

Alonzo said, "Let's go outside, where we can hear ourselves think."

We walked to the edge of the school and then through a gate

onto the sidewalk outside. It was a beautiful day, and I enjoyed strolling under the trees that hung over the sidewalk.

We ambled past the administration building, where my grandfather was probably sleeping soundly again.

Alonzo said, "I really respect how much effort you put into your family even with such a high-profile job. Your grandfather is rightly proud of you."

The thought of Seamus telling people he was proud of me made me smile. Even if he never would say it directly to me.

"I appreciate how you take care of him. God knows it's not always easy."

He smiled. "It works both ways with Seamus. The Church has been a big adjustment for me. Seamus understands that better than most. You're lucky to have had him in your life so long."

I let out a laugh. "I never thought of it as luck. But I have him in my life just the same. All over my life." I didn't say it out loud, but I thought, *And thank God for it.*

CHAPTER 41

I COULDN'T REMEMBER hearing anyone talk about sports at Holy Name with such enthusiasm. If we could bottle Father Alonzo's positive attitude, all the world's problems would be solved.

We walked almost to the next block, then as we were about to turn around and head back to the administration building, I noticed two men turn the corner toward us on the sidewalk. Nothing seemed out of place. The calm atmosphere around the church and the cool breeze were too serene to pose a threat.

Now the two men were directly in front of us on the sidewalk, about fifteen feet away. One of the men, about forty-five, with sleeves of tattoos on both arms, casually reached under his shirt as the other man, younger and thinner, reached behind him.

It was a classic gesture of pulling a gun. I was embarrassed I let them get so close to us. I just hadn't noticed the danger.

The men kept moving and were almost in front of us. I only had time to deal with one of them. It was a dangerous choice to make in a split second. My hope was that the other one would be scared into running away.

I closed the distance on the tattooed man just as his blue steel revolver came up in front of him. I blocked his arm with both hands quickly, then lowered my shoulder and hit him with everything I had.

I don't know if he planned it or if it was just luck, but at almost the same moment, the man swung the gun wildly to get enough room to fire. The butt of the gun grazed me across the temple. I literally saw stars, like I was a cartoon character.

Now I had both men right next to me. Someone was either going to beat me again with the revolver or shoot me. Either way I was in deep shit.

I was dizzy from the blow to the head and backing away, trying to buy time. That's when I saw a movement to my right. It took me a moment to realize it was the graceful form of Father Alonzo as he stepped into the fray.

He took out the younger man with a hard right cross, knocking the gun out of his hand as he did it. The young man bounced off a tree and fell onto the sidewalk.

That stole the attention of the tattooed man right in front of me. Now that I was already leaning down, I followed through by throwing my entire body weight into him. He stumbled over his friend.

Alonzo faced off against the man with the tattoos, but I yelled, "Gun!" The single common police command whenever a cop sees someone with a gun. It was like a smack in the face to Alonzo, who, realizing the man was still armed, darted to the other edge of the sidewalk.

Now my head was clear, and I reached back for the pistol on my hip. Both men were on their feet and running toward the next block. They realized this was not going to be their day.

A green Chevy came around the corner. I focused on the man with the gun running from me.

The driver of the Chevy opened fire with a small-caliber machine gun. As a bullet pinged off a car and broke a window behind me, I ducked behind a parked Lincoln. Alonzo managed to leap over the wall at the edge of a courtyard between two buildings. I was shocked at how quickly he could move. Automatic gunfire tended to have that effect on people.

I did a quick survey of the area to make sure there were no civilians in the crossfire. Two women across the street were scurrying away, and some young men walking near the avenue knew it was time to lie flat on the ground. That came from experience.

I fired one round from behind the Lincoln, then the Chevy sped up. When it was parallel to me, and the man with the machine gun had taken a break, I sprang out of my position and popped off two more rounds.

The men who had attacked us piled into the car.

All I could do was stare as the green Chevy Cruze with no license plate navigated the street.

I was panting from the excitement and exertion. My head was pounding from the blow. I was wondering at what point I needed to start worrying about repeated blows to my head causing some kind of serious trauma.

Then I realized I might have a chance. The car was slowing as it approached the nearest intersection. I knew this neighborhood. Even on foot I might be able to at least get into a position to identify them later. Right now I didn't relish the idea of explaining to a detective that I couldn't get a license number or a decent description.

With great effort, I stood up, but as I started to run, I felt a hand on my arm. My head snapped to my left, and I saw Father Alonzo.

"Don't be stupid, my friend. You'll get them later."

I looked at the priest who had just beaten back a couple of armed men and dived for cover like he was one of the X-Men, and said to him, "Who are you?" My voice cracked from my confusion. He was like no priest I had ever met.

The tall Colombian smiled and did a theatrical bow.

"Alonzo Garcia, at your service."

CHAPTER 42

AFTER I GOT quizzed about the attack by a precinct detective named Toby Reed and his partner, Brian Wong, and after I had answered a few questions from Harry Grissom, I knew exactly what I had to do. I tried not to broadcast my next move. I always like playing my cards close to my vest. So I eased away from my lieutenant and the detectives, who were now badgering Father Alonzo, and made a beeline for one of the places I least liked to go in New York.

I headed south to lower Manhattan, past Little Italy. The FBI office was in Federal Plaza, on the corner of Broadway and Worth Street. The towering glass-and-metal building was a typical federal structure without much flair or imagination. Subtle two-foot-high decorative metal barriers surrounded it to thwart any potential suicide bomber in a vehicle.

Three NYPD Suburbans carrying armed SWAT team

members sat outside the building as an off-duty security detail. They were there twenty-four hours a day.

I needed to keep my visit as quiet as possible, so I had made a phone call first. I never did a favor for someone and expected it to be repaid. But in this case, I had to at least ask.

Three years ago, when Marion Wan's estranged husband kidnapped their five-year-old son, she did what any smart FBI analyst would do and went to the NYPD immediately. I happened to be speaking with one of my old friends in the 105th Precinct, near Floral Park, in Queens, when Marion came in, nearly hysterical.

I was able to short-circuit some of the paperwork and figure out that her estranged husband, who worked for the New York City fire department, listed an emergency address on Long Island. It was the girlfriend he had left Marion for.

An hour after Marion had come into the NYPD, I was honored to see a tearful reunion between Marion and her son.

That's why she came out the front door of the office building and walked with me to the McDonald's across the street. After we had coffee and caught up for a few minutes, Marion read my anxious glances at her notes.

She gave me a sly smile and said, "Okay, I guess you want to talk about your best friend, Alonzo Garcia."

I said, "You may think you're being sarcastic, but right about now he *is* my best friend. The son of a gun saved my life. But he did it with skill and experience. I'm just worried about where he might have gotten that skill."

Marion pulled open her notes and said, "I did all the usual stuff. Public records. Searched media databases in Colombia and New York. No arrests, and he's here on a work visa through the Catholic Church."

"Huh. Never even occurred to me that he'd have to have an immigration status. I guess I assumed the Catholic Church could fix anything."

Marion said, "I had to go an extra couple of steps. I called our legat office in Bogotá. The FBI has more than a dozen agents there. One of their senior people knows Garcia personally."

"You have my complete attention."

"The agent in Bogotá knew Alonzo because he was a captain in the Colombian national police. Early in his career, he fought the FARC rebels—some people call them the People's Army. Then he focused his attention on narcotics. He worked closely with our DEA and has a ton of commendations."

"How does a guy like that end up in the Catholic Church?"

"He was engaged. They were the power couple of the Bogotá social scene. Then she dumped him. She dumped him for a bigwig in the Medellín cartel.

"The agent in Bogotá said it shattered Alonzo. He sort of disappeared, then a year later turned up as a priest. Apparently the Catholic Church was worried about someone taking revenge on him, so they transferred him out of the country."

"So he really was trained in self-defense and tactics."

Marion looked at me and said, "He is a certified badass."

I chuckled. "And he saved *my* ass."

"From what I hear, it's not the first time he's saved someone's ass."

"Thanks. I owe you big-time."

Marion reached across and held my hand as she shook her head. "No. We'll never be even. I owe you my whole life. And this didn't even violate policy."

I felt my face flush as she leaned across the table and kissed me on the cheek.

CHAPTER 43

I STOPPED BY the administrative office at Holy Name. For the first time ever, I wasn't there to talk to my grandfather. I wasn't even there to check on my kids. I was there to speak with Alonzo Garcia, former captain in the Colombian national police, recipient of countless commendations for bravery and hard work.

I led Alonzo out into the courtyard between the church and the school, knowing we would get some privacy there. He wore his clerical collar with a whistle dangling from his neck.

Once we sat on the hard cement bench, I said, "I did some checking and know your history and what you did before the priesthood."

Alonzo said, "I wasn't trying to hide anything. I'm just trying to move on with my life. I'm glad I was in a position to help when it mattered."

"It mattered, and you helped. And I appreciate it. All I'm looking for now is some insight into who I'm dealing with. How can I stop these killings?"

"I wish I could help you, Michael. It's not that I'm purposely trying to ignore the issue. But I've seen this so many times before. I know that the killings will stop whenever the contracts are fulfilled. I may even know who the killer is. If they came from Bogotá and they were active when I was working, I might know who they are. But the fact is there are just too many possibilities. The cartels train kids to become killers. They hire contract killers who have a talent. They just have too many people willing to kill for money."

I let out a heavy sigh. I was hoping he might have some detail that could help me.

Alonzo said, "I do know who likely trained this killer."

"How?"

"Many of the sophisticated killers, the ones who went to college and were bored with their former profession or just liked the challenge and the money, trained with a martial-arts instructor in the Chapinero section of Bogotá. He was a legitimate, hardworking karate instructor, and everyone who wanted to make a career as an assassin trained with him. He was known simply as Sensei Don.

"He taught the use of the blade. He advocated only two strikes. One to the brain and one to the heart. I've seen it over and over.

"I never trained with him, but other police have. This killer you face today has trained with him."

"If we went to this karate instructor, do you think he'd talk to us?"

"He died some years ago. But there are many of his students still working today."

I thought about it and said, "That still doesn't explain the ambush and the three men who tried to shoot us on the street. That wasn't a single assassin. They weren't using some kind of stiletto."

"But that falls in line with their profession. Many of the hit men from Colombia use local thugs on some of their hits. It makes sense. They're just subcontracting out the job for a fraction of their pay."

"So now I have an idea of what I'm up against. I just don't know who it is, how they'll try again, or how to stop them."

Alonzo chuckled. "Just like police work everywhere in the world."

CHAPTER 44

I KNEW IT was time to take this investigation to a new level. Harry Grissom listened as I explained everything, and considering that someone tried to shoot me in front of Holy Name, he agreed that I wasn't being dramatic. There *was* a conspiracy. But I had my own gang to help me stop it.

It didn't take long for me to put together a task force of detectives and NYPD forensics people who were familiar with the case. I just needed some input for now.

I made the trip across town to the office of the chief medical examiner on East 26th Street, across from the City University of New York.

I spoke to an assistant medical examiner who had worked on Cassie Max's double homicide in Madison Square Park. He had worked in the ME's office for more than a dozen years and had given me insight on homicides I never would've gotten anywhere else.

He said, "I've made some calculations, and I think whoever delivered the strike stands between five foot seven and five foot ten. They have some understanding of anatomy and are fairly powerful.

"I also looked at the other homicide you showed me, and I would have to say that the alignment of the bullet wound on the body confirms my estimate of the killer's size. What else do you have?"

I said, "Basically, the killer is someone with enough resources to hire gunmen, enough guts to come after a cop, and enough skill to commit a double homicide in a park right in the middle of the city. The killer appears to be very professional by the way they've disabled security video systems and tracked their victims. I need all the help I can get."

The assistant medical examiner laughed. "If you have Cassie Max working on this with you, I think you've got a lot of help. She never seems to wear out. You know what we call her?"

I shook my head.

"The Terminator. Once she has you in her program, she never stops. Plus she's not too bad to look at."

"You getting lonely locked away in here with all the dead people?"

"I prefer it to wandering around a city filled with loud, obnoxious people. I went to Johns Hopkins. I could be a pediatrician in Baltimore if I wanted. I prefer the quiet, comfortable stillness of the morgue."

I looked at him and said, "I can never tell if you're pulling my leg or just plain crazy."

"Do they have to be mutually exclusive?"

That made me laugh out loud. "You got any ideas about my case?"

"I told you how tall the killer probably is. That they're professional because of the precision of their strikes. My guess is that they're very bright as well. I make that assumption based on their knowledge of anatomy. But I also know that detectives like you and Cassie don't let this shit slide. I figure you'll have this asshole in cuffs sometime in the next few days."

I liked his confidence. I was trying to form a picture in my head of how calm a killer has to stay to use a weapon like that, getting in close to deliver such a precise blow to the victim.

I also hadn't forgotten that a woman was probably involved in the murder of one of the gunmen who killed Antrole Martens. There was no telling if she was a local killer or perhaps someone who worked for the cartel.

Once I had a puzzle like this in my head, I tended to shut out almost everything else. This time I had to solve the puzzle before the killer figured out the puzzle of how to kill me.

CHAPTER 45

ALEX MARTINEZ SMILED broadly as she walked along Park Avenue South. She was coming from a lovely dinner with the mounted police officer Tom McLaughlin. He was charming, sweet, and a full eighteen months younger than she was. Not that it made a difference. She wasn't looking for someone she could raise her daughters with. She also wasn't interested in telling him where she was staying just yet. It was their first date.

He had taken her for drinks at a sports bar called the Hill. It was a younger crowd, but she appreciated his showing her new places. Then they strolled down Third Avenue to a little Italian place named Bistango, and she tried not slurp down clams marinara in an unladylike manner.

After dinner, Tom calmly accepted Alex's decision to catch a cab back to her hotel. A quick kiss good night turned into just a little more. Enough to make Alex wonder if she was making the right choice, leaving this handsome, horse-loving man for the evening. But it was for the best.

After they parted, she wanted to walk instead of ride in a cab. That's when it happened. She realized she was getting sloppy. Someone was following her. She knew it wasn't the police. This was a pretty young woman with short dark hair, wearing a skirt no cop would wear, even undercover.

This was something Alex had dealt with once before. In Madrid, two years ago, some members of a local gang started to follow her. They were subtle, but not nearly as subtle as this young woman now. In Madrid, Alex simply kept walking until she found a police officer and chatted with him. It only took about twenty minutes for the gang to lose interest and wander away.

Ironically, this time she was coming *from* talking to a police officer. And she had no idea who would want to follow her.

She worked out a plan in her head anyway. She turned east, toward the river. She wasn't far from the United Nations building. Once she had gone a couple of blocks, she made another assessment. The woman was still back there.

Alex didn't like to commit violence she wasn't being paid for. Especially violence against a woman. She would do what she had to, but she didn't relish the idea of using her stiletto on this woman, who was using a phone to call out Alex's movements to someone else.

Alex led the woman down to the FDR Drive, then found a place to cross.

She had the river on one side of her. Now she focused on what was coming toward her.

CHAPTER 46

ALEX WAS NOW on the banks of the East River, and she no longer saw the young woman who had been following her. That didn't mean she was no longer in danger. She sat on a bench to wait. A few minutes later, she saw the two men.

Both men were young. One looked to be in his midtwenties and a little on the heavy side. The other one was tall and lean with long, straight hair.

Alex needed to draw them closer. She dug out her iPhone from her purse, leaving her stiletto and pistol within easy reach. She pretended to be engrossed in texting, but in fact she turned on her camera and was watching the men as they approached.

Alex made a quick survey of the area to ensure there were no witnesses close by. She even had a moment to enjoy the view of the East River and the relative quiet compared to the rest of the city.

As the men came closer, Alex casually dropped her right hand to her purse and gripped her stiletto. She rested the stiletto in her lap and suppressed a smile as the men came blundering into her trap.

She felt a change in her breathing, and her heart rate picked up. It was more excitement than fear. These were the types of challenges she had to overcome in her profession. One of the biggest things in her favor was the fact that men tended to underestimate a woman. That was their choice. She'd make them regret it.

Now they were close. She could tell they were Hispanic. Her guess was that they were Dominicans.

The heavier one said in Spanish, "Hello, beautiful. Why would you be sitting alone on a lovely night like this?"

Alex said, "Unfortunately, I am not alone. I'm being bothered by a couple of assholes who showed up uninvited."

The chubby man let out a laugh. "Show me where they are, and we'll get rid of them for you." He looked to his thinner friend for support.

The young man drew a long fixed-blade knife from behind his back. His smile told her he enjoyed terrorizing women.

Alex stood quickly, pressing the button to extend her stiletto as she came to her feet. The movement clearly took both men by surprise.

She leaned back as the young man with the knife took a wide swipe at her. After all her training and experience, it felt like it took place in slow motion. But the young man meant business. It was a blow designed to kill her. And he had aimed it at her throat.

Now she felt anger at the way these men would treat a person, not to mention a woman. She took two steps and let the men bump into each other as they tried to grab her.

Now she stepped to the far end of the bench. She needed them to come to her.

"I hope whoever you work for didn't pay you too much. You must be new to this."

It was an insult—and, more important, it was an insult coming from a woman. She knew that would force one of them to come at her.

It was the heavier man who moved first. He stepped forward, still unaware that she had a weapon in her hand. He reached behind him as though he had a gun. She wasn't going to wait to find out if he really did.

Alex took a step to the side and then, almost like a ballerina, shifted her weight and stood up on her toes as she drove the stiletto into the man's solar plexus and up into his heart.

She knew she had hit the target immediately. The way the man stopped midmotion, and the way his eyes went blank, instantly told her he was out of the fight.

As she stepped away, pulling the stiletto from his chest, the man crumpled and tipped over the low seawall into the East River. She couldn't have planned it any better.

She had no time to admire her handiwork and immediately had to parry a lunge from the man with the big knife. It was a good thrust, but all she had to do was turn sideways, and the blade missed her completely.

She grabbed the young man's wrist with her left hand and drove the butt of the stiletto hard into his forehead.

She caught him as he lost consciousness. She said, "Have a good sleep. You're going to need it."

CHAPTER 47

I WAS SITTING on the couch trying to hide how tired I was from Mary Catherine and Juliana. I was recovering, but the long days seemed to hit me hard in the evenings.

I never wanted to say anything to the family, because I cherished these evenings at home with the children. Working on school projects, talking sports, listening to their dreams and hopes. It was magical. Usually.

At the moment, I was in a serious conversation with Juliana. I know that an eighteen-year-old in New York can legally make her own choices. But that's not what parenting is all about. I'm not naive. Sometimes you can't be the fun dad who always cracks jokes. This was one of those times.

Juliana said, "You don't even know Cade."

I said, "You mean Carter?"

"I mean the man I'm currently dating."

That stung a little bit. I didn't like to think of my daughters dating. But I was realistic. She was a beautiful girl, and now she was going to be on TV. I had to watch what I was going to say.

"You mean the twenty-six-year-old man you are currently dating." So much for watching what I said.

"I'm legally an adult. It doesn't matter how old he is."

Now Mary Catherine leaned in and said, "This isn't getting us anywhere. Let's take a break and talk about it tomorrow."

With that, Juliana stood up quickly and said, "Fine." She stormed out of the room and left me shaken.

I looked at Mary Catherine and just shook my head.

She put an arm around my shoulders and said, "She has a point. She *is* an adult. Maybe it would be better to give her a little space and not push too hard."

"It's just that I don't like to see my children make mistakes. I'm trying to save them from going through the same things I did."

"But we all make mistakes. I would think a man of your advanced years would know that by now."

That made me smile. Only for a moment. Mary Catherine was absolutely right, but I was still a father worried about his daughter.

Mary Catherine said, "Is there something here I don't understand? Or are you just trying to set a certain bar for the other girls as they get older and start to date?"

I dropped my head into my hands and admitted, "I just don't want to make the same mistakes I made with Brian."

"What mistakes? You're a great father. You did everything you could to be a good father to Brian. Sometimes people make poor choices. They make mistakes. Hopefully they learn from them and move on. I think that's the position you might have to take with Juliana."

"I know. That makes sense. I was just considering my other options."

"Such as?"

"Having one of my buddies arrest this young man and maybe losing him in Rikers Island for a few months. Is that a realistic possibility?"

Mary Catherine let out a short giggle and hugged me. Maybe things might work out after all, if I gave them a chance.

CHAPTER 48

ALEX RELAXED IN a chair near the hotel-room door, watching the unconscious young man tied to a chair next to the bed. It was amazing what a cabdriver would accept when he was afraid your "drunk little brother" would throw up in his cab.

This hotel in East Harlem looked like it was generally used by prostitutes and pushers. There was no hourly rate posted, but based on Alex's interaction with the clerk, any amount of time could be negotiated.

By the time she walked into the hotel, her captive was stumbling along with her. She'd undone her ponytail and allowed her hair to fly wildly around her shoulders and face. The wide dark sunglasses obscured what little part of her face was visible. And the hundred-dollar bill she handed directly to the clerk ensured that he didn't pay much attention.

Now she waited patiently for the young man to completely regain his senses. He had lolled in and out of consciousness since they'd entered the room and she'd secured him with the cord from a lamp.

Then the young man's head snapped upright, his eyes open wide.

He was much younger than she had originally thought. Probably around twenty. He was a good-looking boy with thick lips and a long, straight nose.

She wasn't sure what to expect. Usually it was begging, and sometimes it involved offers of fast wealth if she would let him go. He went in a different direction and surprised her.

He snarled with a remarkably clear voice, "You will release me right now. If you don't, you'll regret your decision the rest of your short, miserable life."

Alex was speechless for a moment. "Did I hit you too hard? You're not making any sense. You're the one who's tied up."

"And you're the one who's not making any sense. I was thinking I might sleep with you until you started acting like such a bitch."

Alex just stared at the young man.

"I'll still let you suck my dick, but you better untie me right now."

Alex said slowly, "I'm confused. Are you trying to scare me or make me think you're crazy?"

"I *am* crazy, and you *should* be scared. You have no idea what I've done to other women who disrespected me."

"I probably have an idea. But I'm not one of those women. The only reason you're not dead is because I have a few questions. There's a chance, if you answer my questions, that you'll see the sunrise in the morning. But if you're going to keep up this attitude, I will not waste any more time." She stood up and made a show out of opening her stiletto. It still had his friend's blood on the blade.

Alex saw his eyes open wide and realized she was on the right track. She knelt down in front of him and unbuckled his pants. She thought that was all she'd need to do.

Then the young man said, "You better start sucking or you'll be the one who regrets this."

She couldn't believe how some men acted toward women. She jabbed him in the leg with the stiletto. Nothing too serious. But she still had to put her hand over his mouth to keep him from screaming. Then she tilted the chair back so his head banged against the bed.

Alex put the point of the stiletto onto his groin and pressed slightly.

The man let out a yelp.

She knew he'd tell her anything she wanted now.

"Why were you and your friend after me?"

"We know you killed Cesar Ramos in his hospital bed."

"Who is *we?*"

"The boys in our crew."

"The Dominican gunmen?"

"There's no way you get away with this. One word from me and you'll live in misery for a week before they let you die."

"Then I guess I better not let you give the word."

When she was finished, she left the DO NOT DISTURB sign on the door and casually walked out the hotel's rear exit.

Now she had another complication with this contract.

CHAPTER 49

I ARRIVED AT the hotel in East Harlem about two o'clock in the afternoon. No one in this neighborhood seemed terribly surprised to see police activity around the building. There were a few hotels in every neighborhood that attracted people interested in doing their worst.

I chuckled at the cheap neon sign. FINELLI BUDGET INN. FBI. It had to be on purpose.

I saw the young homicide detective I was looking for. Roddy Huerta was a solid investigator and had proved his reliability over the past few years. He wasn't particularly big on imagination or finding creative ways to solve cases, but he was a good cop. He was the new breed. Young, fit, smart, and college-educated. But he went by the book. On everything.

I came from the school of investigation that said you had to clear cases and actually get murderers off the street. And to do that, sometimes you had to take chances.

But this was his show, and I was just trying to gather information.

Roddy glanced up from his notebook and pushed his glasses back onto his nose. He looked surprised and said, "Hey, Detective Bennett. What are you doing over here?"

"Just curious to see if it's related to something I'm working on. Whatcha got, Roddy?"

He followed me as I walked into the hotel. Some detectives would be offended to have someone wander onto their crime scene, but I knew Roddy was more interested in showing me how smart he was.

The younger detective said, "I've got a Hispanic male victim laid out in the bed. It looks like he'd been bound at the wrists and died from a single-edge-weapon wound to the chest."

I said, "Technically to the heart."

"The ME will have to determine that. Why are you interested?"

"Not the first I've seen this week."

He perked up. "A serial killer."

"Drug war."

He looked disappointed, and I understood why. He was one of those homicide detectives who worked a very specific geographic area and really didn't want to know about anything else going on. To catch a serial killer in an area like that would be something to crow about. Drug wars were a little more common.

We stepped into the room, and I saw the forensics people, wearing complete biomedical suits, processing the scene.

Roddy said, "It was a little tight in there, and the body had been in the bed at least twelve hours. I did my initial examination and decided it would be better to let the forensics people do their thing."

"Have you canvassed potential witnesses?"

"The clerk doesn't remember anyone coming in, and there's no record of this room being rented. There are so many patrons coming and going that we probably won't get anything useful out of processing it.

"The victim moved from the Dominican Republic sixteen years ago. He has sixteen arrests and four convictions and has never done any prison time."

Roddy looked at me and said, "And please don't just write this off as a Hispanic thing. Not all Hispanics are involved in the drug trade."

"Did I say or do anything to make you think that?"

"Sorry—just a little defensive."

I looked into the room at the face of the young man with a gray complexion staring lifelessly up at the ceiling. I'd been looking at this as a homicide investigation when in fact it was more of a narcotics investigation.

CHAPTER 50

IF I NEEDED to know something about narcotics investigations, I knew exactly who to turn to. Sergeant Tim Marcia. When I explained that I wanted to start looking at the homicides as if they were one big narcotics case, he understood immediately.

That's how we found ourselves on Audubon Avenue, a few blocks from Yeshiva University in upper Manhattan. We sat in a booth in the kind of café where all types of business are conducted and no one pays much attention to who comes and goes.

I said, "Who exactly is this guy we're meeting?"

"John is what people call a regulator."

"And what is a regulator?"

"It's an odd little position in the drug world. Someone respected and trusted by all sides of the narcotics business. His job is to iron out disputes and keep things quiet and profitable.

It's exactly the kind of job the NYPD would create if they understood anything about narcotics."

"So everyone listens to him?"

"Everyone except for the cartels. You can't tell them shit. They think they can run the world."

The front door opened, and as soon as I saw the man step inside, something told me he had to be the regulator. He was about fifty and had spent way too much time out in the sun. His hair was brown with streaks of silver and tied in a long braid that draped over his left shoulder. He was dressed like he lived in the West, complete with cowboy boots and a plaid shirt. In New York, he would be written off as just another colorful character.

A much younger woman stepped in behind him. She was stunning, with thick black hair and curves that seemed almost unbelievable. Even though he walked toward us, she sat at another table on the other side of the room.

The regulator stepped right up to Sergeant Marcia and nodded as he sat down.

Sergeant Marcia said, "Mike, this is the man I was telling you about."

The regulator spoke with the raspy voice of someone who'd smoked since childhood. "Call me John. Everyone does."

I looked across at the beautiful woman sitting by herself. "Is she with you?"

"In a manner of speaking." He looked over his shoulder and waved to the young woman. She smiled and nodded her head. "She was provided to me by the Santos gang, near Yonkers. The idea is to make sure I don't talk to the other side during a crucial negotiation."

I said, "What negotiation?"

"It would be unethical for me to disclose that. It has nothing to do with what you want to talk about."

For the first time I noticed a slight European accent. I had the distinct impression he didn't mind a beautiful young woman following him everywhere.

I said, "I don't mean to throw a wrench into anything, but I'm curious as to why you agreed to meet us."

The man took a moment, as if he was gathering his thoughts. "Sergeant Marcia understands the balance of the streets. You do what you have to do, and I do what I have to. That balance is crucial to a happy life for a lot of people. I know about your issues with the Mexican cartel. Their use of a hit man and Dominican gunmen doesn't involve me at all. Personally, I avoid Dominicans whenever possible."

I said, "You don't like their tactics?"

"No. They don't pay me or recognize my value. Their existence should not affect me one way or the other. But if they try to kill a cop and then the cops crack down on everyone, it hurts my bottom line. My job is to keep things quiet and profitable."

"Do you have any information that might help me help you do your job?"

The regulator chuckled. "I like your view of things. Sergeant Marcia said you were okay. What I've heard is that three Dominicans tried to shoot you in front of a church yesterday. You were too fast for them."

"Do you know any of the men?"

He slid a small piece of paper across the table. "I believe these three men were involved. At least two of them are cousins. They're not the kind of people to take a failure like this well."

"I appreciate the information."

"Use it well, and maybe we'll both have an easier time of it. Good luck, Detective Bennett. You're gonna need it."

CHAPTER 51

BACK AT THE office, I wasted no time running the names the regulator had given me, not seeking assistance from analysts and other detectives. This was a lead I wanted to follow up quickly, without input from anyone else.

All three of the men whose names the regulator gave me had a past with narcotics violations. All three had done time at Rikers Island or upstate. Their photos looked familiar, but booking photos are notoriously difficult to match with faces you see on the street. In the photographs, all the men had facial hair. No one who tried to shoot me in front of Holy Name had any facial hair. But that meant little.

What I found most interesting was that one man, named Julio Laza, had a car registered to him. A one-year-old Chevy Cruze. My guess was that the car was green.

Usually someone trying to commit a crime like murder or

even armed robbery goes to the trouble of stealing a car or using a rental. In this case, it seemed like the suspects were overconfident—thought they could pull off the hit with no issues and save the money they would have spent on a car.

I considered grabbing someone to come with me as a partner. Then I thought about Antrole and decided that one dead partner was enough. This was something I was going to do on my own.

When I had a couple of addresses and some information I could use, I scooped everything up and turned from my desk, then almost ran into Harry Grissom.

My lieutenant said, "What have you got, Mike?"

"Still trying to put some leads together."

"Just don't do anything stupid by yourself."

"I haven't since I was a teenager and discovered girls."

"Very funny. But I'm serious. I don't want you to get all vigilante on me. You've got a job to do. That job should include finding out who killed Antrole. But I don't want to have this talk with someone else working on *your* homicide. Do I make myself clear?"

"Crystal."

Thirty seconds later, I was out the door. As the regulator had said, *I do what I have to.*

CHAPTER 52

ALEX MARTINEZ LEANED in close over the elegant table next to a window at Central Park's Tavern on the Green. The colossal windows provided a grand view. Mostly of tourists strolling in the park, but she appreciated that her new police officer friend, Tom McLaughlin, was trying to impress her. He'd used his connections to get them into the very busy tourist spot.

He dressed well and had impeccable manners. That was hard to find anymore. Especially in New York. He opened doors for her and held her chair. All the things he'd been taught as a child.

She never would've guessed she'd be on two dates in two nights with the same man in New York City. She wasn't complaining. This was fun. A lot of fun. Tom had proved to be charming as well as attractive and energetic. And he loved the NYPD. He was almost an expert on its history.

After their salads, Tom pulled out his cell phone and handed it to the young waiter. "Would you mind taking a quick photo of us with the window in the background?"

Alex thought of all the issues a photograph of her might cause. She scrambled for a quick excuse. Finally she said, "Tom, can we take the photo later? A lady needs to put herself together before she's photographed."

Tom laughed. "Spoken like a true professional photographer." Crisis averted. For now.

They chatted about horses and a little about their backgrounds. From force of habit in her professional life, Alex didn't mention that she had two daughters.

Intrigued by what Alex divulged about her frequent travel, Tom told her about the international reach of the NYPD intelligence office.

Alex said, "How is that possible if they are *New York* police officers?"

"I don't know the terms, but the city decided they were tired of relying on the feds to give them a heads-up on terror threats. After 9/11, the NYPD started to open offices in countries that were tied to threats. Mainly in Europe. We even have some uniformed officers at the Vatican during special jubilee years. It's a cool job for a cop."

Alex said, "Is that something you want to do someday?"

"No. If I'm not going to stay in the Mounted Unit, I'd like to go to Homicide. That's where the sharp detectives are."

"I saw an article somewhere about an NYPD homicide detective. I think his name was Michael Bennett. Have you ever heard of him?"

Tom's face lit up. "Everyone's heard of Michael Bennett.

He's hot shit. He used to be on the hostage negotiation team, and he's the one who solved the case where all the hostages were taken at the First Lady's funeral."

"I remember that. Do you know him personally?"

Tom shook his head. "I've seen him around a couple of times. He's got a great reputation. And he's kind of famous for having ten adopted children as well."

That was information Alex could use. She smiled and took a sip from her glass of Chardonnay. This was turning out to be a great date.

CHAPTER 53

I STRUCK OUT at the first couple of addresses for my potential suspects. I decided to call it a day and get home at a reasonable hour, though I wasn't nearly as tired and sore as I had been. I was finally starting to heal.

I wasn't greeted by young children right at the front door. That rarely happened. As I stepped into the entryway that led to the living room, I was surprised by another man in the house. It took me a minute to register his face.

He smiled, stuck out his hand, and said, "Hello, Mr. Bennett."

I stammered, "Carter, how nice to see you. I didn't know you were coming over." I could be polite, even to a twenty-six-year-old man dating my eighteen-year-old daughter. I was still surprised to see him in my home.

Just then, Mary Catherine hustled around the corner and said, "You see we have a guest for dinner tonight. Your grandfather couldn't make it, and Juliana thought it'd be nice for Carter to meet the family."

"Yeah, sure. It's great." I tried to put some enthusiasm in my voice but failed.

The young man melted back into the living room to talk to Trent.

Mary Catherine stepped into the hallway and gave me a look that simultaneously said, *I'm sorry* and *Don't say a single mean word to that boy.*

I nodded in acknowledgment. She seemed satisfied and disappeared to supervise the process of setting the table and getting dinner ready.

Once we'd said grace and everyone had been served, Chrissy, who was sitting next to Carter, looked at him with her innocent eyes and said, "You are old."

I coughed up a little water trying to stifle a laugh. Mary Catherine looked horrified, and Juliana spoke up.

"That's not very polite, Chrissy."

Mary Catherine changed the subject and got Juliana talking about the production.

She said, "We're going to have our first media interviews in the next few days. Someone is supposed to come by the set and take some photographs and interview us for an entertainment magazine."

Bridget perked up. "Like *Entertainment Weekly?*"

"Something like that."

Fiona chimed in. "What's the magazine called?"

Juliana hesitated, but Carter said, "The *Brooklyn Studio Newsletter.*"

Mary Catherine quickly said, "That's wonderful. It's so exciting. I could really see things coming together when I visited the set."

I listened to the evening unfold. I understood that I had to get used to the idea of the dating world. I mean, I have six daughters, for Christ's sake. But the idea of this good-looking, midtwenties millennial dating my oldest daughter bothered me.

It made me think of all the stories I'd heard from other cops who had chased off boyfriends for one reason or another. My favorite was from a sergeant in Queens who answered the door with no shirt on and a badge pinned through his bare chest. That was hard-core. I needed to take another route.

I said, "Carter, what are your acting goals?"

All actors, like writers, love to talk about their future. To most of them, that future doesn't factor in family or romance.

And off he went. "Oh, I'm moving to Los Angeles after the first season of *Century's End* is complete. I've spoken to an agent out there about representing me."

The look on Juliana's face told me this was nothing he had discussed with her.

CHAPTER 54

ALEX MARTINEZ WAS worn-out. In a good way. She sprawled in the king-size bed in the tiny lower Manhattan apartment of Officer Tom McLaughlin. Aerobic energy could be as useful in sex as it was on the job. She was still smiling, listening to the gentle snores of her new lover.

The whole night had been wonderful. Dinner at the Tavern on the Green. The stroll through Central Park, which included a visit to the stables. He was really a special guy.

But one thing stuck in her head. She had asked about Michael Bennett, which might have been a mistake. It probably wasn't a big thing to Officer McLaughlin. He had gone on and on about the homicide detective.

Now she tried to calculate all the ways that might come back to haunt her after Detective Bennett was dead. Would Officer McLaughlin remember the conversation and discuss it with the detectives investigating the murder? If so, did he know anything about her that could be useful? She never did let him have a photograph.

She rolled it over and over in her brain. The sooner you handle a problem, the better things work out.

She wondered if Officer Tom McLaughlin could be a loose end. A loose end that could expose her later.

She rolled over and slipped out of bed silently. She got dressed in the cramped space between the edge of the bed and the wall.

She looked down at the sleeping form of Officer McLaughlin and reached into her purse for her stiletto. She hit the button, and the blade popped straight out of the handle with just a little mechanical click.

She ran through her options once again. This man had done nothing wrong and did not deserve to die because of the mistake *she* made. But she couldn't risk someone coming to the ranch one day to arrest her and separate her from the girls.

She closed her eyes and listened to the sounds of the city in the dark apartment. Sometimes she wished she was someone else.

CHAPTER 55

ALEX STOOD IN the dark room with the stiletto in her hand, ready to make a drastic decision. Then she was startled by Tom McLaughlin's voice.

"Do you have to go?"

"I'm afraid so."

"I need to tell you something. Just so I feel good about where we are. And I don't want you to think I'm keeping any secrets."

Alex just stood in the darkened room wondering if she should say something like, *It doesn't matter.* Because it wouldn't in just a few seconds.

Tom kept talking anyway. "I didn't tell you that I have a daughter."

"What?"

"I don't want you to think I was trying to hide something. I also don't want to freak you out. But I have a three-year-old named Emily."

"Are you married?"

"No. I asked Emily's mother to marry me when we found out she was pregnant, but she wasn't interested. Now I have to fight hard to make sure I'm as involved in Emily's life as I want to be."

Alex didn't know what to say.

Tom said, "I hope this doesn't change anything. I had a great time, and I hope we can see each other again."

To Alex it did change something. It added something to her careful calculations. Suddenly she thought of a girl, not much younger than Gabriela, calling out for her absent father. Her father, who was a decent, hardworking man and didn't do anything wrong.

He sat up in bed and reached for the light on the nightstand.

Alex quickly dropped the hand with the stiletto into her purse.

Tom said, "Let me walk outside and get a cab with you."

"It's really not necessary."

"I can't let a defenseless woman stand alone on a street corner in New York."

A smile spread across her face. "I guarantee you won't be letting a defenseless woman stand on the street. Go back to bed. Dream happy dreams."

Alex leaned down until she was just a few inches away, the stiletto still in her hand. He looked up at her from the bed, exposing the underside of his jaw.

She hesitated for a moment, then kissed him on the lips. She didn't say another word as she slipped out of the apartment.

CHAPTER 56

I WAS STILL looking for the men whose names the regulator had given me. I had an address on 129th Street for one of them, Julio Laza, on the second floor of a run-down apartment building.

As I circled the block to get a feel for the area, I noticed a green Chevy Cruze parked by the side of the building. When I got out and looked the car over, I found a bullet hole just in front of the driver's-side door. Jackpot.

Normally I would call in assistance and arrest someone who tried to shoot me. In this instance, I thought it was more important to find out who had hired Julio.

Not only would finding out who hired him be a bigger coup, I might also find some way to tie the information in with what Brian had told me earlier. Maybe that way, with a better lawyer, we could have his sentence reduced. I saw it happen all the time. That's why I was willing to take a risk today.

A few minutes later, as I headed up the raw concrete front steps, I saw someone coming out the sturdy metal door. Immediately I realized it was my man, Julio Laza. He looked up and recognized me, too. Why couldn't all cases be this easy?

He wasted no time. Julio leaped off the entryway, jumping down four feet to the spotty grass surrounding the building. He landed on his feet and started to run. And he ran fast.

I yelled out to him, "I just want to talk." But he didn't believe me. Why should he? If I ran into someone I'd tried to shoot, I'd probably flee as well.

When I was a rookie, I used to chase fleeing suspects on foot all the time. Then a veteran, not much older than I was but with four years on the job, showed me the wonders of patience. He said it was always better to let rookies chase on foot, while he preferred a patrol car.

I knew how jerks like Julio thought. He was going to run away and come back for his car. Guys like this never wanted to leave their rides.

I acted like I was chasing him. I even let him look over his shoulder and see me fading in the distance as he turned a corner. Then I casually walked back toward his building and sat down behind a tree not far from his car. The rough bark of the trunk was covered in dozens of carvings. Mostly hearts with names inside.

I was not disappointed. About five minutes later, I saw Julio Laza jogging casually toward the Chevy.

I waited until he was in an awkward position. He hadn't

stuck the key into the lock of the door yet. Then I stood up. He didn't notice me.

I stepped around the tree. He still didn't notice me.

I was starting to get a complex. Finally I cleared my throat and said, "I wondered how long it would take you to get back here."

It startled Julio so much that he dropped his keys under the car. He stood up, shaky from his run, hair plastered to his forehead.

He said, "Whatchoo want, man?"

"Exactly what I told you before you went on this marathon. I just want to talk."

He looked around nervously. No one wanted to be seen talking to a cop in this neighborhood.

I said, "Come take a walk with me. We'll get out of public view and have a little chat."

As he took a few steps with me, I put my arm around his shoulders as if I were comforting a child after he lost a football game.

Julio said, "What do you want to talk about?"

I stopped and looked at him. "You're joking, right?"

Julio just shrugged and walked along with me.

CHAPTER 57

INSTEAD OF TAKING Julio Laza to a comfortable café or a McDonald's to sit and chat over a drink, I put him in the passenger seat of my police car.

He was shaking and sweating as if he were working a coal furnace. We drove to a parking lot several blocks away so no one would notice us. But Julio didn't care. He figured he was going to jail shortly—if I didn't shoot him before that.

Hell, he's the one who pointed a machine gun at me. And at a priest! When I mentioned that, I thought his eyes would pop out of his head.

He said, "I'm sorry. I'm sorry. I'm so sorry. It was just business. And I didn't even realize the other guy was a priest. I never shot at him. I hope my mom doesn't find out."

"Your mom is the least of your concerns. You shot at a New York City detective. And then you were stupid enough to be caught almost right away. Not only are you looking at a shit-load of jail time, any kind of street cred you had is ruined."

Julio was about thirty and average in every possible way. His brown curly hair could've used a shampoo, and the acne on his chin and nose made me think he didn't wash as often as he should. I said, "You're sweating. That doesn't do much to recommend a hit man."

"Hit man! Hit man! You can't be serious."

"You tried to shoot me yesterday. I can only assume you did it for money, since we've never met and I never made a case on you."

"Look, man, I don't think I want to talk to any cops right now."

It was time to get serious. "You're already talking to a cop. Your options are very simple. You talk to me and tell me what the hell is going on or you end up in Rikers Island. And I spread it around that you're a snitch."

"What?" He yelped like I'd slapped him across the face.

"The inmates will hate you because you're a snitch, and none of the cops will help you because you tried to kill a cop. I've never met anyone who was stuck between such a rock and a hard place."

I saw him consider exactly what I was talking about. I sat back and let him think up the worst possible scenario himself.

After almost two minutes, he looked at me and said, "Okay, what sort of information are you looking for?"

"Who hired you to kill me and why?"

"I don't know all the details. It was my cousin who hired me. He needed someone to drive. I pulled out my old MAC-10 when I saw you were kicking his ass. I swear to God I was just trying to keep you away from them so they could get away."

"Who's your cousin?"

"Willie. Willie Perez. But he was hired by someone else. I swear I don't know who."

"What did Willie say about who hired him? C'mon—I know he had to talk about it to get you to help."

Julio stared at me like I was a witch who could read his mind.

He looked down at the stained upholstery of my police-car seat and mumbled, "It was a chick."

"What?"

He spoke up. "A woman. It was a woman who hired Willie."

"What did she look like?"

"I don't know. He just said she was beautiful. That was all he said, I swear."

"Where's Willie now?"

"I don't know. He lives in the same apartment as me, but I don't see him that much. He's got girlfriends. Lots of them."

I said, "I'll tell you the truth. I'm not sure how much of this is bullshit."

"None. I swear. I'm just sorry I shot at you."

"For once I'm going to say it doesn't matter that you shot at me. The only thing that will help you now is to help me find whoever hired your cousin. I'm not making any specific deals. I'm not doing shit. Nothing until you help me."

I let him digest that. Often someone's imagination will do your work for you.

Julio looked at me and said, "Okay, I'll tell you everything I know."

"And I'm going to need you to try to set up a meeting with whoever hired your cousin."

"I can't do that from a police car."

"I'm going to go way out on a limb and give you a day to set that up. Don't say anything to your cousin about me yet. I'll tell you something: you don't want to cross me. You believe me?"

"I swear to God I believe you."

CHAPTER 58

ALEX MARTINEZ SPOKE to Oscar, her contact from the Mexican cartel, on her throwaway phone to confirm that the contracts on the Canadians were complete. She threw in Alicia Toussant's bodyguard for free. Now she was just tying up loose ends—like Detective Michael Bennett.

Oscar said, "This is all good. We don't need to make statements with these Canadians in New York. They know someone is tracking them. If we need to, we'll send you to Quebec in a few months. Then we'll make a statement, like killing one of these pricks in front of his family or cutting off a few dicks. That will show them how far we're willing to go."

Alex said, "That's another conversation. I was just calling to say things are almost wrapped up here in New York."

The conversation was brief. All he said was, "Very good. That's why we pay you so much."

When she told him she was tying up loose ends, she didn't go into details. The Dominican gang that had tried to kill her was the biggest loose end she'd ever had on a contract. She had an address for one of the men, and it would make a statement to kill him in his own apartment.

This was as close to a personal reason for killing as she'd ever had. She was angry. The young man she'd killed in the crappy old hotel in East Harlem had been vile. His attitude and comments made her shudder.

The fact that they thought they could eliminate her made her livid.

Finally she found the apartment, on 129th Street in East Harlem. It looked like most of the other run-down apartment buildings in this part of New York. The city had planted a few trees in the grassy swath around the sidewalks, and about every other apartment had an air conditioner hanging out of its window.

She stood on the corner for a few moments and took in the whole block. There was nothing out of place. Some children played in the green space in front of the building. Alex didn't want to be seen entering through the front door.

She walked another block to look at the rear of the apartment complex and checked for video cameras. The surge in video surveillance and security had made her job more difficult. One of the reasons she was paid so well was that she knew how to adapt. In a neighborhood like this there wasn't nearly as much video surveillance as there was in more affluent and commercial areas.

The rear door locked automatically as soon as it closed. She watched as a couple of people came and went, each using a key to get back inside.

An elderly woman carrying two heavy bags of groceries slowly moved alongside her.

Without thinking, Alex said in Spanish, "Let me help you with that." She took one of the bags from the woman's skinny arms.

The older woman smiled and said, "You have very nice manners. I don't see that much around here anymore."

"I'm not from around here."

The woman reached up and touched Alex's cheek. "Good for you, sweetheart."

After they walked for a minute, Alex realized she was headed toward the back door of the apartment building. Perfect. Sometimes luck did favor those who were prepared.

It was natural to follow the woman in the door with a bag of groceries in her arms, and she even helped take it inside her first-floor apartment.

The woman tried to hand Alex a dollar bill as a tip.

Alex smiled and refused as she backed out of the apartment. She turned as if she was headed back out the door, then took the stairs to the second floor.

She found the apartment right next to the stairs and listened carefully for several minutes. There was no sound or movement from inside.

She quietly tried the handle. The door was locked but loose in its frame. The old story: a cheap landlord who never wanted to repair anything.

Alex retrieved her stiletto and popped it open. It only took one push in the right place by the lock to slip the door past the frame. She let it swing open silently.

She stepped inside the empty apartment.

CHAPTER 59

SOMETIMES EVEN I was amazed at the turns my days could take. An hour ago, I was talking to a guy who tried to kill me. I cut a deal no sane cop would make. I gave up an immediate arrest that would probably lead to two other arrests for the chance to land the big one. As long as I didn't tell anyone about it, I probably wouldn't get in trouble. Now I was downtown and meeting Mary Catherine for lunch.

I had gone from talking to a guy who tried to kill me to talking with the woman who had saved me.

It was a spur-of-the-moment decision. I called her and asked her to meet me on the seventh floor of the Bergdorf Goodman department store, in the little restaurant. She sounded shocked by the invitation, then blurted out, "I didn't know you realized there was a restaurant up there."

The BG Restaurant was fancy by my standards, with big, ornate windows and stiff, formal chairs. The menu prices made me flinch a little, but I rationalized the midday splurge. The croque monsieur made that rationalization easier.

We sat at a small table overlooking Central Park near 57th Street. The view was spectacular. And so was Mary Catherine. Her beautiful face, framed by that lovely auburn hair, and those clear green eyes that seemed to take in the whole world made the view pale by comparison. It's too bad I could never put that kind of shit into words around her. Instead I said, "You look great."

She blushed slightly and smiled. "You always say the right things."

We chatted about subjects we normally don't get to chat about. Current events. Where the kids might end up going to college. Where we might go on vacation this coming summer. It was great.

Then we ended up on the topic of Juliana.

Mary Catherine said, "I really think you need to give her more room. By the way, that was a sneaky trick, getting Carter to admit he was planning on moving to LA."

I smiled. "Sneaky or brilliant?"

She shrugged and said, "I guess it's a little bit of both."

"When you get a little older, you have to get sneakier. It's our only advantage."

Mary Catherine wasn't swayed. "I want you to let her live her life. At least within reason. Carter seems like a nice enough boy."

"I wouldn't have a problem with him if he was a boy. But the fact that he's closer to thirty than twenty bothers me."

"Do you really think anyone would try to do anything stupid to any of your daughters after they met you?"

I thought about it. Maybe I did come on a little strong sometimes.

I changed the topic. "Have you thought about a date for us yet? A spring wedding might be nice."

"No, I haven't thought about it."

"I could be sneaky and trick you into it."

"There's no need. It's just that I have so much to keep up with running the house. It's hard to take time to plan anything. I can't even think about a wedding right now."

I said, "It doesn't have to be big and elaborate."

"The hell it doesn't. If I'm going to marry the man I love, it's going to be way over the top. I mean Barbra-Streisand-as-entertainment big."

I chuckled as I said, "What do you mean *if* you're going to marry me?"

She reached across the table and took my hand in hers. "*When* I marry the man I love. But right now I want to focus on Bridget and Fiona as they get ready for their first boy-girl dance. And Trent, the forgotten kid, who never does anything wrong. And Chrissy, who is taking this baby-of-the-family thing a little too far."

I thought about what she was saying. "I know you end up getting a whole family with me. A giant family. I don't want to stress you out any more."

"Oh, you silly, oblivious man. That's just it. I do get the whole family. The whole fantastic family. It's not a negative. I get to adopt each of the kids, just like you and Maeve did. It's thrilling. It's more than I ever wanted. But right now I have cookies I have to get to Shawna's class for history day, and then I'm taking Seamus to the eye doctor."

I leaned close and kissed Mary Catherine. I had never loved her more than I did right then.

CHAPTER 60

BY THE TIME I got back to the office I was on fire. I had more information—specifically, that a woman hired the Dominicans to shoot me. I wanted this whole ordeal over as soon as possible.

Some of my ad hoc task force was already there, and I called in Cassie Max and Roddy Huerta.

When we all gathered in a conference room, Roddy was the first to say, "You do realize you're not my sergeant. You can't just order me into the office any time you want to talk to me."

Cassie casually turned toward Roddy and said, "Shut up and maybe learn something."

I appreciated that kind of support. I hate to admit it, but I got a kick out of seeing Roddy brought down a peg or two.

I said, "I think I have something that'll change how we look at this case." I glanced around the table. The detectives and the three forensics people were all staring at me intently.

"I have a tip that a woman hired the Dominican gunmen who tried to shoot me. They describe her as beautiful."

Roddy shook his head. "You called us in to tell us that? An attractive woman is trying to murder you? Are you bragging?"

"No, numb nuts. I'm telling you this because it's a lead. I know we've all looked through surveillance videos trying to identify a suspect, but I've been looking for a man. Not only is that sexist, it's also the biggest trap a detective can fall into. I got tunnel vision. Now I'm hoping you guys can help me out. If we all start reviewing surveillance videos, we might be able get an image of this woman."

Roddy said, "And what if she's just a go-between? Maybe the killer really is a man."

"I'm not sure how you want me to respond to that, Roddy. Are you saying we should ignore this lead? I think we should run it down, and if we find her, see if we can't get her to identify who she's working for. It's kind of basic police work.

"Also, this fits in with the murder at the hospital. The corrections officers who were guarding the murdered gunman both said they spoke to a woman. They just couldn't give any description and didn't know exactly how she was involved. She may have just been a distraction."

Cassie said, "I have hours of video from businesses around Madison Square Park. I didn't have any idea what to look for, but I'm willing to give it a shot."

Roddy said, "That shitty hotel purposely doesn't want anyone knowing who comes and goes. And there are no businesses at the entrance that would have surveillance. I did grab a tape from an electronics store not far from the rear entrance to the hotel. I looked at it but wrote off the females who were leaving as prostitutes."

Cassie let out a laugh and said, "Typical."

I intervened before Roddy got too bent out of shape. "Unless anyone else has anything useful to add, I would recommend we all get to work. There are other pieces of this puzzle that might fall into place."

As the little meeting broke up, I looked over to my lieutenant. Harry Grissom hadn't said a word during the meeting as he leaned against the back wall with his arms folded.

Now he looked at me like he was about to speak. Instead he just nodded and grunted something that could've been "Good job."

CHAPTER 61

ALEX TOOK ADVANTAGE of being alone in the Dominicans' apartment. She didn't just sit on the couch and wait.
She did a good, thorough search of the place, putting everything back where she found it. To Alex, planning was a part of
the job she enjoyed. With attention to detail and preparation,
she felt ready all the time.

The kitchen drawers gave up something that really interested her. This creep had a photograph of her from the time
when they had sat at the White Castle talking about things. It
was clear that his friend had taken it somehow when she wasn't
paying attention. They had printed out at least two copies.

From a photographer's point of view, the picture wasn't that
bad. He had been lucky to catch the light just right, and her
hair was over her shoulder, away from her face. It was really
quite flattering.

From another point of view, the fact that these men were serious enough about killing her to hand out photographs made her angry. She didn't know how many were in the group, but it was definitely suffering some serious casualties. And it was only going to get worse.

In the next drawer there was an old-fashioned Smith & Wesson .38 revolver. It was the kind of weapon you used up close, for protection. It was small, simple, and reliable.

She took it out of the drawer and stuck it in her purse. She'd find a way to use it sometime.

The apartment had two bedrooms, and from what she could tell, at least two men lived there. They weren't particularly tidy, and a nasty odor of stale beer and cigarette smoke hung in the air. She didn't care for it at all.

She also found the photograph she had given them of Detective Michael Bennett, which she'd found on the Internet, but it was clear and showed the handsome detective's face in full.

Her recent research on the Internet had turned up quite a bit of information about the detective. Since it was obvious she was the one who was going to finish the contract on him, she wanted to know everything she could.

Alex respected a man who adopted ten children. He'd been very smart and careful not to let any of the children's photographs appear on the Internet. No news story carried any information about them. Several articles referenced the fact that he had adopted a number of children, but there was no mention of names or descriptions.

It was a shame someone felt that a man like this had to die, whereas no one really cared about incompetent idiots like the men who lived in this apartment. She hated doing something like this for no money, but she couldn't risk their trying to kill her again. The answer was to send a strong and serious signal that no one should mess with her.

Just as she placed Bennett's photo back in the folder on the cheap, shaky table, she heard the floor creak just outside the door.

She froze in place.

Then she heard the key slip into the lock.

The door started to open.

CHAPTER 62

AS THE DOOR swung open, Alex was ready. She stood in the corner of the main room, perfectly still. The gun she'd taken from the drawer was in her right hand. She watched as a man stepped into the apartment, but it wasn't the person she was expecting. This man was too young and too tall. He had a little acne on his face and thick, curly hair.

He shut the door and tossed a plastic bag of groceries onto the kitchen counter. He walked across the room and flopped onto the leatherette couch, then clicked on the TV.

Alex knew she was stealthy, but this was ridiculous. All he had to do was turn his head a few degrees to the left and she'd be in plain view. Instead his eyes were glued straight ahead as she heard the ESPN intro music on the TV.

It was an odd feeling to be in a room with someone who had no idea you were there. It was almost like watching a movie. It was like some new, fantastic interactive television.

It sent an odd thrill through her, and she savored it for almost a full minute. The longer she waited, the greater the surprise. This man was clueless. It was embarrassing that he and his associates thought they could kill her.

Alex just watched the man until he unbuttoned his pants and started to slip his hand down them. Then she stepped away from the wall and said in a calm tone, "Who are you? Where is Willie?"

"Jesus Christ," he shouted as he sprang to his feet and tried to close his pants. "Who the hell are you? What are you doing here?" Then recognition set in, and he said, "Oh, it's you. Willie isn't here."

"Who are you?"

"His cousin Julio."

"The driver he mentioned." She thought about it for a moment and said, "When will Willie be home?"

Just as he started to answer, she raised the revolver and pointed it at his face. It had the effect she wanted.

Julio said, "He usually comes home in the afternoon about now. When I talked to him on the phone earlier, he said he'd be here."

"Good boy. You're using your head."

"You're not using yours. Willie is a really bad man. Everyone knows him. Everyone's afraid of him. If you shoot me, he'll know who did it."

Alex said, "I hope so." Then she fired once, striking Julio in the dead center of his chest. He took a slight step backward, then tumbled onto the couch. He let out a raspy breath and tried to say something. He never got it out.

His eyes didn't close, even after his heart stopped. Those lifeless brown eyes seemed fixed on Alex.

She shook off the unnerving stare of the dead man and surveyed her work for a moment. She lifted his right leg onto the couch and crossed it over his left. She straightened his body against the pillow so that it looked like he was reclining on the couch.

Then Alex stepped back and looked at the room again. A plan popped into her head.

This could work out.

CHAPTER 63

ALEX MARTINEZ COULD hear her second target trudging up the stairs and through the hallway for twenty seconds before he reached the door. She'd been sitting in the apartment with the dead man for almost a quarter of an hour. This came as a relief.

She stood behind the door when it swung open and immediately saw the heavily tattooed left arm of Willie Perez. He was chatting on the phone in Spanish.

"Yeah, baby. I know. No, you can't come over here. My cousin wouldn't like it. Okay, I'll talk to him."

Alex didn't have to be a mind reader to tell what the conversation was about.

Willie called out to his cousin on the couch. From this angle, all he could see was the top of his cousin's head and the TV playing in the background.

When he got no response, he called out louder, "Julio."

Behind him, Alex said, "He's not going to answer you."

She couldn't hide her smile when Willie flinched and spun around to see the barrel of a gun right in his face.

Willie said, "I guess you're not here to pay me."

"Do you really think you earned anything?"

Now Willie focused on the gun for a moment. He said, "Is that my revolver?"

"It is."

While keeping the snub-nosed revolver pointed at Willie's face, she used her left hand to pat down his waistband. She felt a gun hidden in his belt and pulled free a Taurus 9mm pistol.

She placed the revolver on the kitchen counter and pointed the newly acquired semiautomatic pistol at Willie's head.

She backed him up past the couch so he could get a good look at his cousin.

Willie just stared at him.

Alex said, "A single gunshot in this neighborhood doesn't draw any attention. I doubt your neighbors like you enough to call the cops if they heard a problem anyway."

"You won't get away with this."

"Who's going to catch me? The police? They'll be glad you're gone."

Willie shook his head and said, "I knew you were trouble the first time I saw you. Who looks like you and then decides to kill people for a living? You've got something very wrong with you, lady."

"The fact that you found it easier to kill me than the person I paid you to kill makes me question your judgment."

"And what were we supposed to do about you killing Cesar in the hospital?"

"Which is why I have to do this today. I guarantee your friends on your crew will know exactly what happened."

Willie nodded. "I can see your point. Perhaps we were out of line. Maybe we can work something out."

Alex knew it would be easier if she were able to position him before she pulled the trigger. She needed him to move more to his right so he was in front of the couch, as though he and his cousin had had an argument face-to-face.

That was her mistake. She didn't have her full focus on the killer in front of her. Instead she was thinking ahead.

As Willie shuffled away from her, he paused at the low coffee table between them.

Willie said, "Let me say one thing."

As Alex said, "What's that?" Willie kicked the coffee table hard into her shins, distracting her and making her lose her balance. He sprang across the space between them and wrapped a strong hand around her wrist so she couldn't point the gun anywhere but straight up.

Most people would struggle against the power of his grip and try to get the hand free. Alex had too much training and experience for that. She lifted her knee and caught Willie on the thigh, making him step back.

He was strong and tough and jerked her along with him. Then he twisted, and they both tumbled onto the couch.

Alex found herself sandwiched between the dead man and the man trying to kill her.

CHAPTER 64

THEY STRUGGLED ON the couch as Willie used his size and strength to keep the pistol pointed away from him. Alex wished she could get to her stiletto, but she'd have to make do with just her fist for now.

She punched him once directly in the Adam's apple. The shock and inability to breathe made him shrink back and ease his grip on her wrist. Her next blow was to his solar plexus, knocking out any wind he had left.

That sent him off Alex, and he struggled to stand up.

He took a few steps back and ended up in almost the exact spot Alex wanted. She was lying on top of his dead cousin. It didn't line up any better than this. She fired once, and the bullet hit him in almost the same place where she had punched him.

He slapped both his hands over the wound in a futile effort to ease the pain and stem the bleeding. He stood staring at

Alex, as if he couldn't believe she'd do something like that in his own home.

Willie just stared at her, trying to form a word. He wheezed and coughed. Blood mixed with his spittle as it flew onto the coffee table.

The ESPN music blared from the TV again.

After what felt like hours, but was really only ten seconds, he dropped to his knees, then fell forward.

She got off the couch and checked his pulse. It was weak for a few beats, then faded out completely.

Alex listened carefully for any movement in the hallway or any signs of concern from the neighbors. There was nothing. Just as she expected.

It was a little more difficult than she had anticipated, but the results were exactly what she wanted. She slipped on the plastic gloves she always kept in her purse. The one time a date had found them, she told him the oval case contained a diaphragm. Of all her professional equipment, gloves were the easiest things to hide in a purse or suitcase.

Now was the time for her meticulous nature to come out. She had to arrange the crime scene. She put the Taurus semi-automatic pistol in Julio's hand. She found the spent casing the gun had ejected when she shot Willie and rubbed it on Julio's hand and arm, then tossed it back onto the floor. She thought that would be enough to fool people if they bothered to test the dead men for gunshot residue.

Then she picked up the revolver, removed the spent casing from the cylinder, and rubbed it on Willie's right hand. Then she returned the casing and nestled the revolver in his hand.

She stepped back and admired her work. The time of death

was close enough to make it hard for the medical examiner to determine that the shots came fifteen minutes apart. The longer the two bodies stayed here undetected, the more difficult the task would be.

She spent another minute making sure the apartment was in order and wiping down any surface she'd come in contact with.

Alex slipped out of the apartment. That familiar exhilaration sweeping through her. She may not have been paid, but she'd handled something vital, and she had done it well.

As she came down the stairs, Alex noticed the woman she'd helped with the groceries earlier standing in her doorway.

Alex waited a moment until the woman turned back into her apartment. Then she scampered down the last few stairs and darted out the back door without anyone seeing her.

There were no police cars racing to the apartment, so no one had been alarmed by the two separate gunshots. She knew people in a building like this wouldn't cooperate much with the police. Even if they figured out it was a staged double murder, they had nothing they could pin on her.

She walked along the sidewalk down 129th Street. Now she could focus totally on Michael Bennett.

CHAPTER 65

I WAS SITTING at my desk in Manhattan North Homicide when I noticed a message on my computer alerting me to an active homicide investigation up on 129th Street in Harlem.

Normally I keep my eyes open for homicides in general just so I know what's going on in the city. I found enough to keep me busy on the homicides I was assigned to, so I didn't run off to every crime scene.

But the address made me take a second look. It was Julio Laza's building.

I had a bad feeling.

I arrived on the scene about half an hour later. Before I could pull out my ID, I saw Roddy Huerta step out from the apartment and say, "It's okay. This old geezer is with me."

I carefully stepped into the apartment, avoiding the crime-scene techs and photographers.

Roddy stood next to me and said, "Happened sometime yesterday. The neighbors said they were so used to loud noises and men coming and going all the time that they ignored it."

I said, "They ignored gunshots coming from the building?"

"These two were dope dealers. They were bullies, too. Everyone in this building is just relieved they don't have to worry about them anymore."

Roddy pointed across the room and said, "The guy on the floor is Willie Perez."

He brought up a booking photo of Perez on his cell phone. Then he brought up a photo of the other man.

Roddy said, "The dead man on the couch is—"

I mumbled, "Julio Laza."

"That's right. How'd you know that?"

I looked at the younger detective, with his sharp suit and his reputation for following policy to the letter. I had done nothing by the book. I should never have cut a deal with someone who tried to shoot me. I wondered if this would be the last conversation I'd ever have as a detective with the NYPD.

I could see Roddy was angry, so I led him out of the apartment, away from the cops working the scene.

At the far end of the hallway, I had to sit on the stairs as I filled him in on my conversation with Julio and the fact that he and his cousin had tried to shoot me.

Roddy rolled his eyes. "Are you trying to tell me this is all part of your assassin conspiracy? The woman from Colombia who no one in New York ever seems to see coming? Give me a break, Bennett. I think you're starting to go senile."

"I wish it was as simple as that. But I have a couple of years of experience, Roddy. I do something the book never tells us to: I follow my gut instincts sometimes. Maybe you should try it."

"Maybe, but I get good results, and I've never been disciplined. Can you say that?"

"Is a letter in your personnel file that important? I know I'm doing what's right."

"Cutting a deal with killers? That's not right. Our job is to arrest assholes like that."

"Our job is to protect and serve. All you seem to be protecting is your reputation."

After a few moments, Roddy said, "I'd say for a hot-shit homicide dick, you really screwed this one up."

Finally I said, "Look, Roddy, I've got a lot of reasons to stop this Colombian woman. Not just because of Antrole or that she's trying to kill me. Someone went after my son in prison. She might be able to lead me to the person who ordered it."

"Does Lieutenant Grissom know about all this?"

I didn't answer. I didn't want Harry in trouble, too.

Now Roddy was showing his outrage. "Do you guys understand anything about best practices? I know you laugh at me because I follow procedures on everything, but those procedures were created for a reason. We don't stop and frisk anymore because some officers took it too far. We have our cars inspected so often because some detectives never kept up with maintenance. And we don't get involved in cases with a personal connection because it could affect our judgment and it's a conflict of interest."

I was about to rebut his argument, or at least ignore him, when I realized he was right. That hurt.

I mumbled, "Any fool can make a rule, and every fool will mind it."

Roddy said, "What's that?"

"Henry David Thoreau." It was a quotation I used to live by, thanks to my philosophy degree.

Roddy said, "Henry who?"

"That Syracuse education of yours didn't include philosophy?"

Roddy's surly look told me all I needed to know.

I sighed, stood up, and said, "You going to tell IA about my trek off policies and procedure?"

Roddy glanced down the hallway to make sure no one was close enough to hear anything. The longer he took to answer, the tighter the knot in my stomach became.

Finally he said, "Not just yet. Maybe we can both learn something on this case."

CHAPTER 66

I SAT ON my couch, staring out the wide windows at the Upper West Side of Manhattan. I had a hard time believing that a squabble between Julio and his cousin resulted in both of their deaths.

Willie Perez was a terrible person. All the records I could find on him indicated that he was involved in several murders, even though he'd never been charged. Julio Laza wasn't much better. His records were for narcotics trafficking, but I had no illusions about what he'd do if he had to.

It didn't matter now, because they were both gone. I hated to be selfish, but that mainly meant they couldn't help me with my case anymore.

I was at a loss.

Then Trent strolled into the room and plopped down on the couch next to me. If there was such a thing as a ray of sunshine, it was Trent. He was the youngest of my boys, with bright brown eyes and the darkest complexion of any of the kids. When we adopted him, there was very little information about his family or circumstances. He was only three weeks old at the time.

From the first days, Maeve and I just fell in love with him.

He had a real sense of humor, too. More than once I found him lining up his brothers, then standing between them and singing the *Sesame Street* song: "One of these things is not like the others."

Trent said, "Whatcha doing, Dad?"

"Nothing, bud. Just enjoying the view."

"Is something wrong?"

I smiled at the boy and rubbed his head. "No. Just thinking about work."

"You always tell us that family is more important than work."

I said, "It is."

"Well, we're doing great as a family." He smiled and held up an algebra test. It looked like a foreign language to me, but I understood the teacher's comment at the top. Sister Agnes wrote, "Very impressive, Mr. Bennett. We need to find something more challenging for you."

The nuns could be formal, but they never gave false praise.

"That's great, Trent. You never fail to amaze me. I love that you have your own way of doing things. It's very logical. You'd be a good philosopher."

"But I like math."

"You could be a philosopher like Pythagoras. He was also a mathematician."

"You mean the Pythagorean theorem?"

"Yes, exactly. I have no idea what the theorem is, but I've heard of it a couple of times."

Trent said, "It has to do with a triangle. The square of the hypotenuse is equal to the sum of the squares of the other two sides."

I just stared at him. Eddie was so brilliant that sometimes I forgot how smart some of the other kids were as well.

"Now, there's good news and bad news, my boy."

"What's the good news?"

"I'm gonna buy you that new baseball glove you've been looking at and take us out for a nice dinner. All of us."

"Super Tacos?"

"I guess, if that's where you want to go. We live in New York City. There are a thousand great restaurants, and you want to go to a taco place."

"Is that okay, Dad?"

I laughed. "Of course. It's your night."

Trent gave me a sly smile and said, "Okay, what's the bad news?"

"I'm going to have a talk with Sister Agnes, and your work is going to get a lot more difficult."

Trent gave me that beaming smile and said, "Bring it."

CHAPTER 67

ANNOUNCING NEW PLANS for dinner caused quite a stir in the household. Mary Catherine seemed relieved that we were all going out. I pulled her aside to tell her about my conversation with Trent.

Mary Catherine said, "That little shit."

"I beg your pardon?"

"He acts like all he cares about is baseball and sports, but he's been hiding this from us for so long. He lets us focus on Eddie being some kind of genius, while he's smart enough to coast along."

"Why do I think we're looking at this from two entirely different points of view?"

"Don't be silly, Michael. I'm thrilled. I just like to think I'm the slyest one in the family. I'll have to keep an eye on that one."

No one could ask anything more than to have a fiancée with

a great sense of humor. It was just one of the many things I was grateful for. And she took my mind off my problems for a few minutes.

We were going to make the trek to Super Tacos on foot. It was only a few blocks away, on West 96th Street. I was going to throw in a surprise visit for dessert at 16 Handles. Everyone loved the frozen yogurt there.

Just as I had the younger kids lassoed and ready to get on the road, I noticed Juliana sulking on the balcony. The wind whipped her beautiful long hair behind her. She looked like a model, which I was sure hadn't escaped her.

Mary Catherine stepped out onto the balcony, and I just watched the two of them interact for a minute. Mary Catherine put her arm around Juliana's shoulders and gave her a squeeze.

As they stepped into the living room, I innocently asked, "Everything all right?"

That made Juliana cry and rush into her bedroom.

Mary Catherine waved me off and said, "For a change, it's not your fault."

"What is it?"

"Her boyfriend, Carter, broke up with her."

"I didn't realize they were actually boyfriend and girl-friend."

"Apparently, neither did he. Juliana found out he was dating other girls. Two of them right from the set of their show."

"I better go talk to her."

"Do you think that's a good idea?"

"I'm her father. I never have any good ideas. But I'm going to do it anyway."

I lightly tapped on the door to Juliana and Jane's bedroom.

I heard a muffled sound and eased into the room. Juliana was lying facedown on her twin bed. I think I heard her say, "Please leave me alone."

As a father, I took that to mean, *Sit on the side of the bed and talk to me for a few minutes, Dad.*

After I sat silently at the foot of her bed, she rolled over and looked at me. She said, "I guess you were right about Carter."

"No, sweetheart, I wasn't. I was worried about him being too mature for you, but he proved he was not mature enough. I just hope you see that you deserve much better than a guy like that."

She sat up on the bed next to me and leaned her head against my shoulder.

Juliana said, "It just hurts so bad. I thought we had something real."

"You did. He was just too stupid to realize it." I put my arm around her and wiped a tear off her cheek with my finger. "There's nothing I can say right now that's not a stereotype of something every dad would say. But you are so beautiful and so smart that you'll have your choice of men across the city. And you've always got this guy, who loves you no matter what."

She squeezed me, then mumbled, "Thanks, Dad."

I patted her on the back and said, "Do you feel like going to Super Tacos with us? It's up to you. No one will force you."

She sniffled and said, "I heard Trent might be some kind of brainiac like Eddie. I can't miss a celebration for that. Can you give me a few minutes?"

"As long as you need, sweetheart."

I kissed her on the top of her head, and somehow I was the one who felt better.

CHAPTER 68

MY AD HOC task force on homicides had attracted some attention. While I was briefing the forensics people and some of the detectives involved, I noticed Internal Affairs inspector Alice Witcroft slip into a seat at the rear of the conference room.

Roddy Huerta had been true to his word and not mentioned to anyone that I had cut a deal with Julio Laza just before he was murdered. He sat, in his usual suit and tie, making notes as I spoke.

I had to give him credit because he didn't even shoot me any sidelong glances when I talked about the murders and failed to mention Julio and his cousin Willie Perez. Of course, there was no evidence that the two Dominican gunmen were murdered by our suspect. But I still believed it deep down.

When I asked if anyone had anything new, Cassie Max was the first to speak up.

She said, "I've done nothing but look through surveillance videos in the areas of my two homicides. I have a couple of shots that don't show a face but do show a woman with long brown hair, about five foot seven, who seems to have something strapped across her that's not a purse."

Cassie handed out photos taken from the video. She had described it perfectly.

Roddy said, "I have a similar-looking woman coming out of the East Harlem hotel."

"Can you see her face?"

"No. Just long hair, nice legs, and high heels. I discounted her the first time I saw her. Once you gave us more information I zeroed in on her immediately."

A plump forensics tech named Harry said, "I think she has a camera on a strap around her."

I said, "How do you know?"

"Because I have one strapped around me most of the day. No one ever even notices."

Now, with a new perspective, I saw it, too. "It does look like a camera."

Cassie Max said, "Do you think she takes trophy photos?"

I said, "Or is it a cover?"

The meeting broke up on its own. Everyone had things they wanted to get done immediately.

I thought I might slip out of the conference room without having to talk to Alice Witcroft. I had nothing against her personally. It was just a general feeling that it was best to avoid Internal Affairs.

The tall and fit fifty-year-old woman nearly blocked the door to keep me from escaping.

She smiled as she said, "C'mon, Bennett. You really think you can evade me that easily?"

"I thought I'd try." I matched her gaze. I'm sure many a cop had melted under those intelligent blue eyes. "What are you doing here, Alice?"

"Internal Affairs just wants to make sure one of the department's most well-known detectives is not too close to a case."

"I'm just helping out with a series of homicides. Technically I'm not even the lead on any one homicide investigation."

"As I understand it, you think these murders of Canadians could be related to the death of your partner, Antrole Martens. Am I right?"

There was no sense in denying anything. But there was no reason to admit it, either. "Possibly. We really don't have much yet."

"Look, Mike, I get it. The public is never that outraged by the murder of a cop. They remember every shitbag shot by a cop in the middle of the night, but aside from a few headlines and a high-profile funeral, no one remembers the names of cops killed in the line of duty. Except other cops.

"No matter what you think, Internal Affairs is still staffed by cops. I don't want to stand in your way. I just don't want you to get in the trick bag, either."

"Since when is Internal Affairs so worried about my job security?"

"Since the *Post* called you the best detective the city ever produced."

"So it's more of a PR issue than a desire to catch a cop killer."

The slick IA detective said, "Why can't it be both?"

CHAPTER 69

ALEX MARTINEZ FINISHED her conversation with both her daughters over a static-plagued cell-phone line. Her daily conversations with Gabriela and Clemency just made her miss home that much more. It didn't help that her mother called every other day and made her feel guilty about staying so long in New York.

She sat at a computer in a café a few blocks from Times Square. She'd been making notes from articles and posts about Detective Michael Bennett on the Internet.

Normally this was the part of her job she really enjoyed, but now she was ready for some time with her daughters and her horses.

As she was reading yet another article about Bennett's involvement in the famous case of hostages taken at the First Lady's funeral, her phone buzzed. Only a few people had the number. For a moment, she was scared something could be wrong at home, even though she'd just spoken to the girls.

When she looked down, she recognized the number as that of her mounted police officer, Tom McLaughlin. She let the phone go to voice mail. As sweet and fun as Tom was, she had a job to do, and she wanted to do it as quickly as possible.

She still could find no photographs of or information about any of Bennett's children. Not that she would ever hurt a child, but the kids could be a trail to the detective's weakness. Or perhaps she could use one as bait. At this point she didn't care, as long as she was able to finally close the contract on Bennett.

She decided to start serious surveillance, which meant she had to rent a car. The first place she watched was his office, on Broadway and 133rd Street.

Unless you knew what you were looking for, there was no way to tell that this was an official police office. There were a lot of Chevrolet Impalas and Ford Crown Victorias parked on the street around the building and under the elevated train track, but the building itself was unmarked and innocuous.

Alex was peering out her open driver's-side window when a rap on the trunk of her car startled her. When she looked into the rearview mirror she saw a tall black woman, a traffic enforcement agent, strolling to her window.

Alex smiled and said, "I'm sorry. Do you need me to move the car?" The woman didn't say anything but leveled a stern glare at Alex.

She said, "It's too late. The signs posted all around here clearly say no parking or stopping." She pulled out her ticket book and started writing.

Alex said, "I'm still in the car. I never got out. I was just stopping for a few moments to check my phone."

"I saw you sitting here for more than six minutes. That's six minutes of breaking the law. That's an awfully long time to be checking your phone. I don't care how pretty you are." She stepped to the rear of the vehicle and noticed from the tag that it was a rental. "Where you from, young woman?"

Without hesitation Alex said, "Philly."

"I don't know if Philadelphia enforces the law, but here in New York we do." She wrote something else in her ticket book, then continued to lecture Alex.

"If you don't pay attention to the signs, you get a ticket. Just as simple as that."

Alex didn't like the position she had been put in and couldn't afford to be readily identified by someone who worked for the city. Her pistol was stuffed next to the seat for tactical purposes. She always carried it there when she was driving.

She was prepared for situations like this.

The traffic enforcement agent said, "I need your license."

Alex sighed and retrieved her wallet from her purse. She pulled out a valid Pennsylvania license in the name of Michelle Pagan and gave it to the agent.

It was legit except for the photo. It also would cost her $2,600 and was now useless. She'd have to toss it as soon as she was free of this overzealous agent. It was too bad. She had started to build this identity up nicely.

As the woman finished writing the ticket, Alex noticed Detective Michael Bennett walk out the main door of his building with another man. The man was almost as tall as

Bennett and had an eighties mustache. He had to be another cop.

Alex needed to get going and felt her anxiety rise.

She was careful not to snatch the ticket from the parking attendant when she signed it. There was no sense in pushing this woman any further.

She scribbled her false name, then darted into traffic with the rental car. She could see Bennett's Impala a few blocks up and fell into her surveillance mode again.

CHAPTER 70

I WASN'T THAT crazy about meeting the regulator again. I understood he had a certain image and wanted to project that he was quirky and odd and that everyone could trust him, but he was nevertheless involved in the drug trade. I didn't care if he talked about curbing violence and making everyone happy—he still lived off other people's misery.

Sergeant Tim Marcia had once again set up a meeting. We had to find out more information, because the last lead the regulator had given us was a dead end. With Julio Laza out of the picture, I had nowhere else to look.

We met in the lobby of the Aloft Hotel, a little south of our office. The bar tucked in next to the side entrance was empty, and we sat at a table where no one could hear us. A skinny young waiter delivered my Coca-Cola and a glass of Scotch for John, the regulator.

Today John was a little more dressed up, with a long-sleeved plaid shirt and a bolo tie. His long silver-streaked hair was tied back in a tight ponytail, and the beautiful woman who had been sent to keep an eye on him was nowhere in sight. I didn't ask any questions about it.

He insisted on paying for his drink, and I noticed the first name Johann on his American Express card. Again, I wasn't going to ask any questions.

The regulator said, "I heard what happened to the Dominicans I told you about. Did you have anything to do with their deaths?"

"Not at all."

"You realize that no one on the street or in their crew believes they shot each other in an argument."

"I don't believe it, either."

"The whole crew is running scared. Whoever they crossed has no sense of humor whatsoever."

I said, "I was hoping you might have another lead for me or some information I could use."

The regulator shook his head and said, "I was lucky to get those names. Things are odd right now with this unpleasantness going on between the Mexicans and the Canadians."

"So you have no idea why they would want to kill me?"

The regulator said, "The question is, what would lead them to you? What connection do you have to the Mexican cartel?"

I thought about everything that had happened in the recent past. Brian being arrested. My being forced to shoot a teenage hit man named Diego in the Columbia library. The man who had corrupted Brian.

I snapped my fingers.

The regulator said, "There's always a moment when things become crystal clear. What have you recalled, my friend?"

"Caracortada."

This time it was Sergeant Marcia who said, "The guy we arrested in his underwear? What's Caracortada mean again?"

The regulator said, "Scarface."

I said, "He's a dealer for the cartel. I locked him up a few months back, and he's in Rikers Island right now."

The regulator took a sip of the Scotch and said, "Perhaps he could help."

CHAPTER 71

ALEX MARTINEZ SAW Bennett pull to the curb near the Aloft Hotel. She slipped her car into an overpriced lot and followed him and the other tall police officer into the lobby. Alex had been there before. She headed right for the lobby bar, where she almost ran into Bennett and the other detective, seated at a table tucked in behind the bar. There was something familiar about the man they were meeting.

Alex picked up her camera and snapped a few photos inside the lobby, as if she were cataloging the architecture.

A little girl in a pretty blue dress smiled and waved a tiny hand at her. Alex smiled back and knelt down so the little girl could see her camera more clearly.

The girl's mother said, "Don't bother the nice lady, Susanna."

Alex said, "No—it's fine. I miss my own daughters, so it's nice to see a friendly little girl."

It was true that she missed her daughters, but the little girl also provided her with better cover. No one would suspect her if she was kneeling down to chat with a little girl in the lobby.

Alex also used the opportunity to snap a quick photo of Bennett and the man he was meeting in the bar, an older man with long, graying hair.

Then Alex realized who it was. Johann Batterberg. He called himself John and claimed to be some kind of drug-world negotiator. She had once heard him referred to as "the narcotics whisperer." He brokered deals between rival gangs, avoiding unnecessary violence.

Suddenly she realized that Bennett was working hard at trying to figure out who had ordered the hit on him. He must have reasoned that it was someone in the narcotics business. He was definitely a smart detective.

It was interesting that he was talking to the regulator. While the Austrian-born man was involved in a lot of different negotiations, the major cartels tended to ignore him completely. They gave no credence to the idea that anyone besides them wielded power in the business. She wondered what kind of information Johann could provide to Bennett.

Suddenly this was getting very interesting. She might have to move her schedule for eliminating Bennett ahead, before he figured anything out.

When the little meeting broke up, she already had her car ready to go. She watched Bennett and the other police officer as they stepped onto the street.

CHAPTER 72

I DIDN'T BRING Sergeant Tim Marcia to Rikers Island with me. I was a little embarrassed that I had missed such an obvious link as Caracortada. His real name was Albert Stass, and he had been born in Uruguay, then raised in Mexico. I had barely even met the man, even though I was part of the team that arrested him and sat in on his early hearings.

That didn't mean I didn't know a lot about him. He'd ruined my life. At least ruined it as much as any one man could. He had set up a network of high school students to sell various forms of methamphetamine and ecstasy. The Mexican cartel considered synthetic drugs the next logical step in their business plan.

Unfortunately, my son Brian was one of the kids Stass had corrupted. That's how it started, anyway. Later he had used terror tactics to keep the kids in line. My son was so scared that he ended up going to prison without revealing any information.

Now this creep was a link to the person who was after me. Talking to him would also give me an idea who ordered the attack on my son in prison.

I met a friend of mine, corrections lieutenant Vinnie Mintus, who came with me to a special interview room where Stass was waiting. I had to calm myself down before entering, because the idea of seeing Stass in person made me think about committing a crime of my own.

When I was ready, I went in and sat down on a hard metal chair at a flat, scarred wooden table and looked across at Albert Stass. He was in his forties, and he really did have a fairly significant scar on his face. Other than that, there was nothing remarkable about the man.

He looked back at me with flat brown eyes.

I said, "Do you know who I am?"

"I know."

"You know why I'm here to talk to you?"

"It doesn't matter, because I'm not telling you shit."

I shrugged and looked over my shoulder at my friend, who worked at Rikers Island every day.

Lieutenant Mintus said, "You could help yourself out if you talked to us."

"I've got a lawyer for this case. I got nothing to say to you."

Lieutenant Mintus smiled and said, "I'm talking about the potential assault case for the guy you attacked in the cafeteria last week."

"You mean the black gangbanger? All I did was shove him."

"Shove, tried to choke—who could say?" The lieutenant

gave him a grin that even made me nervous. "You know how things work around here. You could be isolated and secured until trial."

"That ain't right, and you know it."

I said, "Is it right to lure kids into selling drugs?"

"*Allegedly* lure kids into selling drugs."

It was my friend the lieutenant who said, "Cut the shit. If you want to avoid some additional charges, just listen to the questions Detective Bennett has for you. You may not even think they're important."

Stass thought about it for a few seconds, then looked at me without much interest and said, "Go ahead."

I said, "Who put out the contract on me? And why?"

"All I have is hearsay. It could never be used in court."

"No one will know we ever spoke to you."

He waited a bit longer, then finally said, "The mama of that kid you shot in the library. Diego something. She's the one who pressured the cartel. I heard they even hired some hot-shot killer from Bogotá. The killer is supposed to take care of some Canadians and I guess you, too. From what I hear, the killer is really good. You might not live long enough to talk about our conversation." That made him grin, revealing yellowed, uneven teeth.

I had a few more questions, but he didn't know anything that could help me. At least I felt a level of satisfaction for having tied a lot of this case together. Now we had to figure a way to find the woman from Colombia who was committing these murders.

That was always the toughest job: stopping the killer.

CHAPTER 73

THE VISIT WITH Albert Stass had shaken me. Over the previous months, I had experienced a number of revenge fantasies about him. That was not the way I was raised or what my upbringing in the Catholic Church had taught me. It wasn't how I operated as a police officer. But I still fantasized about killing the creep, and that scared me.

I had to clear my head. Some people might call it centering myself. That meant I needed contact with my family. Some men rushed to alcohol, some men to drugs, but in times of trouble, I needed my family.

I didn't hesitate to head south toward Brooklyn. I hadn't been to the set where Juliana was filming her TV show in several days. Just seeing her would make me feel better.

As I parked near the nondescript warehouse in Brooklyn

Heights, near the East River, the first person I saw was Juliana. She was standing outside the main door using her phone.

As I walked up, she covered the mouthpiece of the phone and said, "I get lousy service inside. And by coming out here I get a little air and a few minutes away from Carter."

I waited a few seconds while she finished her call. She was trying to register for some acting class in Greenwich Village. Then Juliana slipped her phone into her purse and gave me a hug.

She said, "What brings you down here?"

I shrugged. "I just needed to see one of my kids. And I was curious about what was going on here on the set."

"You were curious how I was handling Carter since he dumped me."

"I'm more curious to know if you want me to do something to him." I gave her a smile to let her know I was kidding.

Juliana said, "Ugh, Carter. I don't even want to think about that jerk."

I was glad to see that anger had replaced sadness—the natural progression in breakups.

Just then, the front door opened and Carter popped his head out. He said, "C'mon, Jules, don't be like that—" Then he saw me and went silent.

I looked at him and said, "Like what?"

He didn't say a word as he slipped back inside.

Juliana laughed, and it lifted my whole world.

I turned to her and said, "What are you filming today?"

"Just some scenes with the star of the show."

I liked the way she put air quotes around *star*. The woman was an older actress whose name I didn't know.

Juliana said, "Sometime this week I'm supposed to do three different interviews."

"That's exciting. Maybe I can come and distract you during one of them. It will make you tougher."

She laughed and said, "Dad, thanks for worrying about me."

"Honestly, I don't know why I do. You seem to have everything under control."

She hugged me.

I said to her, "I came here for me, not so much for you. You don't have to thank me."

Juliana said, "Then I'll just tell you that I think you're a great dad."

CHAPTER 74

ALEX MARTINEZ HAD a difficult time keeping up with Bennett's car after he left Rikers Island. Surveillance was difficult, especially with only one person working it. But this was a part of the job she really enjoyed.

Now she was definitely on her own. She didn't want to involve anyone else or use any other accomplices. The Dominican gang had illustrated the problems of using local help. She had done it a few times over the years, but never again.

Alex considered a simple drive-by shooting while conducting the surveillance. Everything would have to fall in place just right, and she'd have to worry about witnesses and security video if she did it that way. It was better to work out a plan and stick to it. That's what she was good at.

Her research on the Internet had told her a few things about Bennett the man, including his adoption of ten children. She still didn't have a photo of any of them.

She stayed back about six cars as Bennett crossed over the East River by way of the Brooklyn Bridge. A few blocks later, in Brooklyn Heights, she saw the Impala pull into a lot across from a warehouse.

For a moment, she wondered if everything had lined up just right. When he came through the parking lot she could work it out so her car would not be far from him. But she remembered how quickly he reacted with the Dominican gunmen. They'd tried basically the same thing, and it didn't work out for them.

Still, just in case, Alex drew her semiautomatic pistol from her purse and slid it into its normal spot next to the driver's seat. She kept her right hand wrapped around the grip.

She rolled down her window so she'd be ready if she got the chance.

Bennett walked across the street in front of her quickly and was greeted by someone at the front of the building.

As she drove down the street slowly, Alex saw Bennett speaking with a young woman standing outside the front door. She was tall and pretty with long, dark hair. She gave him a quick hug as soon as she was done on her phone.

Alex recalled that one of Bennett's adopted children was named Juliana and was about eighteen years old. It was a pretty good bet that this young woman was Juliana. It looked like the oldest Bennett child had found a job on some kind of TV show.

Now that Alex had a lead on one of the kids, she could explore it.

It was sweet to see the father and daughter interact. Bennett was basically a good guy. But her profession didn't give her the option to ignore contracts just because the targets seemed like good people. Sometimes she had to just do her job.

CHAPTER 75

ALEX FOUND A fancy coffee shop with Wi-Fi near Columbus Circle. She could've spent more time following Bennett around, but now she knew exactly what she was looking for.

She had to discourage the young man working the counter, who wandered over to her in an effort to flirt. As soon as he said, "So where are you from?" Alex scared him off with a perfect Colombian glare.

Alex had walked around to check out the warehouse where she had seen Bennett greet the young woman. A card on one of the doors said that it was a set for a TV show called *Century's End*. A quick search on the IMDB database told her that the show was in production and scheduled to be released next year.

The description said: "A drama set in the late 1990s, revolving around young people making life decisions as a new millennium approaches."

Didn't sound promising from the description, but it might work if the writing and acting were good.

It listed the director and a producer and six of the series stars. One of the photographs was the girl she had seen—listed as Jules Baez playing the role of Noreen Harwood. She looked up information for Jules Baez on several databases and found very little. It was interesting to note that she had received her Screen Actors Guild card very recently.

Then she found an early description of *Century's End* on a different website, a gossipy industry-insider newsletter. Alex pulled up the newsletter and found a short blurb about the TV show listing the actress hired to play Noreen Harwood as Juliana Bennett.

Excellent.

To Alex, finding something like this was nearly as important as the hit itself. Anyone could point a gun, but only a true professional delved deeper and figured out how to complete the hit and live to enjoy the rewards after it was all done.

On the IMDB database, Jules Baez was listed as "not represented" in the section showing agent and management. That was one weakness all actors had: they lusted for good representation.

Then she had a great idea.

Tomorrow could be the turning point on this contract from hell.

CHAPTER 76

I DIDN'T KNOW if it was the mounting stress of having someone trying to kill me, worrying about Brian in the hospital, or all the other little things a father has to keep track of, but I didn't feel refreshed when I woke up. I'd tossed and turned all night, and now I really felt it.

I'd also hit some dead ends in my investigation. We still didn't have a clear photograph of the killer or anything that might identify her. Roddy Huerta had proved to be a better detective than I had originally thought. He also hadn't ratted me out to anyone about my using Julio Laza as a snitch before he was killed. That told me something about the man.

Cassie Max was her usual blur of activity, and I noticed that she sent me an e-mail every night around eleven o'clock, updating me on everything she had done. I was never that organized, even when I was her age.

I had a little time this morning and wanted to show my family some support. First I was going to go by Holy Name and talk to Sister Agnes about Trent. I thought I might work in a visit to my grandfather as well. If I had time I wanted to shoot down to Brooklyn and visit Juliana again—I knew she was still smarting from the breakup.

As I walked to my police car in the garage across the street from our apartment, I was paying a lot more attention to cars passing me on the street and other pedestrians. I don't want to say that I was starting to get paranoid, but I definitely had my reasons.

I was trying to change up my regular routine in case anyone was watching. I gave Mitch, the homeless man who always sat near the entrance to the garage, two dollars before I went in instead of handing it to him from the window of my car, as I did on most days.

I engaged the sixty-five-year-old Vietnam veteran in some conversation.

"Mitch, have you seen anyone unusual hanging out around here?"

His voice was deep and raspy. "You gotta give me more than that. This is New York. Everyone is unusual."

"Any women you don't usually see?"

"It's funny you ask. I see everyone, but only a few people see me. I appreciate that you even bothered to ask me. You always talk to me."

I said, "What about it? Have you seen anyone?"

"Seen anyone do what?"

I patted him on the shoulder and said, "Keep up the good work."

It was time to head over to Holy Name and make sure Trent never had an easy math assignment again. That thought made me chuckle like a villain in a Disney movie.

CHAPTER 77

I ENTERED THE Holy Name school through the main door and quickly found Sister Agnes in her office. She was busy grading tests at a comfortable-looking desk while balancing herself on a blue yoga ball.

The NYPD had tried various chairs and desks in an effort to stop some of the back problems and health issues related to sedentary jobs, but I didn't care for stand-up desks. Then again, my job involved a lot of activity—maybe too much.

Sister Agnes was dressed casually by nuns' standards, in a simple black shirt and skirt. She was a young-looking forty and taught advanced math classes. She also coached the girls' basketball team.

She was tougher than any cop I had ever met. Her brown eyes could make you wilt if you were in the wrong. She'd turned that look on me a couple of times over the years, the first time after I suggested a little less homework and a little more recess. More recently, there was a string of three days in a row with a late arrival by our entire family. I thought accepting full responsibility would save me. Instead she set those eyes on me and said, "Now I can tell how much influence Father Seamus has had on your life. We'll see if we can fix that. Once a student at Holy Name, always a student."

Now she glanced up from her tests when I stood in the doorway and simply said, "Ah, Mr. Bennett. I thought my little note on Trent's algebra test might bring you in quickly for a chat."

"You could have just asked me to come in for a parent conference."

"Based on the way you sometimes sneak the kids in when they're tardy, and based on the behavior of your grandfather, I thought it was best to use a little subterfuge. Call it a fun game on my part."

I liked her.

She motioned me to the seat, then twisted on her ball so she was sitting up straight. I could see the muscles in her forearm and wondered how much she could bench-press.

She said, "I was hoping to talk to you about moving Trent forward quite quickly in some of the math classes. I also was wondering if perhaps we could pair him with Eddie in a special computer class we're going to put together with Columbia University."

I just stared at her as if I didn't understand. Truthfully, the information and request were a little overwhelming. She wanted my boys to take a class with Columbia students? They were just little boys in my eyes.

Somehow I managed to mumble, "Yes, of course. Whatever you think is best." After a moment, it all sank in, and I said, "I don't think I realized Trent was so good with computers."

"Eddie is clearly a whiz with anything related to Windows-based and Linux-based computers. We feel our computer lab is no longer sufficient to support his interests. But it's Trent's mathematical ability that we think this computer class could really enhance. Often we find that an ability to work with computers is tied directly to mathematical comprehension."

"That all sounds great. What can I do to help?"

"There may be some financial issues and costs, but nothing too extreme. If you need any kind of financial assistance, we feel this is important enough for the Church to provide it."

"Thank you. I think I'll be able to come up with whatever we need. Is there anything else I could do to help?"

She hesitated. That was unusual for Sister Agnes. Finally she said, "Perhaps it would be best if your grandfather didn't know exactly what was going on. Sometimes he tends to get overinvolved in your children's studies. I don't think he would ever admit that he may not be up-to-date on the latest technology. And I know he'd be afraid we're pushing the boys too quickly. Sometimes I think he would have each of your children held back just so he could see them every day here at school."

I smiled because it was true. I also smiled because apparently Trent wasn't the only one hiding his abilities.

Sister Agnes was much more astute and understood the subtleties of family relationships better than I had ever imagined.

I said, "I'll talk to Seamus."

CHAPTER 78

I CUT THROUGH the tidy courtyard from the school to the church administration building. I was beaming, at least on the inside. What parent doesn't want to hear that not one but two of his children are gifted? And gifted in an area that's so difficult?

Clearly I hadn't helped the boys with their computer or math skills as they grew up. I could go on about philosophers and their contributions to society, from the Greeks to the formation of the United States, but technology and math were not my strong suits.

Holy Name had been such a big part of my life that sometimes I took the church and school for granted. Not only were my children going to school here, where we attended services every Sunday, but the church was also essentially harboring my grandfather and giving him a strong purpose late in life. The idea of Seamus living with us as a retired bar owner with no purpose in life was the stuff of nightmares.

God knows what would have piqued his interest. He was a great organizer, a talent the church utilized. He could have just as easily organized a gambling ring or some other semi-illegal endeavor, which would've caused me grief at every turn.

Sister Agnes had just shown me how much she and the school cared about my children and their education. To say they were going above and beyond the call of duty was an understatement. The only thing they were asking in return was that I keep Seamus on his side of the church and out of Eddie's and Trent's educational plans.

Now I was walking into his clean, organized office and felt confident I'd find him in good health and with a worthwhile activity occupying him.

I had two ways I could handle this. I could lie to him or just tell him to mind his own business.

I found Seamus leaning back in a chair sipping coffee.

He looked up at me from the desk. "What are you doing here, Michael?"

"Just had an interesting conversation with Sister Agnes."

"What could that Ivy League snob want to talk to you about?"

"Why do you call her that?" My grandfather was not usually malicious.

"She's got a degree in some kind of mathematics from Harvard, and she thinks I have absolutely no role in the school whatsoever."

"You don't. You work at the church. Why would you have a role in the school?"

"I have ten great-grandchildren at the school. That's reason enough right there."

This was not going to be as easy as I thought.

"Am I missing something? Do you have a personal issue with Sister Agnes?"

"I gave up personal issues when I entered the priesthood. I have never once faltered on the vows I made to the Church."

I caught the somber tone and edge of outrage. I said, "Not that kind of personal issue. I mean some issue you have with her at the school."

He looked down at his desk for a moment, then said, "Okay. She might have nixed my suggestion that I teach a class on Irish history."

"I can't imagine why a reasonable school administrator would turn down a chance to have a class taught by someone with no background in history or teaching."

"Don't be a smart aleck. It doesn't become you. I learned oral history growing up in the old country. But she wasn't interested in any of that. She said there weren't many kids with an Irish heritage at the school. She said even my own great-grandchildren weren't technically Irish. At least most of them."

I had dealt with Sister Agnes for years, and I knew she wouldn't have used the tone that Seamus was using now. But I saw her point. The kids here came from varied and interesting backgrounds. They probably wouldn't fully appreciate fables told by an elderly priest who still had an Irish accent.

I waited for him to calm down a little, then said, "I'm sorry she shot down your idea. But you have to recognize there's great opportunities coming for Eddie and Trent. And I don't want you to cause any heartburn about it. Understood?"

He bowed his head and mumbled, "Understood."

I joked with my grandfather quite a bit. We traded jabs on

a regular basis. But I never liked to see him disappointed. And that's how he looked right now. As usual, though, in a couple of minutes he was past it. He looked across at me as I sat at the other desk and thought about my day.

My grandfather said, "What's wrong, Michael? I know that look."

"Just general stress. Someone trying to kill you tends to do that."

Seamus chuckled. "They tried to kill Alonzo, too. Unless I'm mistaken, he's tickled pink by it. Something about missing the action from his old life."

"That makes him insane."

"He may be insane, but he has reenergized the school and brought out a whole untapped population of students who never had an interest in sports before. It's not just soccer. He understands basketball as well. I think his real genius is in motivation."

"I won't soon forget how he helped me when those men tried to shoot me the other day. I'm glad he's a good coach, but I'm even happier he was a tough cop."

Seamus put down his coffee and straightened some papers on his desk. "What have you got planned for today?"

"I'm going by to visit Juliana in Brooklyn at the TV show set." I saw him perk up immediately.

"Let me come with you."

He sounded like a kid pleading to go with his parents.

I said, "I'm just going to say hello, then get back to work."

"You won't deny an old man the chance to see his great-granddaughter, will you? I'd love to see what the set looks like."

"Give me a break. 'Old man'—that's laughable. You get around the city better than I do."

Then Seamus said the one thing that always got him his way. "Please."

I let out a heavy sigh and said, "Okay, but dress in civilian clothes. We don't want to freak out the movie types. Or maybe they'll think you're an extra from another set who wandered over. Either way, don't wear the collar."

He sprang from his seat and called out, "C'mon, Alonzo. Michael is taking us to Brooklyn."

I mumbled, "What the hell—the more the merrier."

CHAPTER 79

ALEX MARTINEZ WAS in a good mood. She could see the light at the end of the tunnel on this job, which seemed to go on and on. All she wanted to do was go home to her ranch and her daughters and live her life.

She'd already turned down a job offer she'd gotten earlier in the morning. A Swiss banking cartel needed her to clean up a mess in Marseille, France. They had a bank president who had showered his family with gifts paid for through embezzlement. News of the scandal would cripple the stock price. But a fatal hit-and-run would solve everything.

She politely turned the job down, then they offered her more money. She turned it down again, and they said what everyone says: "It's an easy job. You could phone it in."

Alex said, "If it's that easy, why don't you handle it yourself?" She felt invigorated when she hung up the phone.

Now she was walking onto the set of *Century's End*. Dressed in a very sharp skirt with a very conservative blouse, she walked through the hallway with purpose and drive. Not one person questioned her presence.

Sitting at the far end of the set in a director's chair was the young woman she was looking for. She ran it through her head one more time to make sure she called her Jules, not Juliana. She wanted this to move quickly and smoothly. She just needed to lure the girl away from the set, then make contact with her father.

Alex didn't like using a stunt like this. She was not much for traumatizing a young person not involved in any crime. But she had to make a choice. Bennett had proved to be resourceful and dangerous. And she wanted to get home. Immediately.

The other issue was the girl herself. She'd be able to identify Alex if anyone could find a photo. Alex wasn't too worried about that. First she had to get Bennett into the right position. Then she'd worry about witnesses.

Juliana Bennett was having a serious conversation with an attractive young man. The name on the back of his chair was Cade Jason. She had no idea who he was. She'd only done research about Juliana.

Both young people looked up as she came to a stop in front of them.

When she concentrated, Alex had almost no accent when she was speaking English. She looked directly at Juliana and said, "Hello. Are you Jules Baez?"

The girl hesitated, then said, "Yes. Yes, I am."

"I'm Alice Marshall with the Suzanne Grossman Talent Management Company. Have you heard of us?"

Juliana's face lit up as she said, "Of course I have. You guys are one of the biggest agencies on the East Coast."

Alex didn't rush it. She felt a surge of confidence in her plan. She said, "If you have a few minutes, I'd love to talk about representing you."

The girl smiled from ear to ear. "Yeah. I don't have a stage call until after noon."

"Great. Can I take you out to an early lunch somewhere close by?"

"Absolutely." She was standing, gathering her purse.

As Alex started to turn, the young man who was sitting next to Juliana said, "I'm Cade Jason. Would you like to talk to me, too?"

Alex could recognize the smugness on this young man's face. She couldn't resist saying, "No, thank you."

She was rewarded with a snicker by Juliana.

Everything was going as planned.

CHAPTER 80

I ALMOST REGRETTED my stop at Holy Name. Not only did it give traffic a chance to build, I also had two passengers I'd have to drop off at the church again on my way back.

Sometimes dealing with my grandfather was like dealing with a child. It was easier to just give him his way.

Father Alonzo, sitting in the backseat, leaned forward and said, "How goes your investigation? Any leads on the men who tried to shoot us?"

I didn't know how much I should say.

Father Alonzo said, "I'm sorry, but it just gave me a glimpse into my past life. Perhaps I miss the action more than I thought."

I said, "Don't worry about it, Alonzo. I know exactly how you feel. The biggest problem with the case is that, at the heart of it, it involves two organizations. The Canadian mob and the Mexican cartel."

Alonzo said, "I have studied trends in organized crime for many years. Although Canadians don't cause a great deal of problems in Colombia, I still know that they can be as ruthless as anyone. They're also constantly underestimated. The stereotype of the polite Canadian doesn't help them when they're trying to scare people."

I said, "But they're no match for the Mexican cartel."

"Agreed. Especially if the Mexicans are importing killers from Colombia. They have too much money and too large of an established network. I'm just sorry they decided to throw you in with their list of targets."

"I've got a great team working on it with me. We'll find this killer and keep her from causing any more havoc."

Father Alonzo said, "It has been my experience that just as people underestimate the Canadian mob, they tend to underestimate female killers. There's a reason she has this job. She has to be extremely smart and resourceful. This may be a tall order."

"I'm not going to give up on it."

"No—that's not what I'm suggesting. You need to be ready all the time. She'll try to hit you when you least expect it. Or she'll be very sly and somehow lure you into a trap. You won't know what happened until it's too late.

"You must make use of your advantages. This is your territory. You know the city. Use what you know and she doesn't."

I thought about his Zen-like advice. I *did* have resources here and knowledge of the city that I doubted this killer possessed.

I just hoped when the time came, I would remember that.

CHAPTER 81

DRIVING WITH MY grandfather in the car is like having an uninvited know-it-all tour guide with you. He kept saying he didn't get to lower Manhattan and Brooklyn much and wanted to see the sights. Not the Freedom Tower or the bull on Wall Street, but the little markets he used to frequent and the restaurants he knew were no longer in business. He said he just wanted to see the facades of the buildings.

He also explained everything we saw to Alonzo in minute detail. Like the history of how Little Italy evolved and the construction details of the Brooklyn Bridge. Finally I had to tell him I was on a schedule and that the NYPD expected me to work occasionally. But that didn't stop him from making me circle the building where the TV show was being filmed.

Seamus said, "I've been here. I remember this place. It was

a restaurant-supply distribution center I ordered from when I owned the bar."

I said, "When's the last time you were here?"

"Probably twelve or fifteen years ago. It brings back a flood of memories. I'd sometimes buy cases of beer that 'fell off' actual beer trucks. I could buy them for about 30 percent of the regular cost."

"So you're telling me you bought stolen beer and sold it in your legal bar?"

"Sometimes I'd tack on an extra fee, saying that there was a shortage of the beer and I was able to grab some of the last cases." He wore a mischievous grin that made him look like a leprechaun.

It made me smile because it reminded me of when I was a child. How we would go on adventures together and he'd tell me wild tales that even then I knew weren't true.

I was surprised to see that the side of the building facing the river housed a beautiful glass-enclosed set of offices with a receptionist at the front. The grassy park between the building and the river made it that much nicer. I wondered if this had anything to do with the TV or movie business. Maybe it was a separate part of the building the owner rented out. With the East River in front of it and some nice landscaping around the park, it was definitely upscale.

Seamus rolled down his window and said, "I don't care what anyone says about the East River—I like the smell of it. Reminds me of home. The sea."

As we slowly turned at the corner of the building and were driving next to the sidewalk, Seamus said, "I can't wait to see Jules."

I said, "Juliana."

"She likes to be called Jules on the set."

"How do you know that? Have you been on the set before?"

I stopped the car to stare at him as he looked sheepish and wouldn't meet my eye.

A stagehand carrying a box on the sidewalk looked over and said, "Hey, Father."

It was rare to catch the old man so cleanly. Now I gave him a good nod and said, "Explain that."

Without missing a beat, Seamus said, "He's your illegitimate uncle."

"Funny." I did note that Father Alonzo was laughing in the backseat. "You just said it had been a dozen years since you saw the building."

Seamus said, "I meant it had been a dozen years since I saw *the front* of the building, by the river. I saw the rest last Friday when I watched them film a scene with Jules. She was fantastic. She's really talented."

Then I saw two women come out of the building's door about fifty yards from us. It took me a moment to realize that one of them was my daughter.

Seamus said, "Who's that with Jules?"

I didn't recognize the striking woman with the long dark hair. She was chatting casually with Juliana, but there was something about her that seemed familiar.

I started to get an uneasy feeling. I pulled to the curb.

CHAPTER 82

ALEX MARTINEZ SMILED as she listened to this captivating young woman speak. She was very poised for an eighteen-year-old. She was also very excited that an agent was interested in talking to her about representation. Alex was sorry the girl's dreams were about to come crashing down.

Getting her to leave the building had been remarkably easy. Even the timing was good. She was on a break, so Alex didn't have to stand around and chat with someone who might know she didn't work for the Grossman talent agency.

They were just coming to the heavy security door that led to the outside. Her plan was simple from there. Get the girl to her car, then make her call her father.

Alex had no intention of killing an innocent girl—unless she found herself in a situation where there was no other choice.

Just as they stepped out the door, the sun caused Alex to raise her hand and let her eyes adjust. Juliana said, "Would you mind if I called my dad real quick?"

"Not at all. In fact, if you'd be more comfortable, invite him to lunch with us." Could she be this lucky?

As Juliana reached into her purse for her phone, Alex reached into her own to make sure her stiletto and pistol were within easy reach.

Juliana pulled an iPhone from her purse and paused. She looked across the front courtyard and said, "I think that's my dad's car right there."

Alex saw the Impala and kicked herself for not noticing it immediately. It wasn't like she'd never seen it. She'd followed Bennett around most of yesterday.

This plan was so much less complicated than the original one. She slipped her hand into her purse and wrapped her fingers around the grip of her 9mm pistol. She'd wait until he was so close there was nothing he could do.

As soon as she was done, Alex intended to hop in her car and be back in Manhattan before the first patrol car arrived.

CHAPTER 83

I FOLLOWED MY instinct and left the car idling by the sidewalk. I started to walk quickly toward Juliana and the other woman. Nothing appeared to be out of the ordinary as I cut across the grass and looked straight ahead. Still, I picked up my pace.

Juliana smiled and waved. The woman stood next to her and made no overtly threatening movements. Maybe I'd let my paranoia get the best of me again. I felt like an idiot.

I stepped onto the walkway that led to the door where the two women were standing. I looked over my shoulder quickly to make sure my grandfather and Father Alonzo were still in the car.

They had both stepped onto the sidewalk.

Now I relaxed slightly, as it appeared that Juliana was just coming out the door with someone from the production company. Most of the people working on the set looked like electricians or plumbers.

When I was about twenty feet from Juliana, she said, "What are you doing here during a workday?"

"I'm never too busy to see one of my kids." I was waiting for an introduction to the other woman as I walked toward them.

The woman reached in her purse casually. When she pulled out her hand, I could clearly see the small semiautomatic pistol in it.

Right at that moment, I knew exactly who this woman was.

CHAPTER 84

ALEX HAD TO struggle to control her impatience. She didn't want to act too quickly as she watched the tall detective make his way across the courtyard and onto the walkway leading to his daughter.

She trusted her ability, but anyone who'd been around guns knew that every couple of feet of distance from a shooter added a degree of uncertainty to a moving target. Plus he had proved he was wily and fast when the three Dominican gunmen tried to shoot him in front of the church.

It was important that she maintain her composure and allow him to walk into the ambush. That's what it really was—an ambush. She may not be hiding behind a door with a gun, but there was one in her purse, and she intended to draw it when he was about ten feet away.

She felt that twinge of excitement mixed with nerves. She

had a minute tremor in her right hand. This was everything she had worked for on this contract, which had kept her away from home for too long. She could feel the sweat build on her forehead and her heart start to pound.

Did the girl standing next to her notice? If she did, she didn't acknowledge it.

There would be almost nothing Bennett could do, and the closer he got, the more effective the gun would be. She would have to put two into his head just to be sure. At least she wouldn't have to hurt the girl.

Unless she did something really stupid.

Alex's hands felt clammy from sweat.

The girl called out to her father. He answered with a smile. This was embarrassingly easy.

She reached into her purse with her right hand. She concentrated so that it wouldn't be a rushed, suspicious movement. Now she found the perfect grip for the pistol and pulled it out of her purse casually.

Alex didn't want to risk blowing this wonderful chance. Her first shot would be well aimed.

Once the pistol cleared her purse, she extended her right arm and started to sight down the barrel to the center of Michael Bennett's face.

She took a breath and started to squeeze the trigger.

CHAPTER 85

JUST AS ALEX Martinez extended her hand fully and began to get a clear view of her target, everything went haywire.

She squeezed the trigger just as Juliana bumped her arm. The bullet went high and wide.

Suddenly she realized it wasn't an accidental bump. The girl had realized what was happening and took action.

What the hell!

Now she had to fight the daughter as well as the father. She couldn't waste time and give Bennett a chance to close the distance.

Juliana grabbed hold of Alex's arm and threw an elbow into her face, knocking her back toward the door. Alex saw stars, then felt a trickle of blood seep out of her nose.

Alex's face throbbed from the blow. Apparently the apple didn't fall far from the tree. This girl was tough.

Alex moved fast and jerked the girl toward her. Somehow she

had managed to retain the pistol in her right hand. That was the only thing that kept Bennett from charging them right then.

Alex had to think quickly. She used her left arm to pull the girl close to her, twisted her right hand, and put the gun to the girl's head. She wished it was the stiletto, because a small cut and drop of blood would've stopped Juliana's father in his tracks.

Alex started shuffling backward quickly and whispered into Juliana's ear, "Open the door unless you want your brains all over your father."

She turned her attention to the advancing detective and didn't say a word as she shoved the pistol into Juliana's temple. She wanted the girl to cry to out to make a point. The girl kept quiet, but the message was sent, and Bennett froze in place.

Bennett stared at them. He had already drawn his pistol and was shuffling slightly from side to side, clearly trying to get a better shot.

When he saw that Alex meant business, he backed away slightly and took the gun off target. But it was still in his hand.

Juliana opened the door, and they backed into the darkness of the corridor that led to the stage. Alex moved away from the door quickly. This was not what she had planned, but perhaps she could still salvage it.

Her excitement and nerves had been forgotten during the action. Now she had to think clearly.

She had researched the building, cased the area, and she knew she could flee through this corridor into the business offices and out the exit near the East River.

She was about to give up hope that she'd have a chance to fulfill her contract when the door opened and Michael Bennett stood outlined by the sunlight.

CHAPTER 86

I DON'T KNOW if I'd ever felt this kind of pure panic. Seeing my daughter with a gun to her head made me sick to my stomach. Literally. But vomiting wasn't an option. That wouldn't help anyone.

I had my gun up as I sprinted into the fatal funnel of the doorway. This is where cops are most likely to be shot. Outlined by bright light. I slipped into the corner near the door. It was dark, and I took a moment to let my eyes adjust.

I also had to let my breathing calm down. If I had to shoot, it might be a tight shot past Juliana. What a nightmare.

The woman continued to walk backward, dragging Juliana along with her. My daughter's eyes showed the terror she felt, but she wasn't crippled by fear. Seeing her like that almost crippled me.

I wasn't sure where this dark hallway led, but I didn't intend to let them get to the end of it.

Now I crept along the wall with my gun up in front of me and saw them again. The woman stopped, and I saw Juliana's face clearly. She was terrified. So was I.

I made a decision, planted my feet, and took aim. As I let out my breath and focused over the front sight, I saw the woman's dark eyes. We were fairly close, maybe twenty feet apart. I shut out every distraction: my pounding heart, the sweat in my eyes, my shaky hands, and the noise from the set.

Then the woman spoke. She said, "Get back. Lower your weapon or I'll pull the trigger."

It wasn't just what she said; it was *how* she said it. She wasn't panicked. Not ranting. She was calm. Professional. I had no choice.

I'd never surrender my gun, but I lowered it slightly. I couldn't risk her harming my Juliana. I kept the gun in the low, ready position so I could pop it back on target quickly if I needed to.

I was trying to buy time. I knew that if Seamus and Father Alonzo were inside the building someone had called 911. The cavalry would be here soon.

I could feel a tremor in my arm, and it scared me. No parent could ever imagine being in a position like this.

The woman said, "Stay there," in the same professional tone. Then she began backing away.

I let her go. All I wanted was Juliana safe. I watched as they reached the next door down the dark hallway. The woman eased the gun away from Juliana's head slightly.

I felt a flicker of hope.

Then they were through the door and out of sight.

I had to get back to Juliana.

CHAPTER 87

ALEX HAD A good grip on the girl as they slipped through the next door in the corridor and let it slam shut. At least she had something solid between her and Bennett. She could feel the girl trembling.

Alex's face throbbed where the girl had elbowed her. But she was unharmed, had the right position, and was prepared to act. That gave her the confidence to think she'd be able to escape. She'd worry about Bennett another day.

She considered her options. Take the girl with her as a hostage, forget the girl and run, or kill the girl and leave her body to distract her father.

Almost immediately she ruled out the third option. She didn't kill for enjoyment or to be vindictive. She killed for money.

Just as Alex was about to turn around so she could move faster, the door they had just come through burst open, and Michael Bennett stood there with the gun still in his hand. This guy never gave up.

Alex yelled, "Stop."

She liked that the cop froze in place.

Then she said, "Put your gun on the floor." He didn't move. Even his eyes didn't give away his intentions.

Alex sweetened the pot. "Put your gun on the floor and I swear to God I'll release your daughter."

Bennett said, "Then you shoot me and it'll be over?"

"The only promise I make is that I'll release Juliana."

She waited, knowing a man like this might decide to give up his own life for his daughter. She saw a flicker of doubt, or maybe it was confusion, cross his face. Then he held up his left hand to show it was empty as he slowly bent with the gun in his right hand, as though he was going to place it on the dusty hardwood floor.

She tightened her grip on Juliana just in case the feisty girl tried to escape at the last moment. She had proved to be as bold as her father.

From the awkward, stooped position, Bennett said, "Please release her now."

From way down the hallway Alex heard someone call out, "Michael, where are you?"

Bennett shouted back, "Don't come down here, Seamus. Everything will be all right. Just stay away."

Alex wondered if another police officer was in the building. She said, "Who was that?"

"My grandfather. I brought him down here to see the set and visit Juliana. He's no threat to you or anyone else."

It was a reasonable story, and the detective certainly didn't sound like he was lying.

Now it was time to fire the pistol once and be on her way.

CHAPTER 88

I KEPT SLOWING my movement to place the gun on the floor, hoping I'd see an opening or that this assassin would drop her guard. But she was good. Really good. She kept the gun screwed in tight to Juliana's temple and kept her eyes on me.

It was the idea of a gun to my baby's head that affected all my thinking. I didn't care what happened as long as she was safe.

Even when Seamus called out, it didn't break the assassin's concentration. She kept the gun right where it was and managed to stare me down. Now I just hoped Seamus didn't blunder into this shitty predicament.

I could see the woman getting impatient, and I wasn't sure what to do. In every NYPD training session I had ever attended, instructors shouted at us, "Never surrender your gun." Some of the old-school instructors were more colorful about it. The lesson had hit home and been seared into my personality.

The gun was part of me. If I surrendered it, I surrendered any chance I had to play a part in this drama. Not only would I be at the mercy of this killer, Juliana would be, too. But if I gave the gun up, the assassin said she'd release Juliana.

Then, behind the woman and Juliana, I saw movement. It was subtle. A shift in the light and shadow. It was plain that someone was close by.

Then hands wrapped around the woman's shoulder and knocked the gun slightly away from Juliana's head. The gun went off right in front of Juliana's face. The noise was shattering. The flash illuminated Juliana's eyes. Eyes filled with fear.

In the flash, I also saw Father Alonzo as he fell back with the woman in his grasp.

Through the din from the gunshot, I heard Father Alonzo yelling, "Grab Juliana."

I did as I was told and grasped my daughter's left wrist and pulled her so hard that I felt her whole body slam into mine. I lost my balance, and we both tumbled to the floor. It didn't matter because my daughter was in my arms. And I still had my gun.

Father Alonzo and the woman wrestled on the floor. In the dark, I saw the flash of another muzzle blast an instant before I heard it. Once again, the sound bouncing off the solid walls of the hallway was incredible. It shook my whole body.

There was a brief scuffle after the gun went off, then the woman came off the floor in a sprint, running away from Father Alonzo, still on the floor. She was out of sight before I could even raise my pistol.

Quickly I came to his aid and knelt down next to him. He was starting to curl up in the fetal position. In the dim light, I could tell he'd been shot in the abdomen. He was already trying to stop the bleeding and keep his cool.

He looked up at me and said in a weak voice, "Juliana?"

"She's safe. Thanks to you."

"Old instincts die hard. I had to do something." He winced and coughed. Some of his spittle was tinged with blood.

Juliana came up alongside me, and Seamus appeared from the hallway.

Seamus looked down and muttered, "Oh, God." Then he also dropped to his knee, immediately took a handkerchief from his pocket, and told Alonzo to move his hands.

Seamus looked at me and said, "Help is on the way."

Alonzo said, "You can't do anything here. Go catch her and end this nightmare."

I was running just as hard as she was in an instant.

CHAPTER 89

THIS WAS NOT how Alex Martinez had imagined the hit would go. But the mark of a professional is to make adjustments and come home alive at the end of the day. That was her goal right now.

She had no idea who'd grabbed her from behind, but he gave a good fight and barely let go even after she fired into his stomach.

She had run from the shooting and wandered for a few seconds inside the studio. She had turned from the main hallway and now was in a maze of corridors and storage rooms. She knew if she kept heading away from the door she had come through, she would find a way out. Going back through the same door would be suicide.

Alex wasn't panicked. She never panicked. But she had never been in quite this situation. She wiped the sweat from her face several times and got control of her breathing. Every pillar and curtain looked the same. Was she going in circles?

She passed two different people in the patchwork of hallways and kept the gun in her hand, hidden in her purse.

She stopped the second man, apparently some kind of lighting technician, carrying a long pole with a set of lights on the end of it.

Alex said in a very calm and quiet voice, "Excuse me. I've gotten turned around. I want the exit facing the East River. Which way is that?"

The man put down the pole, which wasn't a good sign for brevity.

Alex restrained her desire to screw the pistol into his neck and tell him to speak.

The man pointed behind him and said, "If you take this hallway to the end and turn left, I think there's a door that takes you into the executive offices in the back of the building. The door may be locked."

She mumbled, "Thanks," as she kept heading that way. She picked up her pace and, as soon as the man was out of sight, broke into another run.

Alex wasn't even thinking about laying another trap for Bennett. That guy was either really lucky or really sharp. She was afraid he was really sharp, but she knew he had a soft spot. She hoped that he had stayed to help the man she had shot in the abdomen.

She found the door the man was talking about and, as he said, it was locked.

Alex was going through it anyway—the only question was how much noise she would make. She knocked on it lightly and felt how sturdy it was. The hinges were on the other side.

She checked the lock, then pulled her stiletto from her purse. Unlike a regular knife, it didn't have a perfectly flat blade, but it was still able to fit between the doorjamb and the door. Just that little bit of room allowed her to wiggle the knife and cause the locking mechanism to slip.

After a moment of playing with it, Alex was able to pull the door open. She saw brighter lights in the hallway beyond the door and knew this was where she wanted to be. She took a moment to straighten her blouse, then took a napkin from her purse and wiped it across her face to clean up any sweat.

Then she walked through the offices as if she were the supervisor. No one paid any attention to her as she walked toward the sunlight coming through wide bay windows facing the East River.

CHAPTER 90

I RACED THROUGH the hallway with my pistol up in front of me, aware of the fact that this woman could be waiting behind any corner with her pistol ready to fire. At that point it was a risk I was willing to take.

The terror I felt at seeing Juliana with a gun screwed to her temple had mutated to resolve. And anger. Any time people thought they could stir up shit in my city without any repercussions, I got mad. Now I was determined to stop this killer. If I didn't, who knew when this nightmare might end and how many more people she would kill?

I ran all the way to the stage area, and of course the first person I saw was Carter Javits.

He was shaken to see me out of breath and with a gun in my hand. In my frantic state, I fairly shouted, "Carter, did a woman with long dark hair run through here?"

He just stared at me like a little kid. He didn't say a word.

I called his name out sharp and loud. "Carter!"

He shook his head no.

"You haven't seen anyone unusual?"

"A woman like that walked out with Jules a little while ago. She's a talent agent."

"Keep everyone in here. She's dangerous. She has a gun. Help should be coming any minute."

When he just stared at me again, I said, "Do you understand what I'm saying, Carter?"

This time he nodded.

I was running back down the hallway looking for turnoffs. I found one door that was unlocked and led me into a series of storage rooms and hallways that ran in several directions.

I pulled my badge from my back pocket and held it up to a guy carrying a pole with lights on it. I shouted, "NYPD. Have you seen a woman come this way?"

The guy was stunned, like most people are when confronted by an anxious cop. But he managed to get out, "She went down this way and was asking how to get into the main office."

"How do you get in there?"

"End of this hallway, to your left. Heavy door that's usually locked."

I was off to the races again. I was beginning to feel panic. I didn't want this woman to get away. I thought of Father Alonzo. I wanted to sit and comfort my daughter. And God knows what my grandfather was going through.

I came to the door, and sure enough, it was locked. I had no time to waste. I lifted my left foot and threw my whole body behind a kick. I felt the door shake and the frame crack. I hit it again, and it opened at an odd angle as one of the hinges came loose.

I burst into the bright hallway and immediately startled a woman carrying an armload of papers. She jumped back, and they fluttered to the ground in every direction.

"NYPD. Has anyone you don't know come through here?"

The woman shook her head. "Not that I noticed."

As I started to move past her, she said, "What's wrong? Is it a terrorist? What should we do?"

I took a moment. "Just stay in your office. No one should bother you. Where's the exit?"

She pointed me down the hallway that led to the lobby.

I sprinted ahead toward an astonishing view of the East River.

CHAPTER 91

THE RECEPTIONIST, A young woman with a bright smile and blond curly hair, turned to me with a questioning look.

Before she could say anything, I held up my badge and said, "NYPD. Did anyone come through the lobby?" I worked hard to keep my voice even, but I needed answers.

The young woman just stared at me for a moment, then said, "Yes. A woman I didn't know came from—"

Facing the receptionist, I didn't even register the sound of the gunshot behind me. And that's how I had a view of her face virtually exploding in front of me as a bullet struck her just above the nose.

The impact cut her off midsentence and made her stumble back against the decorative wallpaper. As she tumbled to the carpet, she left a smear of blood on the wall.

I leaped to one side, looking for any cover I could find. I knew the bullet had been meant for me, and the shot gave me a general idea of where the assassin was hiding—behind a column near the front door, with the wide bay window behind her.

I rolled to a stop behind the counter where the young woman had been standing. Her blue eyes were wide open and seemed to stare at me.

Another person I'd failed to protect from this killer.

I was behind the counter and hoped it was thick enough to stop a bullet. I peeked around it once and could see the reflection of the assassin, crouched behind the column, in the window. Her long hair flowed down her back. Behind her was a tranquil view of a park with the river beyond it. A tour boat slowly passing by.

I called out, "It's time to give it up. You've got nowhere to run, and I'm no longer a sitting duck."

I waited for an answer but got none.

"Surrender now, and I can guarantee no one will hurt you." As soon as I finished talking, there were two blasts from the gun, and bullets hit the counter just above my head. One of them punched through and came to a stop in the wall behind me. That answered my question about whether the counter would protect me.

I leaned away from the counter and returned two rounds just to keep her head down. I wanted to remind her I had a gun, too. I also realized that time was my friend. The longer I held her in place, the more likely it was that help would arrive.

She was smart and professional. It did her no good to answer me. She was trying to protect her position while I just kept giving mine away with my big mouth.

I stole a look around the counter again to make sure no one had wandered into our gunfight. I noticed a couple of people trying to hide in the corner of the room behind a table. I was quite sure everyone in the business offices was cowering in a corner or under a desk. On the bright side, there had to have been dozens of calls made to 911.

Time was on my side. The problem was the assassin realized that as well. She would have to make a move soon.

I just hoped to God I'd be ready.

CHAPTER 92

ALEX HAD MADE it as far as the lobby without anyone questioning her. She even said hello to the pretty blond receptionist behind a tall counter. Then she heard the sound coming from the hallway to the business offices. Someone was pounding something hard. Her guess was that it was Detective Michael Bennett knocking down the door.

That gave her an idea. One last chance to salvage something from this miserable day. She eased forward as though she were headed toward the front door, then ducked behind a thick decorative column a few feet from the exit.

She was out of sight when she heard Bennett say to the young woman behind the counter, "NYPD. Did anyone come through the lobby?"

That's when Alex leaned around the column with her pistol up and fired quickly. Too quickly. The bullet missed Bennett and struck the unsuspecting receptionist in the face. Alex couldn't see exactly what had happened, but she knew she had killed an innocent woman. Shit.

The idea made her angry at Bennett. He had forced this. He wouldn't let her just get away. She had to kill him. Now.

When she leaned around the column again, she saw Bennett tumble out of the way and roll behind the counter. He yelled to her to surrender, and she used his voice to approximate his position so she would know where to shoot.

After a couple of her shots missed, he returned fire.

They were in a stalemate, but she was the one who had to move. She had to get away. She wanted so desperately to end this contract and kill Bennett, but she had to consider all her options.

If she sprinted for the exit, she'd be away from cover, and it would take time to open the glass door. That would give Bennett time and a clear shot. She had no doubt he'd take it.

She leaned back against the column and looked out at the East River. No one was racing from that direction to help the detective. She could see a park and open sidewalks. That was where she needed to be. Out in the open. At least making an attempt to get away so she could head back to Colombia as soon as possible. She could picture her girls squeezing her when she came back to the ranch.

She raised the pistol and fired three rounds into the wide glass window. She knew the sound of the gunshots would keep Bennett behind cover. This was not safety glass. It was more decorative and cracked uniformly between the three bullet holes.

She stood up and risked it all by throwing her body against the crack in the window.

She braced for a brutal impact, not knowing what the shattered glass might do to her skin. But it gave way, and she tumbled onto the sidewalk, virtually unharmed.

Alex considered running to the river, but then it might be easy to cut her off. She decided to stay on the studio property and come out in a place where no one expected her. She wasted no time jumping to her feet and racing along the sidewalk that led to the other side of the building.

She didn't see Bennett in pursuit, so she kept her remaining bullet in case she ran into other trouble.

CHAPTER 93

I NEEDED SOMETHING to happen. I know that sounds crazy, but lying on a carpet next to a dead woman can screw with your head. Then I got my wish. From my cover position behind the receptionist's desk, I heard gunshots and braced for the impact on my thin wall of protection. Then I realized the shots weren't directed at me.

I heard another noise and glass breaking. That made me pop around the edge of the desk with my gun up. I didn't have a clear view of anything, but it looked like the assassin had fled through a broken window.

Then I heard other people in the lobby. Women sobbing and someone calling out for help.

I crawled back and checked the receptionist for a pulse, but I could tell before I even put my finger to her throat that she was dead. I had to check.

I stood up behind the counter and saw a woman helping an older man from the office area. Other people were starting to stand, too. I didn't notice them in my tunnel vision as I ran into the room.

Just as I was about to bolt for the door, the woman with the older man said, "Thank God. The police are here."

I couldn't ignore them no matter how much I wanted to chase the assassin. I could hear sirens in the distance and knew help was on the way. The arriving cops just needed to seal the area before she could escape.

When I stepped around the counter, the woman with the older man was right next to me, and the man almost tumbled over.

I grabbed him before he hit the floor and said, "Were you shot? Are you injured?"

He shook his head feebly and pointed to his chest. I eased him onto a bench, but before I could loosen his collar and really make an assessment, a man who had been hiding in the corner of the lobby ran up to me and said, "The woman who shot Tia ran that way on the outside walk."

I peered out the window in the direction he pointed but didn't see anyone.

A middle-aged woman hustled toward me and said, "Don't let her hurt us. Please—you have to protect us."

"You're safe now. Let me help this man." I had already holstered my pistol, and I could see this man was starting to go into serious distress. But I couldn't help thinking about the killer who was running away without anyone chasing her.

Just then the door opened, and a young patrol officer, in a fresh uniform and with shoulders almost as wide as the door, stepped inside.

He called out, "Are you folks all right? We've had reports of a gunfight going on somewhere on the property."

I yelled over my shoulder, "Michael Bennett, Manhattan North Homicide. Get over here. We need help."

The earnest young man raced to me, never asking for identification.

I even felt a little guilty pawning this whole set of scared people off on him. I said, "Get fire rescue rolling for this man. We're looking for a female with long dark hair about thirty years old. She's armed and has already shot at least two people. Get on your radio and put it out to everyone right now."

I didn't wait for a response. I was up and running out the door before anyone had anything else to say.

I thought about what Father Alonzo had told me. Use my advantage. Understand the city.

Then I had an idea.

CHAPTER 94

AS MUCH AS Alex didn't want to admit it, she was scared. Fear is a killer in this business. It saps your strength and keeps you from thinking straight. She didn't know anyone who wouldn't be a little shaken after what she had just been through.

All she wanted to do now was to put some distance between herself and the shooting scene. When she turned the corner of the long building, she noticed people pouring out into the parking lot. There was no order or supervision.

The idea of someone with a gun spooked everyone. That meant no one was using common sense or paying attention to the surroundings. That was exactly what she needed: chaos.

Alex slowed to a walk and pulled her blouse straight. She spent a few seconds making her hair neat and professional. She mingled with the crowd but continued to walk in the same direction, to the opposite side of the complex. There had to be a street with taxis near there.

She heard sirens, but so far she had only seen one police car, racing directly to the main office she had just come from.

Now all she could focus on was escape. She could have no regrets about what had happened or who had been hurt. She just needed to find a way off this property, then out of Brooklyn.

She eased away from the crowd and started walking along the sidewalk at the far end of the parking lot.

Just as she thought she was clear of any interference, a man in a uniform stepped out from between two small buildings close to the river. He had a radio, and as he approached her, she heard someone giving a description. "The suspect is a female with long hair and may be posing as someone in the entertainment business."

The man looked up when he was right in front of Alex. He was young, black, perhaps in his early twenties, and very skinny. And he immediately realized he had stumbled onto the armed woman everyone was looking for.

She drew her pistol from her purse and casually pointed it at his chest.

Alex admired the fact that he came right to the point, raising both hands and saying, "I don't want any trouble."

"Neither do I." She didn't wave the gun to make her point. She didn't have to. "I just need information from you, and I need it fast."

His whole body was shaking. A tear welled in his right eye. She wanted him scared. This was good.

Alex said, "What's the fastest way to get to a street where I can hail a cab?"

He pointed with his right hand and kept his left hand raised. "If you go straight down this sidewalk to the corner of the property, there is a person-size door in the fence. The gate's never locked. There's a busy street right there."

She smiled at the young man and nudged him back with the barrel of the pistol so he walked backward to the two buildings close to the river. Then they kept walking through the narrow park to the edge of the river.

Alex said, "That was very informative and very smart. Now I need to make sure you can't tell anyone for a few minutes. You know how we're going to arrange that?" She held up the pistol.

The young security guard's voice broke as he said, "Oh, God. No, please."

"Can you think of an alternative?" Alex had no intention of shooting him. She just needed him quiet.

The security guard said, "I'm going to promise to sit right here and not call out to anyone?"

She reached onto his belt and pulled his radio off. "First we're going to make sure you don't have communications." She chucked the radio over the seawall into the East River.

"Hey!"

"Maybe you should jump in after it."

The young man looked over her shoulder at the seawall and river behind it. "That's okay. I think I can explain it to my boss."

She pointed her pistol. "Jump. Now."

He hesitated and just stared at her.

Alex said, "What's the matter? Can't you swim?" It wasn't an idle question. She didn't want to kill another innocent bystander today.

He raised his voice and said, "That's a stereotype. Of course I can swim."

Alex nudged him in the chest with the barrel of the small semiautomatic pistol. He stumbled back a couple of steps, then turned, crawled onto the low seawall, and hopped into the water.

Alex peeked over to make sure he was okay. He was already floating with the current and wasn't panicking.

Now she forced herself to walk calmly back onto the studio property, then down the pathway he had pointed out. With all the people milling around, it was as good a scenario as she could hope for. Civilians always distract law enforcement. No matter what the mission, civilians just get in the way. And Alex was happy about that.

She turned to her right at the end of the walkway and followed the fence to the corner of the property, where a six-foot chain-link door was built into the fence. She lifted the handle and stepped onto the sidewalk alongside a busy street.

Sweet.

CHAPTER 95

ALEX WALKED BRISKLY along the sidewalk and noticed two more NYPD patrol cars race past, headed for the movie studio. A smile crept across her face. She felt like she was going to make it. Now that she was away from Bennett, the police response didn't seem like a threat. In some South American countries, the authorities might even call out the army to try to seal an area. She greatly preferred this.

A block away, the traffic was light, and no one appeared concerned with what was happening at the studio. A McDonald's looked like a good place to lay low, but Alex needed to get out of the area. She kept walking, trying to blend in. The last thing she needed was to call attention to herself.

At the corner, she saw two cabs turn onto a side street. That's where she needed to be. She stopped for a moment to get her bearings. She could see the Freedom Tower in the distance and the Brooklyn Bridge not far away.

She would take a cab to within a few blocks of her hotel, then walk the rest of the way. Just in case someone put some effort into finding out where she went from here.

She didn't intend to waste any time after that. She would catch a bus south and then a flight out of Baltimore or perhaps Reagan National. It was extra work but would give her peace of mind. No one would be able to figure out who she was or where she went.

Alex kept a steady pace down the street, her right hand just outside her purse for easy access to her weapons. No one gave her a second look. Another police car flew by, followed by a paramedic truck.

She turned the corner and saw three cabs sitting along the curb near the middle of the block. As she approached, she caught the first driver's attention and stepped directly to the rear passenger door.

Her survival instinct told her she wasn't quite clear yet. She grabbed the stiletto from her purse and held it in her right hand.

Just as she grabbed the cab's door handle, she heard someone from behind her say, "Police—don't move."

She let the stiletto rest on the cab's roof in the crease where the door closed.

CHAPTER 96

AS SOON AS I called out, "Police—don't move," I felt an odd mix of emotions. There was that taste of excitement any cop feels at the moment of making a big arrest, but I also felt anger. That was something strange for me. I could usually detach myself at a moment like this.

I saw her freeze, but I wasn't going to take any chances. I aimed my service weapon at her head. The taxi driver was a veteran of the New York streets—he knew to lie down in his seat to keep out of the line of fire.

The woman didn't move and rested her hands on the cab's roof. I knew she carried her pistol in her purse, so I immediately said, "Drop the purse on the ground. Do it now."

She hesitated, then tilted to her right and lowered her right arm. The purse slipped off and plopped on the ground. I could tell by the way the purse thumped on the sidewalk that it had

a gun in it. The same one that killed that young receptionist. The same gun used to shoot Father Alonzo in the stomach.
The same gun she had pointed at my daughter.

Now I stepped a little closer. I kicked the purse away from
her and leaned forward. I used my left hand to grasp her left
arm so I could handcuff her.

Then I felt her weight shift. It was slight, but if you'd been
in a street fight, you would know what it meant.

She pushed hard off the cab, knocking us both back on the
sidewalk. I stumbled but kept my balance.

Then she spun and extended her right arm. It arced through
the air toward my face. I ducked, and the blow missed me.
That was when I realized she had a knife of some kind in her
hand. It took me a moment to comprehend that it was the
stiletto she'd used in the murders.

She wasted no time after the first strike missed me. The
woman threw a front kick aimed at my groin.

I blocked it with my right arm, then tried to bring the pistol
up again.

She brought the stiletto down and slashed my forearm.

My hand opened involuntarily, and my service weapon
clattered to the ground.

The assassin kicked my pistol under the cab and out of my
reach.

Blood soaked the shredded sleeve of my jacket. It took a second to register the pain as it shot up my arm.

I took a step back, a little dazed, then faced the assassin
as she thrust the stiletto at my heart. She let out a grunt, or
maybe it was a *"Kiai"* she'd learned from her Colombia-based
martial-arts instructor.

I shifted a fraction and felt the stiletto skitter across my shirt. That was close.

I lifted my right arm and wrapped my hand around hers—the one that held the stiletto. She was faster than I was and had more pure fighting skill, so I had to use my size advantage. I held on to her hand even as she struck my face with her left elbow.

I lifted her off the ground, then both of us tumbled to the sidewalk. I landed on top of the woman, who, for all her skill, was still seventy pounds lighter than I was.

The stiletto made a clinking noise as it fell onto the sidewalk.

I felt the fight go out of her.

It was over.

CHAPTER 97

IT TOOK A moment to secure the assassin with handcuffs and make sure I had all her weapons. She stood up gracefully even with her hands cuffed. She faced me with a look of defiance.

I held my right forearm in an effort to slow the bleeding from the gash she had given me with that stiletto. Blood dripped onto the white sidewalk in a crazy red pattern.

I felt the anger rise off me. This woman had caused me so much pain.

"What's your name?"

She gave me a pretty smile and said, "At this time, I'm not going to say anything."

"You won't tell me who wants me dead?"

"I think you might have already figured that out." Then she looked at me as if we were having a conversation. "I don't think I've ever met a police officer as relentless as you."

"You gave me plenty of motivation."

"You could've always taken your family and gone into hiding."

"There was another reason why I couldn't let you slip away."

She looked intrigued as she said, "And what could that reason possibly be?"

"Antrole Martens."

"Excuse me?"

"He was my partner who was killed by a hand grenade. Or do you not even pay attention when innocent people are killed?"

"I feel it. After my work is done."

"His wife and two children feel it every day. And now continue to struggle. Maybe the rest of their lives. There's no way I could ever run from someone like you."

The woman shrugged and said, "Too bad. It would've saved a lot of heartache for everyone."

I gave her a hard stare and said, "Will you talk to me? We might be able to do some good."

She shook her head and said, "I'm afraid I can say nothing more until after I speak to my attorney."

It was over. I felt a wave of emotion rock through me. I managed to say, "You're under arrest."

She just nodded. Then, after a moment, she said, "How did you know where I would run to?"

I saw a patrol car down the street racing toward me. I gave her a little smile. "I'm a New Yorker. I know where the tourists will head."

CHAPTER 98

TWO WEEKS AFTER the shoot-out in Brooklyn, the entire family attended a ceremony for Father Alonzo at Holy Name. He had only been out of the hospital for a week, but the city seemed desperate to honor a brave citizen.

The local media had produced dozens of stories about the "hero priest" who'd risked his life. Even the young doctor who'd treated him at the hospital had gained some notoriety, interviewed by the *Today* show and Fox News.

The media coverage, as well as his storied career in the Colombian national police, attracted visitors from near and far. All the bigwigs from the NYPD, as well as the Catholic archdiocese, sat just behind us with the mayor, though he had a rocky relationship with the police department.

There were a dozen members of the Colombian national police who came to pay their respects. They seemed pleased that they could make a claim on the priest who had helped capture a killer.

Father Alonzo was not required to speak to the crowd, only to stand and accept an acrylic plaque from the police commissioner. He looked stiff and had told me he was a little sore from the bullet.

Seamus sat next to Alonzo during the short ceremony. He was beaming as if he had trained Alonzo in his fighting skills. I knew he had some remarks to make.

I noticed that he sat during the entire service, and it made me worry about his health and stamina. But when the time came, he stepped to the microphone and was the picture of solemn dignity.

He looked down and smiled at his great-grandchildren, just as he did whenever he gave the sermon during the regular Sunday service.

He cleared his throat and had every person in the room staring at him.

Seamus started slowly at first. "Alonzo Garcia makes a difference in the world. How many people can say that? He was a respected police officer in Colombia until God called him to service in the Church. No matter how you look at him—as a cop, as a priest, or as a man—he is an inspiration.

"I can tell you personally, few people have meant more to me in my life." He looked down at Juliana, and a tear ran down his cheek.

Then I found a tear running down my cheek. Though I'd never admit it to Seamus.

CHAPTER 99

AT THE RECEPTION following the ceremony, I met many of Alonzo's former comrades from the Colombian national police. Alonzo sat whenever he could, and I was worried he was getting tired. Seamus was watching him like a mother hen, so I figured he'd keep Alonzo from overdoing it.

One of Alonzo's early partners was second-in-charge of the entire force, and he was clearly proud of his friend. He stepped over to speak with me.

The tall colonel said, "We're aware of the woman who was arrested for shooting Alonzo. Alexandra Martinez works on the fringes of the underworld, and there are many rumors. Some people call her the Beautiful Death."

I said, "She certainly had me running in circles. If it wasn't for Alonzo, I'd be dead."

"Every man in this room who came to pay respects from Colombia could say the same thing."

"I'm sure Alonzo appreciates you guys traveling so far."

"We were also interested in gathering any information you have on Miss Martinez."

"She hasn't said much. But at least we have some clear booking photos and she's in some computer systems now."

"You will be able to convict her, correct?"

"I think we have enough. Not just for shooting Alonzo but also for the murder of a receptionist in the building she was escaping from. We're also looking at several other homicides we believe she was involved in. You can never count on it, but this sure seems like a strong case to me."

Almost as soon as I was finished speaking to the colonel, a well-dressed man in his early forties extended his hand and said, "My name is Oscar." He had an accent, but I couldn't tell from what country.

I said, "Are you here with the contingent from the Colombian national police?"

He smiled and shook his head. "No, Detective. I am decidedly not with them. I am from a business organization based in Mexico."

I gave him a sidelong glance and said, "What kind of business organization?"

"The one you're thinking about right now. The one that wishes you to know they would like to have a truce. They will no longer support any efforts to harm you or anyone associated with you."

"And why do I receive such an honor?"

"Purely economics. We don't want trouble. We don't want

violence. Both things cost us money. You got caught up in something that really shouldn't have escalated. You have my personal and sincere apologies. And my assurances that it will not happen again."

"Would you care to share that information with any of my coworkers or the visitors from Colombia?"

"I would not. And I was really just showing my respect. This was a courtesy call. You need not look behind every door anymore."

"And my son?"

"The attack at the prison will never be repeated. He is safe. At least from us."

"And if I believe you and let down my guard, who's to say it's not just a trick?"

"We don't need to use tricks. We have an army at our disposal. We chose not to use that army and hired someone with a good reputation. She was unable to complete her assignment. And now I've completed mine. Choose to believe me or not. But life will continue. Good day, Detective."

I could've stopped him. But what could anyone do? There was no warrant out on him, and it wasn't a crime to say that you may or may not be associated with a criminal organization.

Something told me his message was sincere. I stepped over to Mary Catherine and gave her a hug. I felt the weight lifted off my shoulders.

As I watched the man walk away, a hand on my arm made me jump.

I spun to see the smiling face of Father Alonzo Garcia.

He said, "A little nervous, are we?"

I shrugged. "We can't all be hero priests."

That got a laugh. "You know how silly that is. For men like us, action is the only answer. I took action. That's it."

"And in the process saved my daughter. By extension saved me and my whole life."

I embraced him.

CHAPTER 100

I ATTENDED SEVERAL of the hearings for Alexandra Martinez. Someone was paying for two of the best lawyers in New York. They were arguing everything from her bond to her immigration status. They wanted her out of jail before trial.

Then the prosecutor stood up. For a change, she had a reason to look smug. She said, "Your Honor, Miss Martinez has been charged in two homicides for which we have reliable eyewitnesses. She's currently being investigated for as many as six other homicides in New York.

"But before we even worry about any of that, I have to advise the court and counsel for the defendant that the authorities in Italy have contacted me to say they're currently putting together a warrant for Miss Martinez's arrest in connection with a murder that occurred in Rome two years ago."

It was rare that prosecutors had so much ammo when facing high-powered attorneys with wealthy clients. This had to be fun for her. She even milked it a little bit by continuing to stand after she was finished.

A reporter for the New York *Daily News* slid onto the seat next to me.

He said, "Are there any big cases you're *not* involved in?"

"I'm basically just a witness on this one. Why do you care?"

"I'm not sure I buy that whole story about the hero priest. I'd like to get the facts so people could make up their own minds about who's a hero."

"The facts are the facts. He saved my life and the lives of several others. Why is that suspect?"

"Because suspicion sells more papers and gets us more clicks on the Internet. It's also a hell of a lot easier than trying to investigate some kind of fraud at city hall."

I just turned away and watched the proceedings some more. Life was too short to waste talking to idiots.

I stayed long enough to hear the judge say the words "No bond."

That was all I was hoping for. At least for now.

CHAPTER 101

WHEN I GOT home that evening, I enjoyed my Italian dinner cooked by my Irish fiancée.

Seamus's grace was particularly on point.

Once we were all holding hands, he said, "Heavenly Father, thank you for allowing us all to be together here." He couldn't help but pause and look over at Juliana. "In God's name we thank you."

There was a perfectly synchronized "Amen" said by all the kids, Mary Catherine, and me.

After dinner, when everything was cleaned up and the kids were diligently working on homework assignments, Mary Catherine snuggled up next to me on the couch as I stared out at the lights of the city.

She wrapped an arm around my waist and laid her head on my chest. She said, "Michael, I'm ready to get married."

That was not something I saw coming. It had been one of the foremost issues on my mind until Antrole's death. Now, hearing this beautiful woman, whom I loved more than anything, say she wanted to marry me, I was at a loss for words.

She sat up and looked me in the eyes. "I'd like to do it sooner rather than later. In fact, I'd like to get married as soon as possible."

"Is it because you're afraid that if we wait, Seamus might not be able to preside? He is looking a little frail."

"That's part of it. But you're the rest. You and the kids. I love you, and I can't think of anything I'd want more than to be married to you and raise these kids."

I sat up and kissed her. We kissed so long that the kids started to make noises from the dining room, where they were doing their homework. Chrissy said she might be sick. That meant it was a good kiss.

And it wouldn't be the last one these kids saw.

EPILOGUE

FIVE DAYS AFTER Alonzo's ceremony, the family gathered at our apartment on the Upper West Side. There was a ripple of excitement running through the crowd. The kids had jostled for position on the couch and on the carpet so that they could look into the screen of the new laptop computer I had bought for Trent and Eddie. They were going to need it for the special classes at Columbia University.

Wedged in the middle of the crowd was Seamus, who looked as excited as an eight-year-old at Christmas. I didn't even fool with the computer. I deferred to Eddie and let him set up the video chat. We were looking at a prison administrator on the screen to make sure our connection was stable.

This was our reward for Brian's helping out on the case. Sergeant Marcia and I had written up an affidavit detailing

Brian's help on a case that not only hurt a drug cartel but also captured an assassin who was wanted all over the world.

It wasn't enough to get him released early, but the judge did have him moved to a medium-security youthful offender program at the Mohawk Correctional Facility, in Oneida County. It was closer to us and, after what had happened to Brian, considered much safer. One of the perks was that Brian got to make a weekly phone call via computer. That meant we had a live video feed of him every week.

Brian's face came on the screen. I pumped my fist as if the Giants had just scored a touchdown. It was a tiny victory, but after all we had been through, it made my heart race with excitement. It was great to see his wide smile as he took in the video feed of his nine brothers and sisters, his father, his great-grandfather, and his soon-to-be stepmother.

Each of the kids got to say hello individually and chat with him for a minute. I'm sure when they put the time limits on these calls, no one at the New York State Department of Corrections considered the possibility that an inmate would have nine siblings.

Then the boys talked to him as a group for a minute.

Ricky said, "How's the food in there?"

"A little better than Gowanda."

Eddie said, "What kind of computer are you on right now?"

Brian gave him a quick laugh and said, "It's no brand name, that's for sure. One of the classes here is computer technology. These computers were all built by parts ordered in bulk. It's a big ugly desktop, but it gets the job done."

I realized that prison life had filed off any ideas Brian might have had about luxury. But he looked good. His smile alone was enough to cheer me up.

Seamus chased away the kids and sat down with me on the couch so the two of us could talk to Brian alone.

My grandfather said, "Are you keeping your priorities straight, Brian?"

"Yes, sir. I've signed up for every possible course. I'm trying to read two books a week, and I go to the service in our chapel every Sunday."

Seamus nodded in approval. "Good lad, good lad."

I finally had my turn to speak with my son for a few minutes. I told him, "Don't worry. I haven't given up on getting you out. I have other angles to work on."

"I'm not worried, Dad. I know you'll do your best. Who knows? Like Gramps says, 'God works in mysterious ways.'"

That was enough for me. No matter what happened or what conflicts I faced on the NYPD, I could rest easy knowing my son believed in me.

And there was no way I was going to let him down.

MICHAEL BENNETT, BE GRATEFUL YOU'RE ALIVE.

Someone attacked the Thanksgiving Day Parade directly in front of Michael Bennett and his family. The television news called it "Holiday Terror"— Michael Bennett calls it personal. The hunt is on....

READ ON FOR A BONUS MICHAEL BENNETT STORY, *MANHUNT*

CHAPTER 1

MY ENTIRE BROOD, plus Mary Catherine and my grandfather, gathered in the living room. We'd been told to expect a call from Brian between eight and eight fifteen. That gave us enough time to eat, clean up, and at least start the mountain of homework that nine kids get from one of the better Catholic schools in New York City.

We had the phone set on speaker and placed it in the middle of the group, which was getting a little antsy waiting for the call.

At exactly ten minutes after eight, the phone rang and some dull-voiced New York Department of Corrections bureaucrat told us that the call would last approximately ten minutes and that it would be monitored. Great.

My oldest son, Brian, had made a mistake. A big mistake— selling drugs. Now he was paying for that mistake, and so were we.

Tonight was Thanksgiving eve. Tomorrow we would embark on our annual tradition of viewing the Macy's Thanksgiving Day Parade, and it would hurt not having Brian with us.

My late wife and I had begun this tradition even before we started adopting kids. She'd get off her shift at the hospital and I'd meet her near Rockefeller Center. When the kids were little, she loved the parade more than they did. It was one of many traditions I kept alive to honor her memory.

She even made the parade after chemo had wrecked her body, with a scarf wrapped around her head. The beauty still managed an excited smile at the sight of Bart Simpson or Snoopy floating by.

As soon as Brian came on the line, there was a ripple in our crowd. The last time I'd seen him, he was still recovering from a knife attack that was meant to send me a message.

Tonight, he sounded good. His voice was clear and still had that element of the kid to it. No parent can ever think of their child as a convicted felon, even if he's sitting in a prison. Currently, Brian was temporarily housed at Bear Hill Correctional, in the town of Malone, in northern New York. It was considered safe. For now. Mary Catherine and I talked over each other while we asked him about the dorm and classes.

Brian said, "Well, I can't start classes because I haven't been officially designated at a specific prison. That will happen soon."

All three of the boys spoke as a group. As usual, they took a few minutes to catch Brian up on sports. Football always seemed to be the same—the Jets look bad, the Patriots look good.

Then an interruption in the programming.

Chrissy, my youngest, started to cry. *Wail* is probably more accurate.

Mary Catherine immediately dropped to one knee and slipped an arm around the little girl's shoulder.

Chrissy moaned, "I miss Brian." She turned to the phone like there was a video feed and repeated, "I miss you, Brian. I want you to come home."

There was a pause on the phone, then Brian's voice came through a little shakier. I could tell he was holding back tears by the way he spoke, haltingly. "I can't come home right now, Chrissy, but you can do something for me."

"Okay."

"Go to the parade tomorrow and have fun. I mean, so much fun you can't stand it. Then I want you to write me a letter about it and send it to me. Can you do that?"

Chrissy sniffled. "Yes. Yes, I can."

I felt a tear run down my cheek. I have some great kids. I don't care what kind of mistakes they might've made.

We were ready for our adventure.

CHAPTER 2

IT WAS A bright, cloudless day and Mary Catherine had bundled the kids up like we lived at the North Pole. It was cold, with a decent breeze, but not what most New Yorkers would consider brutal. My grandfather, Seamus, would call it "crisp." It was too crisp for the old priest. He was snuggled comfortably in his quarters at Holy Name.

I wore an insulated Giants windbreaker and jeans. I admit, I looked at the kids occasionally and wished Mary Catherine had dressed me as well, but it wasn't that bad.

I herded the whole group to our usual spot, across from Rockefeller Center at 49th Street and Sixth Avenue. It was a good spot, where we could see all the floats and make our escape afterward with relatively little hassle.

I was afraid this might be the year that some of the older kids decided they'd rather sleep in than get up before dawn to make our way to Midtown. Maybe it was due to Chrissy's tearful conversation with Brian, but everyone was up and appeared excited despite the early hour.

Now we had staked out our spot for the parade, and were waiting for the floats. It was perfect outside and I gave in to the overwhelming urge to lean over and kiss Mary Catherine.

Chrissy and Shawna crouched in close to us as Jane flirted with a couple of boys from Nebraska—after I'd spoken to them, of course. They were nice young men, in their first year at UN Kearney.

We could tell by the reaction of the crowd that the parade was coming our way. We sat through the first couple of marching bands and earthbound floats before we saw one of the stars of the parade: Snoopy, in his red scarf, ready for the Red Baron.

Of course, Eddie had the facts on the real Red Baron. He said, "You know, he was an ace in World War I for Germany. His name was Manfred von Richthofen. He had over eighty kills in dogfights."

The kids tended to tune out some of Eddie's trivia, but Mary Catherine and I showed interest in what he said. It was important to keep a brain like that fully engaged.

Like any NYPD officer, on or off duty, I keep my eyes open and always know where the nearest uniformed patrol officer is. Today I noticed a tall, young African American officer trying to politely corral people in our area, who ignored him and crept onto the street for a better photo.

I smiled, knowing how hard it is to get people to follow any kind of rules unless there is an immediate threat of arrest.

Then I heard it.

At first, I thought it was a garbage truck banging a dumpster as it emptied it. Then an engine revved down 49th Street, and I turned to look.

I barely had any time to react. A white Ford step-van truck barreled down the street directly toward us. It was gaining speed, though it must have had to slow down to get by the dump truck parked at the intersection of 49th and Sixth as a blockade.

Shawna was ten feet to my right, focused on Snoopy. She was directly in the path of the truck.

It was like I'd been shocked with electricity. I jumped from my spot and scooped up Shawna a split second before the truck rolled past us. I heard Mary Catherine shriek as I tumbled, with Shawna, on the far side of the truck.

The truck slammed into spectators just in front of us. One of the boys from Nebraska bounced off the hood with a sickening thud. He lay in a twisted heap on the rough asphalt. His University of Nebraska jacket was sprayed with a darker shade of red as blood poured from his mouth and ears.

The truck rolled onto the parade route until it collided with a sponsor vehicle splattered with a Kellogg's logo. The impact sent a young woman in a purple pageant dress flying from the car and under the wheels of a float.

Screams started to rise around me, but I couldn't take my eyes off the truck.

The driver made an agile exit from the crumpled driver's door and stood right next to the truck. Over his face, he wore a red scarf with white starburst designs.

He shouted, *"Hawqala!"*

CHAPTER 3

I STOOD IN shock like just about everyone else near me. This was not something we were used to seeing on US soil.

Eddie and Jane, crouching on the sidewalk next to me, both stood and started to move away from me.

I grabbed Eddie's wrist.

He looked back at me and said, "We've got to help them."

Jane had paused right next to him as I said, "We don't know what's going to happen."

As I said it, the driver of the truck reached in his front jacket pocket and pulled something out. I couldn't identify it exactly, but I knew it was a detonator.

I shouted as loud as I could, "Everyone down!" My family knew to lie flat on the sidewalk and cover their faces with their hands. A few people in the crowd listened to me as well. Most were still in shock or sobbing.

The driver hit the button on the detonator and immediately there was a blinding flash, and what sounded like a thunderclap echoed among all the buildings.

I couldn't turn away as I watched from the pavement. The blast blew the roof of the truck straight into the air almost thirty feet. I felt it in my guts. A fireball rose from the truck.

The driver was dazed and stumbled away from the truck as the roof landed on the asphalt not far from him.

Now there was absolute pandemonium. It felt like every person on 49th Street was screaming. The blast had rocked the whole block.

The parade was coming to an abrupt stop. Parade vehicles bumped one another and the marching band behind the step van scattered. A teenager with a trumpet darted past me, looking for safety.

The driver pushed past spectators on the sidewalk near us and started to run back down 49th Street where he had driven the truck.

The ball of flame was still rising like one of the floats. Then I noticed a couple of the floats were rising in the air as well. The human anchors had followed instinct and run for their lives.

Snoopy was seventy-five feet in the air now.

Several Christmas tree ornaments as big as Volkswagens, with only three ropes apiece, made a colorful design as they passed the middle stories of Rockefeller Center.

I glanced around, but didn't see any uniformed cops close. The one young patrolman I had seen keeping people in place was frantically trying to help a child who had been struck by the truck.

I had no radio to call for backup. I just had my badge and my off-duty pistol hidden in my waistband.

There had been plenty of cops early, but now I saw that some of them had been hurt in the explosion, others were trying to help victims. It was mayhem, and no one was chasing the perp. I was it. I had to do something.

CHAPTER 4

WHEN I STOOD up, my legs still a little shaky, I concentrated on the red scarf I'd seen around the driver's face and neck as he fled the scene. The splash of color gave me something to focus on.

I looked around at my family, making sure everyone was still in one piece. They were on the ground and I said, "Stay put."

I worked my way past panicked parade spectators until I was in the open street and could see the driver half a block ahead. I broke into a sprint, dodging tourists like a running back.

By this point, no one realized the man running from the scene was the driver. The people this far back on the street didn't have a front row seat to the tragedy. No one tried to stop him. Everyone was scrambling for safety, if there was such a place.

I started to gain on the man because he hadn't realized yet

that he was being pursued. He had a loping gait as if one of his legs was injured. But he was also alert, checking each side and behind him as he hurried away.

I wasn't a rookie chasing my first purse-snatcher in the Bronx. I didn't feel the urge to yell, "Stop—police!" I was silent and hung back a little bit so he didn't pick up on me.

He took the corner, then slowed. He looked around, as if he was expecting someone to meet him. I paused at the edge of a high-end fashion boutique and watched him for a moment. I still hadn't drawn my pistol, to avoid attracting attention.

Finally, the truck driver decided his ride wasn't here and started down the street again. He looked over his shoulder one time as he approached a packed diner, and surprised me by slipping inside.

I looked in the window as I came to the door of the diner. Every patron and server was glued to the TV in the corner of the room. News of the attack was mesmerizing. The room was silent as the news had just broken—the same TV parade footage was on loop as the newscaster started repeating the information he was receiving. No conversation, no clinking of silverware, nothing.

I immediately stepped to the cashier by the front door, held up my badge, and said in a low voice, "NYPD. Did you see where the man who just came in here went?"

The dark-haired young woman shook her head. She mumbled, "I didn't notice anyone." Then she turned and looked back at the TV.

Even though the attack had happened only a couple blocks away, a few minutes ago, watching it on TV made it feel like it was in another country.

I saw the hallway that led past the kitchen. There was a sign that said RESTROOM, so I presumed a back door was that way as well. I hustled, squeezing past several tables crowded with extra patrons. Today was a big day for New York eateries.

Just as I started to pick up my pace, I heard something behind me and turned. The man I'd been chasing was lowering himself from an awkward position above the door. What the hell? It looked like it was out of the movies.

When he dropped to the floor and faced me, I realized he had led me into a trap.

CHAPTER 5

THE TRUCK DRIVER and I stared at each other for a moment. He had taken off the scarf, having used it to trick me. Pretty sharp.

He was about thirty, with neat, dark hair and blue eyes.

I reached for my pistol.

He reacted instantly and blocked my arm. That was from training. That's not a natural move. Then he head-butted me. Hard. My brain rattled and vision blurred.

I stumbled back and kept reaching for my pistol. Just as I pulled it from under my Giants windbreaker, the man swatted it out of my hand. I heard it clatter onto the hard, wooden floor—then the man kicked it.

The gun spun as it slid across the floor and under a radiator.

The man nodded to me and sprinted away. He didn't want to fight, he just wanted to escape.

I couldn't let that happen.

I was dazed and unable to reach my pistol, but I had to do something. I just put one foot in front of the other and followed the man.

My head started to clear.

A moment later, I found myself in the kitchen. The cooks and busboys weren't paying any attention to us. They were watching the news, just like everyone else, but on one of their smartphones. The back door wasn't at the end of the hall, like I had expected, but through the kitchen.

The man was almost to the back door when he turned and saw me. He looked annoyed, and he turned his full attention on me and charged forward.

I picked up a bottle of cooking wine and smashed it across his face just before he reached me.

The driver teetered back. Blood poured out of a gash on his cheek. Just as I was about to subdue him so I could call for backup, his foot flew up and connected with my chin.

That was the second time this asshole had made me see stars.

This time he took the opportunity and ran. He was out the door in a flash.

CHAPTER 6

IT TOOK A minute to get my legs under me. One of the cooks made the connection between the events at the parade and the fight in his kitchen. He helped me stumble out onto the street, but I saw no sign of the terrorist. He had fled back into the chaos he'd created and there was no telling where he was headed.

After retrieving my gun, I'd made my first phone call to dispatch, telling them where I was and what had happened. Now I was talking to a heavyset patrol sergeant and two Intel detectives.

Tom Colgan, the senior Intel guy, had been raised in Queens and now lived on Long Island. I'd known him for too long. We had a lot in common. He was from a classic Irish Catholic family and had four kids of his own.

Now he said, "So after this guy kicked your ass, he just disappeared into the crowd."

I nodded. He had summed it up pretty well. Then I remembered when the truck plowed into the crowd and said, "He yelled something before he detonated the bomb in the truck. I didn't recognize it."

Colgan said, "Allahu Akbar?"

"No. I've heard that before. Frankly, I almost expected him to say that. But this was different."

Colgan said, "They're rounding up all the witnesses now. I'm sure more than a few people caught the whole thing on video." He paused for a minute, then said, "Your family is okay, right?"

"They're coming to meet me here in a little while."

Colgan said, "I'm not kidding when I say I'm surprised someone was able to fight you off, then flee."

"What can I say? The guy had skills." I looked over and saw that Colgan had taken several pages of notes, including the description I'd already given him. The NYPD Intel detectives were some of the sharpest people I'd ever met. He had more information on two sheets of paper already than I take down on a whole case sometimes.

The uniformed sergeant, clearly a Brooklyn native with a long Italian name, got on the radio and gave out the limited description I had of the driver. He was clear and thorough. That's exactly what we needed right now. A patrolman was going to drive me down to One Police Plaza to work with a sketch artist.

I could still hear sirens in the distance. Cops were everywhere. The parade was canceled, and everything in a two-block radius was closed off while the bomb squad made sure there were no other nasty surprises. It was complete mayhem.

This was not the Thanksgiving Day I had envisioned.

CHAPTER 7

I WAS TOGETHER with my family by the time darkness fell. Other than when I was at police headquarters, I had been on the phone just about all day with one person or another from the NYPD. There were several still photographs of the bomber holding the detonator where you could see the kids and me in the background. One photo had already appeared on CNN and ABC.

CNN had named the attack "Holiday Terror." The theme music had just a hint of Eastern influence. I wondered if that was intentional.

Even after seeing all the footage and the news that six were dead and twelve seriously injured, all I could think about was how much worse it could've been. I was standing there. I saw the crowds. Just the truck itself plowing into them could have killed twenty people, but the driver hadn't been able to get to full speed, because he'd had to slow down to get around the dump truck that was blocking off the intersection. Thank God.

The bomb itself caused very little damage. Mainly it ripped apart the truck. The blast didn't cause any additional injuries. Had the explosive been set properly and the blast spread out in every direction, the result would've been very different. Just the idea of it made me shudder. More than one witness interviewed thought it was a miracle the exploding truck didn't kill many more.

Seamus said, "These people are taking it too lightly. It *was* miraculous. God *did* intervene."

Fiona looked at her great-grandfather and said, "Why didn't God stop the truck driver in the first place?" It was a simple question asked by an innocent girl, no trap or guile in it.

My grandfather turned and put his hand on Fiona's cheek. "Because, dear girl, God gave man free will. It's not something he can turn on and off."

Fiona said, "I learned about free will at CCD. Does it basically mean we are responsible for the things we do?"

Seamus said, "Exactly."

I noticed Trent frantically searching something on his phone. Recently he had been making a concerted effort to match his brother Eddie's intellectual output. A tall task by any measure.

Trent said, "C. S. Lewis wrote, 'Free will, though it makes evil possible, is also the only thing that makes possible any love or goodness or joy worth having.'" He turned and gave me a sly smile.

I chuckled and said, "Good job, Trent. Watch out or you might end up studying philosophy."

Trent said, "Why do you say it like that? *You* studied philosophy."

I wanted to say, "Look where that got me." Instead, I just nodded and said, "And enjoyed every minute of it."

Finally, we gathered for our Thanksgiving dinner. When we were all around the long table, with one chair left empty for Brian, as had become our custom, we joined hands and Seamus said grace.

"Thank you, God, for this family being safe after what they witnessed. I can ask no more of you at this moment. The fact that we are all here together makes everything else in life trivial. We thank you for your guidance and understanding as we humans try to figure things out."

The old guy could still make his point in a quick and efficient way.

Later, as I was helping the kids clean off the table, my phone rang. I was prepared to let it go directly to voice mail, but I noticed it was from my lieutenant, Harry Grissom.

I tried to hide the weariness in my voice when I said, "Hey, Harry, how has your day been?" That got the rare laugh from my boss.

"You did a good job out there today."

"You mean except for the part where I let a suspect beat my ass and get away."

"From what I hear, you got a good look at him, you marked him with the cut on his face, and got a few licks of your own in. They all can't be home runs."

"Did you call just to try and cheer me up?"

"You're assigned to work with a joint terrorism task force at the FBI building starting tomorrow."

"Do they know that?"

"Frankly, I don't give a shit if the FBI wants to work with us. But we've gotta give it a chance. By pooling our resources, we have a better chance of catching this jerk-off and unrolling the cell he's connected with. And we gotta do it before they try something else."

CHAPTER 8

I WAS READY to go at six the next morning, but I had been told to arrive at the FBI building at eight o'clock sharp, so I enjoyed having a little extra time with the kids and Mary Catherine. But at eight, that's where I was: standing in front of the Jacob K. Javits Federal Building on the corner of Broadway and Worth Street in lower Manhattan.

The building was the standard, drab government off-white color with an efficient, if not attractive, design. There were low decorative posts all around the property to discourage car bombs.

I had friends here. Agents I'd worked with and analysts who had helped me solve some of my biggest cases. But the Bureau's attitude and ability to work with others was still questionable. Old habits die hard.

A tall, good-looking guy in his mid-thirties took his time

coming down to collect me from the front desk. He stuck out a big hand and said, "Dan Santos. You must be Mike Bennett."

We walked slowly to a conference room behind the main FBI door. I was impressed that the entire office seemed to have shown up ready to work.

As we walked, Santos said, "I thought about joining the NYPD after I graduated from Hofstra."

"What changed your mind?"

"I wanted to make a real difference in the world."

I said, "I hear you. Guess I don't mind just collecting a fat city paycheck without doing anything." I could tell this was going to be a long special assignment.

The conference room was the new headquarters for the investigation into yesterday's bombing. I recognized a few of the agents and a couple of the NYPD Intel people who were also working the case.

Santos walked me over to a woman sitting at a table in the corner. I could tell she was making a complete assessment of me with her pale-blue eyes. Apparently, I didn't impress or disturb her, because she didn't say a word and looked back at a report she was reading.

Santos said, "NYPD Detective Michael Bennett, meet our liaison from the Russian Embassy, Darya Kuznetsova."

The woman extended her hand and said with almost no accent, "A pleasure to make your acquaintance."

Her blond hair muted her hard-edged look. She was athletic, with broad shoulders, and attractive in every sense of the word. But something about her told me I'd never want to tangle with her.

Not knowing what else to do, I sat at the long table next to her. I tried to make small talk, without much success. Finally, I came right to the point and said, "What's your job with the Russian Embassy?"

She turned that pretty face to me and said, "For now, I am the Russian liaison to this investigation."

"I realize that. What is your title at the embassy?"

"I am just an assistant to the ambassador. They thought it would be a good idea for me to work with you because of Russia's own issues with terrorists, and I might see or hear something that American police officers might overlook due to differing cultures."

I said, "Am I missing something? Why would Russian culture be important in this investigation?"

That's when Dan Santos said, "I think all your questions will be answered during our briefing. Believe me, we're going to need all the help we can get."

CHAPTER 9

SANTOS STOOD UP in front of the gathered agents and NYPD people to get everyone's attention. There were maybe twenty-five people in the room now. The tall agent looked confident as he straightened his blue tie and faced the crowd. Of course, few people got to run a case like this unless they were confident. It was a key element to getting people to do what you needed them to do.

Santos gave a recap of what had happened, but he didn't say anything I had not already heard or personally witnessed.

We had several videos taken from bystanders' phones that covered almost every angle of the attack. He played all the videos a few times, ending them all just as the truck came to an abrupt halt and the driver stepped out and yelled, *"Hawqala!"*

Santos said, "Based on our analysis and the attacker's

accent, we believe he is a Russian speaker from Kazakhstan. To help us with language and context, we have Darya Kuznetsova, who will be working the investigation with us."

Suddenly the attacker's neat hair and blue eyes made more sense. Perhaps even his training. This was a wrinkle I had not been expecting.

Santos continued. "The Russians have excellent contacts with the Kazakhstan Security Forces and have a shared interest in working with us to curb terrorism."

We watched another video and some of the aftermath, and then Santos broke us down into smaller groups and explained what everyone would be doing. One group was only following up with interviews of witnesses. Another was working with informants to see if anything was being talked about on the street. A third group, which included analysts, was scouring computer databanks to see if it could find information that might shed some light on the attack.

When Santos said, "Any questions?" I could see the annoyance in his eyes when I raised my hand. He said, "Go ahead, Bennett."

"What, exactly, does *hawqala* mean?"

"Literally it means, 'There is no power nor strength save by Allah.'"

"I've never heard it before. Is it common?"

"Not in attacks like this. We're looking into it." He looked around the room. "Anything else?"

Once again, I raised my hand.

Santos just looked at me.

"Is there some significance to *hawqala?* Could it mean he's after something else or representing a certain group?"

"As I said, we're looking into it." Then he quickly moved on and introduced Steve Barborini from the Bureau of Alcohol, Tobacco, Firearms, and Explosives.

The tall, lean ATF man stood and looked around the room. He didn't use notes when he spoke. That meant he knew what he was talking about and he was confident about his subject matter. I liked that.

The ATF agent said, "Obviously we're still processing the van, the explosive, and parts of the scene. It looks like the device was fairly simple. It contained a five-gallon paint jug with an explosive made up mostly of commercial Tannerite, which is a brand name for the most popular binary explosive on the market. We're not absolutely sure how many pounds were crammed into the paint jug, but we're guessing it was at least twenty."

One of the FBI agents raised her hand. "Where could they buy something like that? How is it legal?"

"Tannerite can be bought anywhere. Even on Amazon. There hasn't been any big move to curb it. It's legal because it's sold in two different packages. Unless the packages are mixed, they are not explosive. That's why it's called a *binary* explosive."

That seemed to satisfy the FBI agent as she made a few notes and nodded her head.

Barborini went on. "There were nuts and bolts taped around the paint jug. The idea is that the explosion should have dispersed the nuts and bolts like shrapnel in a wide circle around the explosion. What we believe happened was that the metal paint jug that was used did not have a secure lid. The detonator was a simple blasting cap on an electronic igniter. When the blasting cap went off and started the chain reaction in the Tannerite, it blew the top off the paint can and the power of the explosion went straight up. That's why the roof of the truck blew off so neatly. An explosion will travel the path of least resistance. That's what saved so many lives."

CHAPTER 10

AFTER ALMOST AN hour of briefing, I wondered if all we were going to do on this case was have meetings. This went against my instincts—to get out on the street and start talking to people. In my experience as a cop, that's what always broke open major cases. People talk. It doesn't matter where they're from or what their reasons are for committing a crime. People always talk.

I couldn't find out what they were saying if I was sitting in a conference room in Federal Plaza.

Dan Santos went through the last few things on his list, explaining how the scarf over the attacker's face had thwarted any efforts to use facial recognition to match the attacker with photographs in the intelligence databases.

Santos turned to me and said, "Turns out that Detective Bennett here is the only one who's seen the attacker's face."

He held up the police artist's sketch of the man I'd described. "This is based on Detective Bennett's description. There's nothing unusual about him except possibly a cut on his left cheek."

Then I had to speak up. "There's no *possibly* about it. The man has a decent gash on his left cheek from a broken bottle across his face." I could still feel the heft of the bottle, suddenly going weightless as it broke against his face.

Santos continued. "We're covering the leads on the step-van truck—which was a rental—immigration, current gripes against the US government, and even city employees. The last group is because the dump truck at the intersection was too far to one side, allowing the attacker to slip past.

"I know we have a lot of different agencies working together, but there will be an FBI agent in each group. They will document everything you do, brief me, and handle evidence."

He closed his notebook and straightened up to glance around the room. "Are there any questions?" He shot a dirty look at me in an effort to keep me quiet.

As everyone broke into their small groups with different assignments, Dan Santos walked over to me and Darya and said, "I'm on your team. We'll be handling a lot of different things. But no matter what we do, neither of you are to run down any leads without me. Is that clearly understood?"

I was preparing a smartass answer when Darya said, "I sorry. My English not so good. Let's hope I make no mistake." She turned to me, winked, and shot me a little smile.

I was liking this Darya more and more.

CHAPTER 11

I FELT LIKE I'd found a kindred spirit in Darya Kuznetsova after she stood up to the FBI agent, Dan Santos. It wasn't just what she did, but how she did it—it was playful yet said, *Don't mess with me.*

That's why I was comfortable sitting down next to her away from everyone else in the corner of the conference room. She seemed pleased that I had chosen to speak with her. She gave me just a hint of a lovely smile, but her sharp eyes didn't miss anything.

She said, "Do you always carry two pistols? I thought the NYPD usually carried only one gun, their duty weapon on the right hip."

"I decided a backup .380 on my ankle was a good idea considering how tough this suspect was. How did you pick up on it?"

"You dragged your left leg ever so slightly and I noticed your ankle holster. Your duty weapon on your hip is obvious."

"You don't approve of guns?"

"On the contrary, it's smart. The Kazakhs tend to be of a rougher sort than most Russians. It would be similar to someone being raised on the frontier in the Old West." She grasped my right hand and held it up to examine it. "Just like I could tell you were not raised on the frontier."

I gave her a smile, though she had subtly just called me a wimp. "New York City is its own kind of frontier."

Darya considered my comment for a moment and said, "Were you ever pressured to join a group and commit crimes?"

I thought about mentioning the Holy Name basketball team when I was a kid. We'd been a tough bunch, and on a dare I'd stolen a bag of M&M's from a grocery store on the corner. But that probably wasn't what she meant, so I didn't mention it. Besides, I had gone back the next day to give old man Rogers, who ran the place, money for the candy.

I changed the subject and said, "I know we talked about this, but how did you get this assignment?"

"Part of it was that I happened to be here in New York and my English is better than most Russians'."

"Your English is better than most New Yorkers'." It was satisfying that the comment earned a smile.

"I was raised in Maryland. My father was in the diplomatic corps in Washington, DC. Then I attended MIT on a student visa."

"What did you study?"

"Engineering. I still get to use it occasionally. What about you? Did you go to college?"

"Right here in New York. Manhattan College."

"What did you study?"

"Philosophy." That one earned a little bit of a smirk.

"Do you ever get to use your degree?"

"That depends. If my studies did, in fact, open my mind to help me better understand the human condition, then yes, I do. If I was merely sucked into the factory of higher education designed solely to make money, I still use it every day."

"What do you think we will be doing on this investigation? Will the FBI try to hinder us?"

"I guarantee the FBI will try to hinder us. Some of the NYPD Intel detectives say that the FBI stands for *Forever Being Indecisive*. But sometimes they're useful."

"Agent Santos did not seem interested in some of my suggestions."

"Such as?"

"Reaching out to Russian immigrants who have an excellent communications network. I'm also looking into the word *hawqala*, to see if it has been used in the past. It seems like an unusual change of pace for someone delivering a message from a jihadist organization. Perhaps this will be the link we need to find and destroy a significant terror group."

We sat in silence for a few moments and then I said, "Do you have some personal beef with terrorists, or are you just focused on this asshole?"

"Russia has seen many more attacks than the US. Some are more public than others. It's a scourge that we would like to see neutralized. If it takes a little effort on our part to teach our friends in the United States how to best deal with extremist groups, then I am all for it."

"Let's hope we don't disappoint you."

She smiled and said, "Don't worry about it. Everyone disappoints me."

All I could say was, "Hard-line. I like it."

CHAPTER 12

LESS THAN AN hour after our first briefing, I found myself playing chauffeur to my Russian liaison, Darya Kuznetsova. She apparently had less use for bureaucracy than me. When Dan Santos said he had to go talk to his bosses and directed us to either sit tight or grab something to eat, Darya said, "I'm going to talk to some Russian speakers who might help us. Do you care to be part of such a conspiracy?"

Not only did she have the right idea, she worded the question perfectly. Next thing I knew, we were driving through Brooklyn on our way to Midwood. There were a lot of Russian immigrants from Midwood all the way to Brighton Beach, but I wasn't sure what information they could offer us.

As we were driving on the Ocean Parkway through Flatbush on our way to Midwood, Darya said, "These are ethnic Russians who lived in Kazakhstan. I don't want to explain why an NYPD detective is with me. Don't show your badge. I'll try to speak in English, but if we speak Russian, just smile and nod."

"Did you just tell me to be quiet and look pretty?" That got the laugh I intended.

"I hope that brain of yours is as sharp when we have to act quickly. I don't have a great deal of faith in your FBI."

"With an attitude like that you could be an *American* cop. We hate the FBI, too."

"I'm not a cop."

I didn't know exactly *what* Darya was, but I didn't get a chance to follow up, because we had arrived at our destination.

The first people we talked to were an elderly couple who lived on the first floor of a five-story walk-up. The man said virtually nothing but glared at me like I had stolen something from his bedroom. His giant, bald head reminded me of a pale watermelon.

The little knickknacks around the apartment could've been from any grandmother in the world. I liked a figurine of a burly man in a fur hat driving a wagon with an ox pulling it. It shouted "Russia."

The woman was better dressed than the man and evidently took care of herself. She agreed to speak English with Darya, and while she had a thick accent, I could still understand her.

Darya told me in a low voice as we walked through the apartment that the man still had ties to Kazakhstan and Russia. That was one of the reasons she didn't want to bring the FBI along with us. They just wouldn't understand.

She was also afraid the FBI would use heavy-handed tactics and threaten these people with everything from arrest to deportation—and ruin any chance of getting useful information.

The woman said, "Living in Kazakhstan can be hard in the best of times. We went with a program to work as teachers at a school for Russian children. The climate is better than Moscow, but as we got older, it was still tough on our bodies. We had a chance to follow our oldest son here and have been quite happy for the past nine years."

Darya said, "Do you talk to others in the Kazakh community?"

"Of course. Every day."

I followed the conversation, but the woman's accent was sometimes tough to understand. I liked the way Darya showed her respect as if she were a daughter visiting a grandmother. The old man just stared on in silence.

Finally, Darya got to the meat of our questions. "Have you heard anyone talk about the attack yesterday?"

"Some. Mostly people just repeating things from the news."

I had considered this question and thought this would be a critical juncture in any interview. Do we reveal the fact that we think the driver was from Kazakhstan? It might make people pay attention.

Then Darya said, "We think the driver was a Kazakh."

The old woman was shocked. "How can this be? The Kazakhs have no real hatred for the United States. Is this some ploy to ship us all out? Do they want us all to move back to our homelands? We live here, but we've never trusted the government."

I said, "Neither do we. Governments try to trick people. But this isn't one of those times."

Then the old man mumbled something. I thought it was English.

I looked at him and said, "Did you say something, sir?"

The old man said it again and I heard it clearly: "Bullshit."

Apparently, he spoke the essential English words.

CHAPTER 13

AFTER WE TALKED to several other Russian families with ties to Kazakhstan, I decided to track down a couple of my informants as well.

Darya said, "I don't understand. If your informants are not Russian, what would they know about this?"

"These are the type of people that hear everything. Small things. Big things. We may get a tip about someone looking for a ride out of the city that could break open the case. The more ears we have listening the better chance we have to hear something."

"But none are Russian?"

"These people aren't Russian, but they're criminals, and criminals often trade in information."

Darya said, "If they're criminals why aren't they in jail?"

I had to shrug at that simple question. "Different reasons.

Some are smart. Some are lucky. Some have good lawyers. You can't tell me all the criminals in Moscow are locked up."

"It depends on who is protecting them."

I laughed. "Here in America, we don't care who protects who. We just found it's easier to let most criminals stay free. Keeps me in a job."

I could tell my Russian guest didn't agree with my flippant logic. I was curious to see how she reacted to some of my informants.

I added, "I also have some Russian mob people who occasionally help me. But these guys are easier to reach for now."

The first place I stopped was a gambling house in Flatbush. It was close and not too dangerous. A good test for Darya.

The small storefront on Foster Avenue looked like a simple diner. Busy, but simple. Few people realized that when you ordered one of only five things on the menu, you also got access to a variety of gambling opportunities from football to soccer in Asia.

I heard someone call out, "Hey, Mike." I smiled and waved at one of the gamblers I knew from somewhere. No one was alarmed to see me. They knew I was a homicide detective and this place was as safe as any in the city.

I ducked into a corridor past a heavy curtain. Darya followed right behind me. When we entered the rear room, a blond man with tattoos smearing his upper arms and neck jumped up in alarm until he recognized me.

He said, "Jesus, Mike, a little notice would be nice. You scared the crap out of me." Then he took a moment and didn't hide the fact that his eyes were wandering over Darya like she was a piece of meat for sale in the grocery store. He flashed a charming smile and said, "And who is this?"

Before I could say anything, Darya gave him a dazzling smile. Better than any I had earned. Maybe she was a softy for lowlife attention and cheap compliments.

My informant held out his hand and said, "Edward Lindell, at your service." Then he winked at her.

Darya grasped his hand and put her left hand over both of them like it was a warm greeting. Then she twisted quickly, put him in an arm bar, and drove Lindell's head into a table that held thousands of betting slips.

To make the point that she didn't care for the attention, Darya ran Lindell's head down the length of the table, using his face to push everything onto the floor.

Then she released her grip and watched him sprawl onto the dirty green linoleum floor that used to be part of the kitchen.

I suppressed a smile as I watched Ed Lindell get up on his hands and knees and shake his head to clear the stars.

"I think that was her way of saying she doesn't have time for your shit."

From the floor, Lindell said, "All she had to say was, 'Cut the shit.'"

"Frankly, I like her way better. But we're wasting time. We aren't here to watch you get the shit kicked out of you by a pretty woman. We need you to put out feelers about anything unusual related to someone trying to get out of the city or trying to buy a gun or explosives."

Lindell slowly rose to his feet and said, "This have to do with the bombing at the parade?"

"How did you know that?"

"Because I went to Penn State and I'm no idiot. That's all anyone is interested in right now. What will it get me?"

The universal question by informants. I thought about it and said, "Depends on what you give us. But it'll save you more lumps from this lady and you'll be in my good graces for a very, very long time."

Lindell said, "That and some toilet paper means I could take a shit."

Still without looking or acknowledging him, Darya raised a closed fist and caught Lindell across the left side of his face, knocking him against the wall and back onto the floor. She walked out without saying a word.

I nodded to Lindell on the floor and hustled out after Darya.

As we walked a block toward the car, she said, "You're not upset that I assaulted that man?"

"He's had worse. *I've* given him worse."

Darya said, "You don't want to know why I did it?"

"I assume you did it to hide the fact that you stole the 9 millimeter pistol he had sitting on the table." I didn't wait for an answer. I just held out my hand.

She slipped the gun out of her purse and laid it in my palm. "This is America. I'll be able to find a gun if I need it."

All signs pointed to her being a pretty good partner. I'd be able to work with her.

CHAPTER 14

THE NEXT MORNING everyone was in the task force meeting rooms early. Even some of the FBI agents seemed a little annoyed at all the planning and meetings we had gone through the day before. As far as I could tell, Darya and I were part of a handful that had actually gone out and done something. Not that we were telling anyone.

And of course, we started off the day with a stupid meeting. At least I thought it was stupid, until things got rolling.

Dan Santos went over some of the information they had learned the day before, including some of the forensic information from examining the destroyed truck.

Santos said, "There wasn't a lot to grab from the truck— mainly chemical residue that will be used to track down the exact manufacturer of the explosive. The ATF did manage to lift a fingerprint off the inside of the steering wheel, so we put a rush on it to every agency and database in the country. No hits came back. But our esteemed colleague from the Russian Embassy"—he turned and opened his hand toward Darya, as if he were a ringmaster announcing an act—"has found the print in a Russian military database."

Santos nodded to Darya, who stood up. She took a moment to gather her thoughts, as if she was trying to make the announcement more dramatic after the dull crime-scene analysis.

Darya said, "The fingerprint belongs to a thirty-one-year-old male named Temir Marat. His father was raised in Kazakhstan and his mother is an ethnic Russian. He spent his early years in Kazakhstan, then bounced back and forth between there and Russia."

I noticed everyone taking furious notes, but I still hadn't heard anything that would tell me where this asshole was.

Darya continued. "Marat served a stint in the Russian army, and that's how we got his fingerprint on file. He has no history of extremism, but the FBI says that's very common. There's little else known about him."

Someone from the back room called out, "Do we have a photograph of him?"

Darya shook her head. "It's printing now. It's five years old. It's from an application to the Moscow police. There is an older photo from when he entered the army, but he is much younger and he has a buzz cut."

I wrote one line in my little notebook. *Applied to police. Why?*

An Asian woman who worked for the FBI said, "I don't think a history of extremist views is necessary anymore. The way some of these groups recruit leads many without previous violent histories to join. In fact, it's a good move to recruit people not on any terrorist watch lists. This guy sounds like the perfect choice. Smart, unafraid of death, and able to blend in with the general population in the US. He could've been recruited from a website."

An Army major in uniform said, "I can see recruiting people inside the US like that, but this was someone living in Russia or Kazakhstan. There were some serious expenses. This is a step above some of the spur-of-the-moment attacks ISIS has inspired."

Dan Santos said, "It's hard to tell exactly what happened until we catch this guy. Our intelligence indicates that shifting to using trucks and cars and simple attacks like this has a major effect on public opinion. Anytime a group uses the fear of something common to exploit terror, they're eating away at our way of life. Berlin and Paris are perfect examples. There'll be kids there in ten years that jump at the sight of a truck. It's important that we move before this guy comes up with anything else to do."

Darya said, "Russia has seen some of this. Several attacks using trucks that plow into crowds."

When she sat down next to me I said, "I haven't seen those attacks in Russia on the news." This was a private conversation, not intended for the others.

"We don't have a need for everything to be public. Perhaps your government should try that approach occasionally."

I said, "Let's not get into a conversation about whose government is more effective."

"You're right, of course."

I said, "This wasn't some kid trying to get famous. I agree

with our colleague in the Army. This attack was organized and funded. It was too big to try and keep quiet in a free country. The US government generally makes information about attacks public. Even if keeping things secret works for Russia, it's not the way we do things."

Darya smiled and said, "I know Americans have a fixation with fame and publicity. You also have many more TV networks than Russia. But sometimes it's better to handle things quietly and not cause a panic. I fear this is a lesson the US will have a chance to learn in the coming years."

I hoped that wasn't the case.

CHAPTER 15

DAN SANTOS SURPRISED me. As soon as our early morning briefing was done, he grabbed Darya and me and said, "I lined up some interviews we can do today."

I withheld any smartass comment, because I wanted to encourage this kind of behavior.

Darya looked bored, but stood up and gathered her things.

Santos said, "Pretty exciting, huh? Your first interviews on a major terror investigation."

I mumbled, "Yeah. Our first interviews. Exciting." I could barely meet Darya's eyes.

She had a wide grin, but Santos was too wrapped up in his own world to notice.

The first stop we made was in lower Manhattan near the NYU campus, a small deli on University Place. It was still early and the place was nearly empty.

I caught up to Dan, who was walking pretty fast from the car, and said, "Are you hungry? What would this deli have to offer us for the case?"

"It's not the deli, but who's working there." He pulled a photograph of a young man with a dark complexion and short-cropped, black hair. "His name is Abdul Adair, he's from the United Arab Emirates. He's studying biology at NYU and works here part-time."

"What led you to him?"

"What do you mean? He's a Muslim, first of all. He attends virtually all of the Muslim student union meetings, and we have intel that he has acted suspiciously and taken a lot of photographs of New York."

That response actually gave me more questions than answers, but I wanted to see how this would go. Santos had just described a college student who likes to sightsee.

We stepped in the doors and no one paid any attention to us, the sign of a good neighborhood. A couple of little kids chased the deli cat, and a young mother lazily followed them while chatting on her cell phone. The smell of the chicken cutlet hero the cook was wrapping up for a customer reminded me I had forgotten to eat breakfast. My stomach growled.

Santos stepped to the counter and asked about Abdul. A minute later, we were sitting at a small table in the corner, next to a refrigerator stocked with smoothies that cost seven bucks each.

The student from the UAE was twenty-one and small. He couldn't have been over five foot five and 130 pounds, which made him look even younger. The kid was already trembling.

Santos spent a few minutes clarifying Abdul's information. The whole process only seemed to make the young man more nervous. I scooted my chair back slightly because I didn't want to be in the splash zone if he vomited.

Then Santos asked a series of questions. "Have you ever had contact with an organization that espouses jihad? Don't lie. I'll know if you're lying."

The young man vigorously shook his head.

"Do you or any of your friends know anyone involved in a group like that?"

This time Abdul thought about it, then shook his head. He said, "I spend most of my time either studying or working here."

Santos said, "What about the Muslim student union at NYU?"

"What about it? I go there to see my friends. Meet women."

"And what do you plan to use your degree in biology for?"

"This coming summer I have an internship at an institute in San Francisco doing cancer research. That might be what I'm interested in long-term." The young man seemed to be getting some confidence.

The FBI agent made notes, but didn't invite Darya or me to say anything at all.

Now Santos moved on to our case. He pulled up our photograph of Temir Marat and said, "Know him?"

Abdul shook his head.

"Where were you on Thanksgiving morning?"

"Having breakfast with the family of one of my professors who lives in the Village."

"We'll need his name and address. Now."

Santos pushed over a notebook for Abdul to write in. He made more notes and asked more questions, which Abdul answered quickly and clearly. Then the FBI man thanked him, but warned him not to leave the city. That was it. It felt more like a schoolyard bullying session than an interview. When Santos stood up and handed Abdul a card, I did the same thing. The only difference is, I smiled and winked at him when I gave him the card. He gave me a nervous smile and nod in return.

Then all three of us marched out of the deli.

Before we even got to the car, I had to say, "What the hell was that?"

"What was what?"

"Treating that kid like that! We have no reason to believe that he's done anything wrong. Why are we wasting time scaring kids to death?"

Santos stopped on the sidewalk and looked at me like I was a little kid who just asked a stupid question in class. "Do I have to remind you, Detective, that this is a *federal* case? It's not some cheap New York City misdemeanor or dead dope addict." Santos looked at Darya to see if she was interested in getting involved in the argument. Then he said, "The FBI has to look at the big picture and see if we can link different terror networks. It may not seem like it's helping much now, but it could pay off big later. Let me know when you solve a major terror case."

That stung a little bit. As I slipped into the Crown Victoria, I felt like I'd been told off pretty effectively.

CHAPTER 16

AFTER THE INTERVIEW with Abdul, I realized my time might be better utilized. I saw my opportunity when Santos was called to a boss's office to give an update on the investigation.

I tried to quietly slip out of the task force office, ready to tell anyone who asked that I was just going to lunch. It would take a while to drive out to Brighton Beach, the Brooklyn neighborhood with a high population of Russian immigrants. But I doubted anyone would miss me, especially Agent Dan Santos.

As I hustled down the corridor away from the office, I heard someone behind me. I turned to see Darya Kuznetsova with a smile on her face.

She said, "Going somewhere?"

"Yeah, I'm going to do my job." Then, for no real reason, I said, "I'm going to visit some Russian mobsters. Do you want to come?"

She didn't say a word but just kept following me.

"Why didn't we talk to these Russians yesterday when we talked to your other informants?"

"Because Russian mobsters are in a different class. They could help us, or they could try to find Marat themselves for a reward."

Darya said, "Do you think every Russian living in the US is a mobster?"

"That's ridiculous. Not everyone can be a mobster. Some Russians work in support roles." I waited until she turned and stared at me, then laughed and said, "I'm just kidding. But if you think no Russians are involved in organized crime, you're just as wrong. I know a couple of them. I know they won't be happy about the attack. So why don't we use that?"

That seemed to satisfy Darya and she stayed quiet, but alert, all the way through Brighton Beach. I pulled off Neptune Avenue a few blocks from our destination.

I parked away from the apartment we were headed to. No sense in alerting everyone by driving an NYPD Impala, whether it was marked or not, into one of the tightest, most isolated communities in New York.

Darya said, "What are you hoping to find out?"

"I just want to see if anyone knows anything about Marat. These guys won't have any loyalty to a terrorist. Terror attacks hurt their bottom line. They'll listen for information if we tell them what to listen for."

We walked up to the second-floor apartment, which offered a glimpse of the Atlantic if you angled your gaze just right.

I told Darya, "This guy we're going to see goes by different names. I'll wait until we see him to tell you what his name is now."

A wiry man with a disturbingly dark tan and a cigarette dangling from his mouth answered the door and just stared at us for a moment. He was about forty but looked older. He said, "What a surprise. I have no idea why you are visiting me now. I've been a very good boy lately." He ushered us inside. It was a surprisingly comfortable apartment, even if it did stink of cigarette smoke and beer. He plopped down in an oversize recliner while Darya and I eased onto a leather couch.

I said, "It's nice to see you too, Mr...."

"Vineyard. Lewis Vineyard. Good name, eh?"

"Yeah, I guess."

The Russian said in accented English, "I like it. I figure I work on my English, no one will ever suspect who or what I am."

I shrugged my shoulders and said, "Except for the fact that you live in Brighton Beach, work at a Russian, mob-run bar, and sell drugs and guns to Russian mobsters, I doubt anyone would ever suspect you of being a Russian criminal. I'm sure everyone will assume you're Swiss."

He gave me a smile and said, "That's my hope." Then he turned his attention to Darya. "And who's this lovely creature you brought to my home? If you're looking for a place for her to live, I agree. She can even have my bedroom."

Darya didn't say a word and I immediately realized she didn't want this guy knowing she was Russian as well. It was also useful for people to not realize she spoke their language.

He held up his arms to show off his tan and said, "You'd love it, baby. I sit on the beach every single day. You would, too, if you were raised in a place like Moscow." He gazed into her face and said, "With soft, white skin like that, you could be a Russian beauty yourself."

I said, "This is my colleague. And we're here about something serious."

"I'm listening." Then he threw in, "And what's in it for me?"

"We're working with the feds on this, so there could be some decent reward money."

He clapped his rough hands together and rubbed them. "Sounds good to me." He stubbed out the cigarette in an overflowing ashtray.

I said, "It's about the attack on the parade Thursday. I'm looking for any information about a Russian-speaking suspect. If there's anyone unusual in the area. If there've been strange requests for guns or explosives. Anything you can think of."

Lewis Vineyard said, "I deal mostly with people I know already. But I'll keep my ears open. No one wants to see shit like that happen. There were little kids killed."

"And we're going to catch that son of a bitch."

CHAPTER 17

WE STOPPED AT a few other places in Brighton Beach, but none seemed as promising as Lewis Vineyard. He knew everyone and dealt with everyone. I was confident he'd come up with something.

Darya said, "I can see why these people leave Russia. They left food lines, and found decent weather and good housing. It's hard to compete with America head-to-head. Even your marketing is better than ours."

"What do you mean?"

"You have *land of the free* or *the streets paved with gold*. We have *plenty of land to farm if you don't mind freezing in Siberia*."

I laughed at that.

She gave me a smile and said, "It would be interesting to work with you on a daily basis."

"Let's catch this guy first, then see where it goes."

"And when we catch him, what happens to him next?"

"The FBI will bleed him for information. On everything."

"That's what we thought."

Before I could ask her what that meant—that "we"—my phone rang. I looked down and saw it was my grandfather. I never like to ignore calls from Seamus because it could be something serious, the fear always associated with an elderly relative's calls.

"Seamus, everything all right?"

His chuckle told me he was fine. "It's not like I'm going to keel over at any minute. I may still be in my prime. It's a new millennium. Age is just a number."

"The fact that you've seen the last few millennia makes me worry about your health."

"For a change, I'm calling to help you with your job."

"How are you going to do that?"

"As a man of the cloth, I have friends in every denomination. One of them happens to be a Muslim cleric. He's the imam of a mosque in Queens."

"I appreciate that, Seamus, but we're not really taking the shotgun approach that all Muslims know about terror attacks."

"But this imam spent some time in Kazakhstan. If I overheard you correctly on the phone last night, Kazakhstan has something to do with your investigation."

All I could say was, "Give me the info."

Twenty minutes later, we were in Jamaica Estates, pulling up to a mosque off the Grand Central Parkway near 188th Street.

As soon as we were out of the car, a small man who looked about sixty-five approached us. He was wearing a suit with a collarless white shirt and a small, white cap.

The man gave us a warm smile as he said, "You can't be Seamus's grandson, Michael, can you? I am Adama Nasir." He had a slight accent that was hard to place. His wire-rimmed glasses gave him the look of a scholar.

I took his hand and said, "I am Seamus's grandson. He's much older than he pretends to be." I introduced Darya as my associate.

We stayed outside and strolled through a playground for the school attached to the mosque. Nasir explained that he was born in Qatar and had traveled throughout the world as a visiting scholar of the Koran. I noted that he had spent two years in Kazakhstan.

Nasir said, "Your grandfather mentioned what you were doing. I think it's important for Muslims to spread the truth that, just like Christians, the vast majority of Muslims just want to worship in peace. Most Muslims are outraged at attacks like the one on the parade."

I said, "I can appreciate the sentiment, but right now I'm only interested in catching who's responsible. It doesn't matter to me what religion he is or even what his motivation was. We need to catch him before he does anything else."

"That's why I asked your grandfather if I could speak with you, because he mentioned that there was a possibility the suspect was from Kazakhstan. There is a bar in Rockaway Park that's a meeting place for ethnic Russians with connections to Kazakhstan. It's really quite a festive place. I have visited it myself because of my stay in Kazakhstan. Of course, I couldn't drink alcohol, but the company was invigorating. If anyone knows about someone from Kazakhstan looking to hide in the greater New York area, it's that crowd."

This was a good lead. Probably more than the FBI had. I thanked him and turned with Darya to head for our car.

Nasir said, "I hope you find who you're looking for. It's a tricky business, these attacks. I've seen it all over the Middle East. Some are based on religious conviction. Some people are forced to do the attacks and some attacks are not what they seem."

I said, "Not what they seem in what way?"

"I used to see it in occupied Palestine. They've been known to kill other Palestinians in attacks so that Israel is blamed. I've even heard rumors that some of the old Israeli governments allowed attacks in Jerusalem so that they would have a reason to respond. There is a certain return on this philosophy."

He was right, but I didn't see the US government allowing an attack like this. I also couldn't see them putting so many resources into catching someone if they had allowed the attack to occur.

All we could do was follow up on the leads we had.

CHAPTER 18

THE STREETS FELT more alive than ever on the drive to Rockaway Park. It was incredible. Even with the cold weather, people were out in the streets, as if telling the terrorists, "New Yorkers don't hide."

The bar was on Rockaway Beach Boulevard, not far from the Jacob Riis Park. As soon as we stepped in the door, I heard conversation in Russian.

Darya was right behind me as I surveyed the long room with booths on the left and stools against the bar on the right. Bright sunlight crashed through the wide bay windows, saving the place from the usual depressing air of a bar in the middle of the day.

It was also surprisingly crowded, with people shouting good-naturedly from one booth to another while the bartenders called out orders in Russian.

I wasn't sure what to do, so without identifying myself, I told the bartender I was looking for someone. I showed him the picture of Marat and told him he was a Russian, speaking Kazakh.

The burly bartender scratched his red beard and shook his head and said in English, "No, no, I never seen this man. Sorry. What you want to drink?"

I bought two beers and settled in at the bar with Darya. There were several other women in the place, but the way they were sitting in booths by themselves or with one man led me to believe they might be prostitutes. I hoped no one would make a mistake and approach Darya. For their sake.

I watched our bartender speaking in a low voice in Russian to one of his colleagues, not far from us.

Darya leaned in close and said, "The bartender just said the two men at the end of the bar are looking for the same man we are."

Having Darya undercover was brilliant. They didn't seem to care if we overheard them speaking Russian.

I looked over to the far end of the bar where there were two men standing, dressed in cheap suits with ties, about my age, but heavy and out of shape. One of the men was burly, with a pockmarked face, and the other had cold, gray eyes, and as soon as they met mine I realized someone at the bar had just told them who I was asking about.

I assumed he made me for a cop, because he made no move to come over to talk. That was fine by me. His interest didn't concern me.

I formulated a plan, and appreciated the fact that Darya didn't ask what it was.

After a few minutes, the two men in suits stepped out the back door of the bar and into the narrow parking lot. We wasted no time going out the main door and into the same lot.

I saw them get into a new Lincoln. Comfortable, but not flashy. Once we got into my Impala, I ran the tag quickly and it came back to a moving company owned by Russians. Shocking.

When it didn't look like they were going anywhere, I said to Darya, "Sometimes we have to make our own karma."

All she said was, "I agree."

As we slipped out of the car, I said, "Whatever happens in Rockaway Park stays in Rockaway Park. Is that a problem?"

"Not unless you expect me to dig a hole if you kill them. I hate to dig."

"I'll keep that in mind."

Both the men were still sitting in the car, looking out at the traffic trickling by on Rockaway Beach Boulevard.

I was careful, trying to approach the car from behind and in the blind spot. As we got closer, I realized they were taking a smoke break with both the windows open.

Neither seemed to be monitoring the mirrors. For a couple of mobsters, they weren't terribly observant.

They couldn't have set it up better for me.

CHAPTER 19

I LIKED HOW both men stayed calm and didn't jump when I appeared in the driver's-side window. I crouched low so my face filled the window, and rested my arms across the door with my Glock service weapon in my right hand, casually hanging into the car.

I said, "Hello, fellas, how's your day going?"

The driver, the burly man with a pockmarked face, mumbled, "No English. Go 'way."

"You think you're the first one to pull that kind of shit on me? There is a universal cure for those who don't want to speak English." Without hesitation, I pulled the door handle, reached into the Lincoln, and grabbed the man with two fingers behind his jaw. The pressure made him hop out of the car with no help from me other than the two fingers on his sensitive nerves that ran there.

I spun him around and slammed him into the car.

I was prepared to order the other man out, but he jumped out on his own to help his friend. Just as he reached the rear of the Lincoln, Darya sprang out from behind the car parked next to them. I had no idea what she did, but the guy was on the asphalt in a heartbeat.

I said to her, "You okay?"

She said, "Good."

She was careful to keep her words to a minimum, because even though her accent is barely discernible, she didn't want these Russians to pick up that she knew their language.

I focused on the man I had in an arm bar against the car. I patted him down quickly and pulled out a Ruger 9mm from his waistband. Holding him with one hand, I holstered my Glock and stuck his Ruger in my pants.

I said, "If you don't speak English, you're under arrest for carrying a concealed weapon. If you do speak English, I'll talk to you for a minute."

He said in a remarkably clear voice, "We speak English."

"Good. See how easy that was?" I eased up slightly on my arm bar, then stepped back and let the man face me. I said, "Now, why were you asking about Temir Marat?"

"Who?"

I grabbed his arm again to show him I could get rough if I had to. That's when he surprised me. He was fast for a big guy. He twisted his body and then landed a knee right on my thigh. It hurt. I mean, in an it-made-me-want-to-pee kind of hurt.

I staggered back and he immediately threw two punches at my head. He had some style and looked like he'd boxed at some point in his life. That's probably how he landed a job like this.

I had done a little boxing myself and immediately had my guard up, fending off his punches. As I stepped back, I saw that Darya, still alert and on top of her man, was watching what was happening.

I let the guy in front of me take a wild swing. I ducked the right fist as it just grazed the top of my head. Then I twisted hard and landed a left, low on his back, right in his kidneys. Ouch—I knew from experience that that location was *painful*.

I spun to his other side and kneed him in the left thigh, making sure things were equal. Then I grabbed him by the groin with my left hand and by the throat with my right hand, and bull-rushed him backward into a parked pickup truck.

He let out an *umphf* as the air rushed out of him. Then I put him on the ground close to his partner.

The partner tried to sit up and Darya blasted him with a forearm right across the back of his head. I could hear his nose crush against the asphalt; blood started to leak out and pool into puddles near his face.

I said to the guy I had on the ground, "This is serious shit. For all I know, you were involved in the attack on the parade. That's why you're about to have the worst day of your life."

The man sputtered, "Wait, wait. It's not what you think."

"Then tell me what it is."

"I don't want to get in more trouble."

"You can't get in more trouble. You're carrying a gun illegally and you assaulted a police officer."

"I don't want to get in more trouble by talking."

I sat there for a moment and thought about it. Darya looked

up at me expectantly. Finally, I said, "Tell me what you want to tell me. Anything you say while I have you on the ground like this is free. Total immunity."

"If I tell you the truth, you let us go?"

"That depends on how much of the truth you tell me."

The man thought about it for a moment, then said, "I don't know your man, Marat. I have the same photo you showed the bartender. Someone contracted us to take him out."

"A mob hit on a terrorist? Why?"

"*Why* is not one of the questions we ask in my line of business."

"Where did you get the photo of him?"

"It was in an envelope with some cash and instructions to find him and kill him." After another moment he said, "That's the truth, the whole truth."

I released my grip and let him sit up. He brushed off a couple of pebbles that were lodged in his face. One of them perfectly filled the biggest pockmark on his left cheek.

I looked at him and said, "Surprisingly, I do believe you."

I got a little more information out of the other, but stuck to my promise to release them. Besides, I had gotten the information through an illegal interrogation. There was nothing I could do to them.

After I stood up, I took his Ruger out of my waistband, took it apart, and tossed two pieces in a sewer drain. He started to object, then kept his mouth shut. I would toss the rest of the pistol, including the magazine, down a few different drains on our way back to Manhattan. I appreciated his groan as the gun disappeared.

I stepped over to the other man standing next to Darya and

started to pat him down. Just as I did, the man said, "She took it already."

I gave Darya a look and she reached in her purse, then pulled out a Smith & Wesson revolver. She shrugged as she slipped it into the palm of my hand.

She gave me a smile and said, "A girl has got to try."

CHAPTER 20

AFTER WE TALKED to the Russian mobsters, I drove us back to the task force headquarters. Darya said she had calls to make based on some of the information we'd found. We agreed to meet up later.

She was very quiet on the ride back, and I found myself wondering what her role in all this was. Dan Santos trusted her, and even though he was a fed I didn't think he'd put someone in the middle of the investigation who couldn't be trusted. But still, something nagged at me. The moment I got to my desk, my cell rang. I didn't recognize the caller, a man's voice with a thick Russian accent. He said his name and I still couldn't place it. Then I realized who it was: the silent husband of the woman we had spoken to in Midwood yesterday. The only English word he had said was, "Bullshit."

Now he spoke in halting English. I guess Darya's idea of not letting people know you spoke their language wasn't a unique trick.

I said, "What can I do for you?"

"When you and the pretty Russian woman came here—we told truth."

He spoke slowly and carefully so I could understand him. Aside from the accent, his English was not bad at all.

I said, "But some of your truth has changed since we were there?" I was trying to think how he had reached me, then I remembered that Darya had written my number as well as her own on a sheet of paper.

"Nothing has changed, except I met someone who might know the man you're looking for. He gave me some information that I thought you might use."

On every big case, there are thousands of leads. God help me, but I was a sucker for someone giving me new information, even if the odds of it being accurate or useful were small.

The old man said, "A man I ran into said he knows the family of the man who did this terrible crime."

"In Russia or Kazakhstan?"

"In New Jersey."

That caught me by surprise and made me pull a notepad from the FBI desk I was sitting at. I couldn't help but look around the room to make sure no one was eavesdropping on my conversation. Technically, all official leads were supposed to be put into a computer program for review before anyone followed up on them.

I said, "It's interesting he has family in New Jersey. That's nothing I had heard."

The old man said, "There are lots of Russians trying to live the right way. Many of us fled terrible conditions and appreciate all the advantages we have here in United States. Most Russians are perfectly respectable. It might not seem like it in your line of work, where everyone is a potential suspect. But this isn't Russia. You can't think that way."

"I don't generally think that way about any group. Nevertheless, I am a cop and I have to follow up on leads. Can you narrow down where his family might live in New Jersey?"

"A little community called Weequahic, in Newark. The name you're looking for is Konstantin Nislev."

"Do you want to give me some details about the person who gave you this information?"

"No. No, I don't." Then the phone went dead.

If nothing else, it gave me another excuse to get out of the Federal Building for a few hours. With Manhattan's usual Saturday traffic, I knew I could be in the car for a while.

A little work in Google and in the New Jersey public records database gave me an address for a Konstantin Nislev, right where the old man said he'd be.

Traffic wasn't as bad as I feared, and I was cruising past neat row houses in the Newark community of Weequahic. I found a parking spot just across from where I was going. I sat there for a minute, checking out the situation.

It was a well-kept row house, and an old oak tree rose up from the front yard and sent branches toward the house like a giant monster. Other than that, the yard was immaculate. Just a few short strips of grass and a lot of decorative stones. It looked like a comfortable home.

I stepped out of the car and tried to look casual as I walked up toward the front door. But I didn't feel casual. If this lead was accurate, it was a big deal. A *giant* deal. So big I might have a hard time explaining to the FBI how I managed to get the lead, not file it in the proper system, not tell anyone where I was going, and then question the suspect's family.

It was probably nothing.

I rang the bell and heard soft chimes on the inside of the house. A moment later, a man who looked about sixty, with thinning hair, wearing heavy-framed glasses, answered the front door.

He smiled and had a noticeable accent when he said, "May I help you?"

I held up my badge and said, "Konstantin Nislev?"

The man said, "I wondered how long it would take the authorities to find us."

CHAPTER 21

I SAT ON a couch with an uncomfortable wooden frame on the back. I took the tea that Konstantin's wife, Vera, offered as we all chatted in a small living room almost overwhelmed with photographs.

Temir Marat's aunt and uncle had heard through the Russian grapevine that he was a suspect in the attack on Thanksgiving. The older couple didn't deny the relation, or that they were worried about their nephew.

I gave them a few minutes to settle down and we chatted about other things before I got to the serious questions on my mind.

I said, "You have a lot of photos of Seton Hall."

Konstantin said, "I have been the facilities manager there for five years. I was an engineer in Russia, and it fit in perfectly with the needs of the university when I started to look for a job here."

"How long have you been in the US?"

"We moved here about six years ago. I had lived in the US before for extended periods, while I worked on different projects for a construction company based in Switzerland. My children and the rest of the family came over four years ago."

"And your nephew, Temir?"

Vera answered that one. "We were hoping he would come with his cousins four years ago, but he had a wife who was pregnant, and already had one young child at home."

"Where was he living?"

"Moscow." I just nodded and let the story continue.

"Temir had a decent job doing something for either the city or the Russian government. He had a nice apartment and a little bit of money. He speaks English so I thought he might want to come. But he decided to stay."

"When's the last time you talked to him?"

"He always sends me mail on special occasions," Vera said. "He loves his aunt Verochka."

"And you had no idea he was here in the US?"

"None at all."

"Do you have any photographs of your nephew?"

Vera stood up quickly and went to a series of framed photographs sitting on a bookshelf. She walked back with a particularly large one that showed a group of more than twenty-five people.

Vera pointed to a young man, no more than fourteen or fifteen, in the corner of the photo. "That is Temir. This was at a family gathering in Moscow about fifteen years ago. His father had died and we thought it was important for him to have male role models. Konstantin's brothers all spent time with him."

"Do you have any idea when he might've become radicalized and interested in attacking the US?"

Konstantin said, "I'm not sure I understand. Radicalized in what way?"

"Had his belief in Islam twisted to where he felt he needed to participate in a jihad?"

Konstantin said, "That's ridiculous. I don't understand any of that. We're not Muslim. We are Russian Orthodox. The whole family is Russian Orthodox. We are all, to my knowledge, devout and law abiding. Are you sure you have the right suspect?"

Suddenly I had some doubts. They had identified their nephew through the photograph I had. The ATF had taken the fingerprint from the truck used in the bombing. I had fought the man in the photograph hand-to-hand. He was the right suspect, but did we have the correct motive?

I'd have a lot of explaining to do when I got back to Manhattan.

CHAPTER 22

AFTER I'D INTERVIEWED Temir Marat's family in New Jersey, I took my time driving back to the Federal Building. I lingered in the lobby and called home to make sure everything was all right. Then, God help me, I sneaked back into the task force office. I felt sheepish, like a dog who had peed on the carpet.

Now I had to figure out how to explain my trip to New Jersey and all the interesting information I'd found out.

Darya was working on some notes at a table on the side. When I sat down next to her, I noticed the report was written in Cyrillic.

Darya glanced up and said, "When I'm in Moscow, I write in English. It's quite convenient. Like my own secret code. Because no one tries to learn anyone else's languages anymore."

I said, "Thanks, grandma, for the lecture. Besides, you've been with me during most of the investigation. There's nothing you could write that I haven't already heard firsthand. Probably from someone with a thick Russian accent."

"Where have you been?"

"Jersey."

Darya gave me a smile and said, "Seeing a girlfriend?"

"Ha, that's funny. Until I think about my Irish fiancée. Then it's scary. If I went to see a girlfriend in New Jersey, it would probably be my last trip to New Jersey ever."

Darya said, "While you have been out sightseeing, your friend the FBI agent and I have come up with an interesting wrinkle."

"What's that?"

"We've found the phrase Marat said before detonating the bomb, *hawqala*, the one that means 'There is no power nor strength save by Allah.'"

I said, "What do you mean you 'found' it?"

Just then Dan Santos strutted up to us and said, "It's a phrase that has been used by people being blackmailed into committing an attack." He looked between Darya and me, then just kept talking. "A Georgian soldier said it before he detonated an explosive vest at a police station, killing eleven, including himself. Turns out his mother was being held by a group that forced him into the attack. Apparently Georgians love their mothers."

"What happened to his mother?"

Darya answered. "They released her. They want people to believe them when they say they'll release someone for carrying out an attack."

Then Santos said, "Last year a former Russian security agent said *hawqala* before he charged a speaker at a meeting of businessmen in Chechnya. He managed to kill the mayor and a deputy with a hand grenade. The mayor was opposed to Russian influence in Chechnya. That attacker survived four bullets by security. He said he'd been told to do it. He regretted it. He also said the reason he shouted *hawqala* was because he heard it would show he wasn't a monster. It's a weird situation. The military and some law enforcement types know the phrase. This is the first time it's been used outside the former Soviet Union. It might be the wave of the future."

That all started to make sense with what I had just learned in New Jersey. Now I had to find a way to tell them I'd been working on my own.

I looked at Darya and realized I wasn't built for keeping secrets. I just started to talk. "I've developed some information I want to discuss with the two of you."

Neither of them offered any encouragement so I kept going. "I got a tip that Temir Marat had family that lived in Newark."

Darya said, "Right here in the US."

I nodded.

Santos said, "Did you put the lead into the system?"

"Not yet." I paused, but I could have been just as easily yelling, *I ignored you and went out on my own.* Instead, I said, "I wanted to make sure it wasn't a prank."

Santos calmly said, "I'm listening."

"So to ensure the information was good, I took a ride across the river."

Santos glared at me and raised his voice. "What?"

It was about as emotional as I had seen an FBI agent.

Santos said, "Was there something not clear about your place in this task force and how the investigation was going to be conducted?"

I shook my head. "All I can say is that it was not a prank. Marat's aunt and uncle moved here years ago and are still in touch with their nephew."

Now Santos slipped into the chair next to me and said, "Tell me everything they said."

"Oh, so I can't break the rules unless I find out something important?"

"No, but this case is bigger than politics."

I ran down the information I had gathered from Konstantin and Vera Nislev.

Both Darya and Santos took notes with interest.

Finally, when I had come clean and told them everything, Dan Santos looked at me and said, "This is good stuff. Now collect your shit and hit the road."

I stared at him for a moment. "What are you talking about?"

"It's a privilege to work on a case like this, on a task force like this. We all have certain procedures and everyone was briefed. Yet you are the only one who decided to go out on his own."

Darya started to come to my defense and I was afraid she was going to mention our earlier interviews. I held up a hand to stop her. I knew when a decision had been made. It didn't matter why it was made.

Without saying a word or acting like a spoiled brat, I picked up my notebook and a few other things I needed and strolled out of the task force with my head held high.

CHAPTER 23

THAT EVENING, I sat on the couch after dinner and doodled on a pad, making a few notes and my own version of a chart that showed the connection between everyone in the case.

The only call to the NYPD I had made since I left the FBI was to my lieutenant, Harry Grissom. I told him exactly what had happened, what I had found out, and that I had been told to leave. His response was pure Harry.

Grissom said, "On the bright side, at least you weren't kicked off the task force for stealing something."

I gave him half a chuckle.

He said, "Seriously, Mike, this isn't going to change anything between us or on the squad. Maybe some bosses will be pissed off, but they're so used to the FBI bullshit that I doubt anyone will care. I'll talk to Santos, then call you back when things have leveled out."

That made me feel better. Seeing the kids and having one last dinner of Thanksgiving leftovers set my head on straight. I also decided that just because I wasn't officially on the task force investigating the attack on the parade, that didn't mean I couldn't do anything about it. I was still a cop.

Now I was a pissed-off cop. And I wanted to find out what the hell was going on. Things were not as they appeared, and my unrelenting need to understand events kept pushing me.

Jane plopped down on the couch next to me and said, "What'cha workin' on?"

"Nothing, really. Just putting a few thoughts down on paper."

She laid her head on my shoulder and pointed at the page where I'd been doodling and said, "I especially like your thoughts about this boat and the giant shark behind it. Did you watch *Jaws* again last night?"

I let out a laugh. "No, but I'll let you in on a little secret."

She turned that beautiful face toward me and looked at me like I was about to explain the meaning of life.

I said, "The only things I can draw are boats, sharks, and swords. Anything else looks like a chimpanzee grabbed the pencil."

Jane said, "That's incredible. I'm in the same boat."

"You can only draw a few things?"

"No. Mine is with reading. I can really zip through novels I like by great writers like Michael Connelly and Tess Gerritsen. But when I read the history books I'm assigned at school, I just can't get into them. Now that I know it's just a family issue, I won't worry about it as much."

Even though I liked her sly smile, I said, "Sorry, that's not gonna cut it. It's an interesting argument and I admire the effort that went into it, but you'll read every history book assigned or I'll try to draw your portrait and post it at school."

Jane said, "I like that kind of out-of-the-box thinking. You're turning out to be a pretty good parent."

That was the kind of praise I needed about now.

I was still smiling at the remark a few minutes later when my phone rang and I heard Harry Grissom's voice. As usual, he got right to the point.

"Mike, it was too hard to listen to that jerk-off Santos. He was jabbering on about you not following regulations. But all I could say was, 'So what else is new?'"

A smile crept across my face, though I'd been dreading this call.

Grissom said, "I've never seen them quite like this before."

I said half-jokingly, "So you don't want me to show up at the FBI office tomorrow?"

"I don't even want you to show up at an NYPD office tomorrow. You've earned a day or two off. Enjoy yourself."

If I was a good parent, Harry Grissom was a great lieutenant.

CHAPTER 24

I SPENT SUNDAY with the family and on Monday was up early to make sure everyone got off to school without a hitch. It was fun. We played a couple of quick games over breakfast and on the short ride to Holy Name. We even arrived more than five minutes early. I was afraid it might give Sister Sheila a heart attack.

She surprised me with a simple smile and wave.

I ran some errands, cleaned up the apartment, and in general sulked about not being at the task force. Then, in the afternoon, I stopped in to say hello to my grandfather. He was busy at his desk when I walked through the front door of the administrative offices for the church.

I said, "What are you working on, old man?" I expected a smart-aleck reply.

Instead, Seamus said, "I've got to get this grant into the city before the close of business today."

"Since when do you worry about grants?"

"Since I want a way to bring kids in the neighborhood, who aren't Catholic and don't attend the school, to an afterschool program that would include a meal and tutoring."

"That sounds like a worthy project."

"At my age I only work on worthy projects." He set down his pen and looked up at me. "Is this how you're going to spend a precious day off? Harassing an elderly clergyman? Do you think you could find something better to do with your time?"

A broad smile spread across my face. "It's odd to have the shoe on the other foot for a change. You know how usually I'm trying to work and you're bugging me about something. How does it feel?"

Seamus said, "You tell me. How does it feel to block my efforts to bring underprivileged kids in for a snack and extra tutoring every day?"

"Okay, you win this round, old man. But I'll be back." Just then, my phone rang. I said to Seamus, "You were saved by the bell."

I backed out of the office as I answered the phone. I didn't recognize the number. "This is Michael Bennett." I shaded my eyes from the afternoon sun.

"And this is Lewis Vineyard."

It took me a second to realize that was my Russian mob informant's new name. At least one he was trying out. "I'm a little surprised to hear from you."

Lewis said, "We need to meet. Today."

I thought about explaining that I was off duty, but I could tell by the tone of his voice he needed to see me. We picked a diner we both knew near the West Side.

I said, "What do you got? Did you find Temir Marat?"

"No. But I know where he'll be tonight."

CHAPTER 25

LEWIS VINEYARD HAD hooked me. I wanted to meet with him right away, but he said he couldn't. He had other commitments. And it would look suspicious if he slipped away right now. He met me four hours later, at a diner near West End Avenue. I knew that meant he was serious. He didn't want to risk any of his Russian friends in Brooklyn seeing us together. I was in the booth waiting for him thirty minutes early. I never did that. It took me a moment to notice Lewis coming down the street toward the front door. I craned my neck to look out the window at my overly tan informant wearing a nice button-down shirt and jeans. He almost looked respectable. He was dark, but not leathery; he hadn't started spending all his time in the sun until the last few years.

As soon as he plopped into the booth across from me I said,

"It's not cool to tease me with important information, then not meet me immediately."

He held up his hands to calm me down and said, "No way around it. I called you as soon as I had the information, but things got hopping around the bar and I couldn't just leave. And there was no way I could have you show up there."

"I believe that the information you have is good, otherwise you wouldn't come all the way up here to see me."

Lewis said, "It's nice to see how the other half lives. Just walking down the street, I'd say you guys live pretty good up here. I prefer Brighton Beach. But that's just me."

I couldn't wait any longer. "If you're done with your monologues about New York City, can you tell me where Marat will be tonight?"

"It's not quite that easy. This is worth a lot."

I said, "What about the time there was a hit on you and I stopped the hitter in Brooklyn Heights? What was that worth?" I just stared at him and waited for an answer.

"You have a point. You've never screwed me, and you help me out. So I'm going to give you this information—if you tell me you'll make the FBI pay. This is so big the NYPD won't have the cash."

"I doubt that."

His smile told me he had some good info. Finally, I nodded and said, "If it's good information, I'll do everything I can to get you paid. That's the best I can promise."

Lewis Vineyard said, "That's good enough for me." Now he took a moment to gather his thoughts and glanced around the diner to make sure no one was close enough to hear us speak.

Lewis said, "Your man, Marat, will be at the Harbor House,

down by Battery Park, at eight p.m. tonight. He may be meeting someone there. A couple members of the Russian mob are going to intercept him."

"How do you know that information so precisely?"

Lewis perked up and said, "I sold them the guns. Two SIG P220s. It's a shame they'll probably toss them in the river after the hit. They're some nice guns just to use one time."

I looked down at my watch and realized I didn't have much time. I didn't have time to verify the information or even scope out the restaurant. But that's how things with informants usually worked.

CHAPTER 26

I RACED SOUTH on West End Avenue until I could slip onto the Joe DiMaggio Highway. It was too late to call in the troops and plan anything worthwhile. Besides, this could still all be bullshit. I'd know soon enough.

I had to catch myself when I realized I was driving like a lunatic. My driving was the reason people always cursed at New Yorkers. I cut off a UPS truck and tried to wave my apology to a heavyset driver who was not happy.

I'd zipped past all the Trump buildings, some with plywood hiding his name. The vents for the Lincoln and Holland tunnels barely registered on my right.

I tried calling Darya, just so someone knew what was happening. No answer. I didn't leave a message.

Now I started to consider the questions that were popping into my head. Why would someone pay the mob to kill a terrorist? Who gained from his death? Were the local Russians worried about backlash? Did they really love America that much, or was it their bottom line? All the same questions any homicide detective would ask.

I didn't know the answer to any of them.

I didn't call Harry Grissom. There was no need to put him in the trick bag if I screwed this up. I had to let things unfold.

And I wanted Temir Marat alive. I had questions to ask him before he was in FBI custody and no one got to talk to him again.

It was true, our last meeting had not gone the way I planned. He was tough and he had skills like no one I had seen in a long time. But I was determined. I had my Glock. And I had a backup revolver on my ankle.

I was as ready as I would ever be.

I exited the highway just before the tunnel that would loop me around to the East Side, parking illegally before I started running through the maze of parks and benches before the water. I scouted the area thoroughly, hoping to see Marat out in public. What the hell, it seemed to happen all the time—fugitives caught by someone who was keeping their eyes open. There had been a baseball hat in my car, left there after the last police league softball game of the season. I'd pulled it on as low as I could, since Marat would no doubt recognize me.

I didn't see him, so as I approached the Pier A Harbor House, I slowed down to take it all in, peering into some of the windows that didn't face the water. I finally stepped inside.

The heat inside the restaurant made me realize how strong the chill in the air was, which I hadn't registered as I ran there.

I scouted for other exits and windows while standing in the corner of the bar, noting that a long bar led to the dining room.

There was no one here I recognized. Lewis Vineyard had told me that one of the hitters who bought the guns from him was a well-built man about my height in his early forties, with a distinguishing characteristic of a purple birthmark on his cheek below his left eye. Lewis said the man worked with a tall female who had long black hair. There was no one that fit either of those descriptions that I could see.

I stepped farther into the restaurant, then saw someone I recognized. And frankly, it caught me by surprise. I might even say it shocked me. Sitting alone at a table by a window overlooking the river was Darya Kuznetsova.

What the hell?

I was about to get her attention when it hit me. This couldn't be a coincidence. What was she doing here? Was she luring Marat to be killed by the Russian mob? Why? Why not do it with her own government people?

That line of questioning led me to wonder—why had she provided a photo of Marat if she just intended to kill him?

Then I understood. At least that part of it. She didn't have a clue where Marat was hiding. The more people looking for him, the better.

She's the one who spread the word in the Russian community. That's how his aunt and uncle knew he was a suspect, why Konstantin said, "I wondered how long it would take the authorities to find us."

Shit. I was a fool.

CHAPTER 27

ONCE I MADE up my mind, I didn't dawdle. I stepped up, crossed the room, and sat down directly across from Darya Kuznetsova. I removed my hat like a gentleman, and smiled as if I were her date.

The look on her face and the way her eyes darted around the room told me she didn't want me there and expected someone else.

Darya took a moment and sipped her water. Then she said, "Hello, Michael, what a surprise."

I said, "Do you mind if I join you? Are you waiting for someone?"

She gave me a flat stare and said, "Why do you ask?"

"Just curious. All cops are curious. I noticed you're quite curious. Are you a cop in Russia? Or a spy? C'mon, you can trust me."

"I've learned I can trust no one."

I shrugged and said, "Too bad. Life's a lot easier with friends."

Darya said, "It's longer if you don't trust friends." She paused. "You're very sharp. I'm used to dealing with FBI bureaucrats. You're not like them at all."

"Flattery won't help you now."

Darya said, "I want this terrorist stopped as much as you do."

"Dead or alive?"

"That's how Russia views all terrorist hunts."

"There's a lot more to this than just hunting for a fugitive." I waited while she seemed to ponder my question and consider whether she could trust me.

Finally, Darya said, "Are there factions within the NYPD?"

"Yes. All agencies have factions."

"So do we. I suspected it was the same everywhere. Some in my government have different ideas about the war on terror. Unfortunately, they've acted on them. You might call them cowboys or rogues."

"What kind of different ideas do these factions have?"

She brought those intense, blue eyes to rest on me. "We all have the same goal: stop terrorism. Some people in the Russian government feel like the US has not participated the way it should."

I couldn't hide my shock. "Are you saying this is a Russian government–sanctioned attack?"

Darya stayed calm and steady. She didn't rush what she had to say. That was the mark of a pro.

She said, "No, just the opposite. Now this is all hypothetical, of course. But suppose a rogue element, which was now neutralized, had forced a Russian agent to carry out an attack like this."

"Temir Marat worked for the Russian government?"

She lifted her hands and said, "I was just giving you a theory. I'm doing this because I know you're actually trying to help things."

I said, "I want to capture Temir Marat and question him. What do you want?"

Darya gave no answer.

Before I could press her on it, I glanced up. There, near the front door, at the end of the bar, stood Temir Marat.

CHAPTER 28

IT FELT UNREAL to have been searching for someone so hard and then see him in person not far away. I guess part of me thought Lewis Vineyard was full of shit.

I stared at Marat. A bandage on his cheek covered the cut I'd given him with the bottle. He wore a NY Rangers baseball cap pulled low. He was gazing around the room, looking for someone. I suspected I knew who.

I eased out of my chair, getting ready to make a casual stroll across the dining room to get next to him.

Then I saw the couple coming into the bar behind Marat. A tall, burly man with short hair, and a woman nearly six feet tall with black hair. The man's birthmark told me exactly who he was. The birthmark looked like a smeared tattoo of a purple house.

All I could think was that the FBI was going to owe Lewis Vineyard a truckload of cash.

If I wanted Marat alive, I would have to act quickly.

Then the mob hitters made their move. It was smooth and professional—if I didn't know what I was looking for, I might've missed it.

The man stepped up right next to Temir Marat, folded his hands across his waist, and casually slipped his right hand under his dark linen coat.

It was subtle, but not too subtle. Marat immediately picked up on the man right next to him. He moved like a cat.

I could clearly see the Russian mobster as he pulled his blue steel SIG Sauer P220 semiautomatic pistol. It was an ugly thing, out of place in a nice restaurant like this.

But Marat was smooth as he turned and used both hands to block the gun before it could come up. He locked the man in close, with the pistol pointing almost straight at the floor.

The killer struggled with the gun under the power of Marat's grip. I could tell he was also struggling with the shock. He'd thought this would be easy.

Marat head-butted him, then ripped the gun right out of his hands. Now the woman got involved, reaching into her Louis Vuitton purse to pull out an identical pistol.

Marat reacted immediately, jerking the dazed man right in front of him as the woman pulled the trigger, shooting her partner twice in the chest.

Marat shoved the motionless man toward the woman. The dead weight knocked her off balance.

This all happened before I could even reach the bar. Everyone was looking around, startled by the two gunshots. The echo had made it difficult to pinpoint. This guy really did have skills.

I was a few feet away from the bar when the female hitter regained her balance and had Marat in the corner. The man with the two bullet holes in his chest was dead on the white tile floor. His blood was swirling into dark red pools and running along the grout lines.

Marat didn't have his pistol up yet. He was at the mercy of the female hitter.

I kept coming full speed and threw my entire body into the hitter. It was just a gut reaction.

We both hit the tile hard, but I landed on top of her.

She was out cold, the pistol loose on the floor.

Marat gave me a faint smile, raised the pistol to his forehead, and saluted me before disappearing out the door.

Darya appeared at my side as I was kneeling to make sure the woman was breathing properly.

I said, "Watch her." Then I was on my feet and out the door.

As soon as I hit the open area beyond the restaurant, I had my head on a swivel. There weren't many people out. Then I caught just a glimpse of someone running. It was the way his head bobbed up and down, and the blue and red of the Rangers cap.

He was running south, along the water. I drew my Glock and started to run the same direction. I fell into a measured pace, not knowing what I might have to deal with once I caught this unusual suspect. At least he wouldn't surprise me with his abilities this time.

The park was flat and relatively empty as it got closer to the street. I would see him if he moved away from the water.

Just as I paused by a cement column that depicted the construction of the World Trade Center, I heard a gunshot. The bullet pinged above my head on the column.

Great. Now this was a gunfight.

CHAPTER 29

I CROUCHED ON the other side of the column and brought my pistol up. There were several low cement shapes in the park designed to be artistic and give people a place to sit and rest.

I crouched low and ran to the first of the concrete structures. It wasn't until I dropped behind it that I realized Marat was just beyond, crouching behind a closed food kiosk.

I leaned from behind the cover and popped off two quick rounds, hoping to scare him out of his position. Instead, I was met with two quick rounds back at me.

I knew the gunfire had to attract attention and if I could just hold him in place, help would be on its way soon. But I still wanted to take this guy alive. A patrol officer rolling up on a gunfight wasn't going to take that kind of care. I wouldn't blame any officer that fired a weapon in this situation.

I popped around the edge and fired twice more. Just to let him know I was here and I wasn't giving up. That's when he used his skills once again. Most people, when they are being shot at, will find cover and stay there. Marat started to move as soon as I fired the two shots. He came low and fast from his cover along the edge of the cement block I was behind.

Next thing I knew, he was right in front of me. I turned and raised my pistol, but he had already twisted and slapped it hard. Then his foot came off the ground in a blur and struck me in the side of the head. I was dazed as I pitched over.

But he didn't want to fight. He just wanted me to stop shooting. He turned and sprinted away toward a series of decorative concrete walls designed to block the wind and give people something to look at. It looked like a tiny maze.

Once again, after I cleared my head, I was running after him as quickly as I could.

I slowed as I came to the walls. I had my pistol up and scanned the whole area, hoping to get a glimpse of Marat. I entered the little maze carefully.

As I came to the last wall, expecting to see Marat in the wide-open space between here and the Clipper City Tall Ship anchored in the water, I spotted some movement out of the corner of my right eye. Just a blur.

Unfortunately, the movement was Marat's fist as it connected with the side of my head. I had to look like a cartoon character with my face twisting under Marat's fist, my eyes spinning, as I tried to protect myself. I thought I was losing consciousness as I dropped my gun and heard it clatter against the rough cement. Then I steadied myself as I bounced off one of the six-foot-high concrete walls.

Marat was on me in an instant.

He threw his whole body into mine, knocking me flat on the ground. Then he picked up my pistol and flung it hard toward the river.

Marat said, "Just stay here. I still have a pistol." He held up the SIG Sauer like I needed some kind of visual cue.

Now he was jogging away again. He thought he had disarmed me. That was his mistake.

CHAPTER 30

I HATE TO admit that I sat on the hard cement for a few seconds just to gather my wits. This guy could've killed me several times over. Why hadn't he?

Now I had an advantage. He thought I was unarmed. I reached down and drew the Smith & Wesson model 36 revolver. I wasn't crazy about going up against a man armed with a .45-caliber semiautomatic while I just had a five-shot .38, but there was no way I could let this guy disappear.

I knew he'd been headed south, so I got to my feet and started to jog unsteadily toward the masts of the Clipper City Tall Ship I could see in the distance.

It was cold and dark, so there were few people in the park or near the ship. I spotted his Rangers cap about halfway between me and the ship. He was walking fast, trying not to draw attention to himself. I knew he was trying to get out of the area. That's what I'd do.

As I closed the distance, I suddenly felt like the .38 in my hand was a BB gun. Where the hell was my backup?

I scanned for cover to get behind before I shouted for him to stop. A drop of blood from a cut on my forehead slipped into my eye. I felt like I'd been run over by a Volkswagen.

The best cover I could find was a heavy, freestanding billboard that advertised tours out of the mouth of the Hudson. I stood behind it, raised my revolver, and sighted from the groove near the gun's hammer to the front sight, with Temir Marat's body taking up my entire sight picture.

I shouted, "Police—don't move!"

He froze.

I spoke loudly and enunciated carefully. "Put the gun on the seawall." He was right next to the low wall with the open water beyond it. If he tried anything, he had to pull the gun, turn in this direction, and then find me in a split second. I liked my position.

Marat just stood there, facing the water. I could still see his hands hanging at his side. There was no telling what a man like this was thinking or how far he'd go.

I shouted again, "Put your pistol on the seawall!" I waited a moment and added, "Do it now."

He never moved his hands as he stepped up onto the seawall and spun to face me. This is not what I wanted to happen. I didn't want him to have a chance to survey the area and see where I was standing. But I didn't feel I could pull the trigger when I saw both of his hands clearly, and didn't see the gun at all.

He glanced over his right shoulder as if he were thinking about jumping in the river. It wouldn't be the first time a suspect tried it. Most people overestimated their swimming ability.

I shouted, "Don't do it, Temir!"

That caught his attention. He just stared at me.

"That's right, I know your name. I know everything about you. I even visited your aunt and uncle in Weequahic. Aunt Vera and Uncle Konstantin."

He was listening. It was a nice change from him punching me.

I stepped out from behind the sign and started to walk slowly toward him. My pistol was still up as I said, "You didn't attack the parade because of a jihad. You're not even Muslim. You're Russian Orthodox like the rest of your family."

Now I was only about ten feet from the seawall. After what this guy had done to me in two different fights, I wasn't about to get any closer.

I was careful how I phrased my next statement. "I think I know who you're working for. We can protect you. All you have to do is surrender."

His right hand twitched and eased toward his jacket's front pocket.

I said, "Don't do it."

The hand froze about halfway to the pocket.

"Surrender and we can work this out."

Then Marat spoke. His voice was even and he clearly had an accent, but his English was good. "If I surrender, you can ignore the people I killed?"

I just stared at him for a moment. I had no answer.

Marat said, "Neither can I." His voice had a catch in it. "I had to do it. They have my wife and daughter."

"Is that why you said *hawqala?*"

"I didn't know if anyone would pick up on it."

I kept the pistol trained on him. I was still expecting someone to come help me shortly.

Marat said, "They told me I had to do this one job. Drive the truck into the parade, then detonate the explosive they had built into the truck. That was my first clue they'd abandoned me. When I hit the detonator, it was supposed to give me thirty seconds to escape. Then there was no one waiting to drive me away like they were supposed to. They've been trying to kill me ever since. Now it looks like they tricked you into doing their dirty work."

All I could say was, "Who? Who is trying to kill you? Who do you work for?"

He looked like he wanted to tell me. Like he knew it was over. He started to speak, then hesitated.

His right hand moved. That's when I heard two gunshots.

CHAPTER 31

AS SOON AS I heard the shots, I couldn't keep from turning to see where they came from. Behind me, partially hidden by a wooden bench, Darya Kuznetsova kneeled with the other Russian mob hitter's pistol in her hand.

I spun back to Marat. He seemed to be frozen. Somehow, in that split second, his right hand had reached the gun in his jacket pocket. Now he held it loosely with the barrel pointed to the ground.

He looked at me and tried to speak. That's when I noticed the two red stains expanding on the front of his jacket. Both were close to his heart.

The pistol dropped onto the seawall. Marat stood for a second longer, then toppled over into the river.

I raced to the seawall and leaned over to look at the dark water. The tide was going out and there was a serious current.

But there was no sign of Temir Marat. The swirling black water would hide anything more than a few inches below the surface.

Darya joined me at the seawall. She carefully placed the pistol next to the one that had dropped out of Marat's hand.

I looked at her and simply said, "Why?"

"I thought he was going to shoot you. You have no idea what men like that are capable of."

"I'm starting to get an idea."

"He would've shot you."

I said, "That's bullshit. He's one of yours. You're just trying to cover his tracks."

Darya shook her head and said, "He's not one of mine. I had nothing to do with anything this man was involved in." She was convincing. Then she said, "And I really thought your life was in danger."

Two patrol cars pulled up to the edge of the park and the four patrol officers started jogging toward us with their weapons drawn.

I immediately set down my revolver, pulled my badge from my back pocket, and held it in my right hand. To be on the safe side, both of my hands were above my head before they got too close.

Darya took my lead and raised her hands as well.

A female patrol officer who was leading the pack charging toward us recognized me. "Do you need a hand, Detective Bennett?"

Immediately, I felt relief wash through me.

It was over. Maybe not the way I wanted it to end, but the manhunt for Temir Marat was finished.

CHAPTER 32

TWO HOURS LATER, I was sitting on the same seawall where Temir Marat stood when he was shot. My feet dangled over the seawall as I watched the search for Marat's body.

A crime scene was set up where Marat had been shot. The three pistols, mine and the two mobsters' SIG Sauers, were still sitting in the same place on the seawall.

Several harbor boats, two NYPD boats, and the Coast Guard rescue ship were shining lights and casting nets into the murky water.

Someone sat down next to me, and I was surprised when I turned my head to see that it was Dan Santos.

He just sat there watching the water with me for about half a minute. Neither of us said a word.

Finally, I said, "How did your interview with Darya go?"

Santos said, "About how you'd expect. She claims she

followed you from the restaurant to help you catch Marat. She picked up a pistol from the floor of the restaurant that came from one of the people trying to kill our suspect. When she found you facing Marat, she thought he was about to shoot you so she fired first."

"But did she say anything about Marat's motive or who he worked for?"

"C'mon, Bennett, give the FBI some credit. As soon as we figured out how *hawqala* had been used in other bombings, and consulted some counterparts at the CIA, we had a pretty good idea what was going on."

"Did you suspect what Darya was up to while she was working with us? I mean, she never intended for us to get our hands on Marat."

Santos smiled and said, "Did you ever see me do, or say, anything classified in front of her?"

I said, "Maybe you're not the dumbass prick I thought you were."

Santos laughed and said, "Once again you're underestimating the FBI. I'm not a dumbass, but I am a prick. Sometimes you have to be in this line of work. Especially when you deal with the NYPD every day."

The only answer I had to that was, "Touché."

CHAPTER 33

I'LL ADMIT TO being a little uncomfortable when Darya asked me to grab a cup of coffee after we were released from the shooting scene. But curiosity got the better of me and I agreed to slip into a coffee shop right at the edge of the financial district.

We sat in silence as I made a show of stirring my coffee until she finally said, "I have no idea why it is important to me that you know I had nothing to do with the attack."

I just nodded. My grandfather had taught me that running your mouth without thought is always a bad idea. When I was a kid I believed he followed all of his own advice.

Darya said, "There is nothing about this incident that I agreed with. I shouldn't even have to say that I'm against terrorism. I'm against any government trying to trick other governments. And I was against the way my government chose to handle the whole situation. And if you repeat anything I say here, I'll simply deny it. I just felt like you had earned an explanation."

"And you didn't want me to think you were a cold-blooded killer."

She shrugged and said, "Frankly, I prefer you think I'm a killer than a liar."

I stared at her, trying to get a feel for her sincerity. She really was striking with those deep-blue eyes and high cheekbones. No matter how I focused, I couldn't get a clear read on her.

Darya said, "I'm pretty certain Dan Santos will never deal with me again, but I would love to hear who hired the two Russian mobsters and tipped them off that I had arranged a meeting with Temir through a mutual acquaintance. If you were able to talk to the woman who survived, is that something you might be able to find out for me?"

I just smiled. There was no way I was going to commit to helping her on anything until I knew more about what had happened during the investigation. I was in a weird no-man's land between the FBI and an official envoy from Russia.

I drank about half my coffee as we sat there and watched the few people on the streets at this time of the night.

Finally, I asked the one question that had been on my mind. "Will the US see any other fake attacks?"

"Not from Russia. Who knows what others have in mind. It's too easy to bend public opinion. Why should a government make a good-faith effort to do the right thing about terrorism or any other hot-button issue, when one incident like the attack on the parade will galvanize the population?"

"What about you? Are you going to stay in New York?"

"For a while. I like it here. I'm starting to understand American police politics and I am certain there will be more incidents where we all have to cooperate."

"I'm afraid of the same thing."

Darya surprised me when she reached across the small table and grasped both of my hands. "I am your friend, Michael. In time, I hope you learn to trust me. I think we could each help the other in a number of ways."

I couldn't deny the logic, but wasn't sure I grasped her entire meaning.

She released my hands and stood up. I immediately stood as well. She stepped toward me, rose up on her tiptoes, and kissed me on the cheek. Then she whispered in my ear, "We'll meet again."

Then she was gone.

CHAPTER 34

THREE NIGHTS AFTER Temir Marat was killed, I sat in the only safe place I knew in the entire world. In my living room with Mary Catherine, nine of my kids, and my grandfather.

Mary Catherine was snuggled in next to me on the couch, with Chrissy and Shawna tucked in on the other side of me. The older kids all sat on the carpet as we watched the Jets on Thursday Night Football. It was a game against the Dolphins in Miami and every camera shot between commercials showed people walking along the beach in shorts. It just didn't feel right to a New Yorker.

Before the game, I had watched the news, where everyone was reporting the attack on the parade as just another terror incident. They went on to say the terrorist was shot by "authorities." Reporters made it a point to say the suspect acted alone.

That seemed to put an end to the terror attack that had rocked the city. Even Ricky said, "So you solved another one, huh, Dad?"

"*Solve* isn't the word I'd use. We *cleared* the case. That'll have to do."

Eddie said, "It's got people on their guard now."

I smiled. "For now, but people forget. Always. It's got to be one of the fundamental laws of the universe."

Mary Catherine said, "You really think the attack will be forgotten?"

"Not totally, but no one will think twice about next year's parade. That's how these things always go. People talk about never forgetting, but they forget remarkably fast. The Free-dom Tower is a good reminder, but you have to be in lower Manhattan to see it."

Shawna looked up at me. "We'll still go to the parade next year, won't we?"

Jane chimed in. "We have to, otherwise the terrorists win."

I didn't know if she was serious or joking.

Shawna still stared up at me. "Can we go?"

I smiled. "Of course we'll go. That's our thing. Your mom loved it. In a way, we're honoring her memory. St. Patrick's and Macy's are two parades we won't ever miss."

There were smiles and cheers all around. Mary Catherine hugged me, then kissed me on the lips.

ABOUT THE AUTHORS

James Patterson is the world's bestselling author and most trusted storyteller. He has created many enduring fictional characters and series, including Alex Cross, the Women's Murder Club, Michael Bennett, Maximum Ride, Middle School, and I Funny. Among his notable literary collaborations are *The President Is Missing*, with President Bill Clinton, and the Max Einstein series, produced in partnership with the Albert Einstein estate. Patterson's writing career is characterized by a single mission: to prove that there is no such thing as a person who "doesn't like to read," only people who haven't found the right book. He's given over three million books to schoolkids and the military, donated more than seventy million dollars to support education, and endowed over five thousand college scholarships for teachers. The National Book Foundation recently presented Patterson with the Literarian Award for Outstanding Service to the American Literary Community, and he is also the recipient of an Edgar Award and six Emmy Awards. He lives in Florida with his family.

James O. Born is an award-winning crime and science-fiction novelist as well as a career law-enforcement agent. A native Floridian, he still lives in the Sunshine State.

JAMES
PATTERSON
RECOMMENDS

JAMES PATTERSON

MICHAEL BENNETT

STEP ON A CRACK

MICHAEL LEDWIDGE

STEP ON A CRACK

I've created some memorable characters in my day, but Detective Michael Bennett is particularly special. He's a loving husband, father of ten, a proud New Yorker—and very much inspired by the real-life heroes of the NYPD. His story starts with a bang in STEP ON A CRACK during the funeral of a beloved former first lady. The world's power elite are all in attendance, which, of course, creates the perfect scenario for a psychopath's genius plan. Enter Michael Bennett. I really wanted a trial by fire for this guy, so not only did I make him face off against the most ruthless man I could have ever dreamed up, but I also threw the ultimate heartbreak at him: his wife's earth-shattering medical diagnosis.

JAMES PATTERSON
"I like this character even more than Alex Cross."
—Bkfaerie.blogspot.com
MICHAEL BENNETT
TICK TOCK
MICHAEL LEDWIDGE

TICK TOCK

Sometimes a setting is so rich, vibrant, and alive that it's very much a character in a book. That's how I think of New York City. In TICK TOCK, she's under attack again, and this time the crime tearing through the Big Apple is so horrifying—so perfectly planned by a deadly mastermind—that Detective Michael Bennett is pulled away from a seaside vacation with his children so he can investigate. Things heat up as Michael comes across one of my favorite twists yet, and you'll see why the city that never sleeps is the city that never stops needing Detective Michael Bennett.

JAMES PATTERSON

GONE

MICHAEL LEDWIDGE

A Detective Michael Bennett Thriller

GONE

In GONE, Michael Bennett and his children are *trying* to start over on a secluded farm in California under witness protection. But Michael Bennett just wasn't made for retirement. Enter: my most charismatic and coldblooded criminal yet, Manuel Perrine. Detective Michael Bennett was the only U.S. official, ever, to put him away. And now that Manuel is out, he's out for blood. Michael's blood. To lure Michael out of his hiding place, Manuel starts a one-man war against America, embarking on an escalating series of assassinations that Michael Bennett and the FBI can't ignore. It's a faceoff between two heavyweight contenders. And only one of them will make it out alive.